NO BOYS?

McCLURE JONES

SCHOLASTIC INC.
New York Toronto London Auckland Sydney

Cover Photograph by **Owen Brown**

ISBN 0-590-33485-9

12 11 10 9 8 7 6 5   6 7 8 9/8

Printed in the U.S.A.   06

NO BOYS?

A Wildfire Book

WILDFIRE TITLES FROM SCHOLASTIC

Love Comes to Anne by Lucille S. Warner
I'm Christy by Maud Johnson
Beautiful Girl by Elisabeth Ogilvie
Superflirt by Helen Cavanagh
Dreams Can Come True by Jane Claypool Miner
I've Got a Crush on You by Carol Stanley
An April Love Story by Caroline B. Cooney
Dance with Me by Winifred Madison
Yours Truly, Love, Janie by Ann Reit
The Summer of the Sky-Blue Bikini by Jill Ross Klevin
The Best of Friends by Jill Ross Klevin
The Voices of Julie by Joan Oppenheimer
Second Best by Helen Cavanagh
A Place for Me by Helen Cavanagh
Sixteen Can Be Sweet by Maud Johnson
Take Care of My Girl by Carol Stanley
Lisa by Arlene Hale
Secret Love by Barbara Steiner
Nancy & Nick by Caroline B. Cooney
Wildfire Double Romance by Diane McClure Jones
Senior Class by Jane Claypool Miner
Cindy by Deborah Kent
Too Young to Know by Elisabeth Ogilvie
Junior Prom by Patricia Aks
Saturday Night Date by Maud Johnson
He Loves Me Not by Caroline Cooney
Good-bye, Pretty One by Lucille S. Warner
Just a Summer Girl by Helen Cavanagh
The Impossible Love by Arlene Hale
Sing About Us by Winifred Madison
The Searching Heart by Barbara Steiner
Write Every Day by Janet Quin-Harkin
Christy's Choice by Maud Johnson
The Wrong Boy by Carol Stanley
Make a Wish by Nancy Smiler Levinson
The Boy for Me by Jane Claypool Miner
Class Ring by Josephine Wunsch
Phone Calls by Ann Reit
Just You and Me by Ann Martin
Homecoming Queen by Winifred Madison
Holly in Love by Caroline B. Cooney
Spring Love by Jennifer Sarasin
No Boys? by McClure Jones

One

I waved good-bye to the camp's bus driver and climbed on the train. Stumbling down the aisle, I lugged my suitcase and the tennis satchel Uncle Jerry had bought for me, with its two outside pockets for two tennis racquets. Their handles jabbed my ribs at every step. After dropping all my gear in the first empty aisle seat, I climbed over it and curled into the window seat, too weary to lift my bags to the overhead rack. As the coach was almost empty, I didn't think it would matter.

Every muscle I owned ached, but at least I was done with one more dreadful summer of camp. In the past six years my uncles, Jerry and Max, had sent me off to music camp; riding camp; hiking camp; drama camp; sailing camp; and this year, tennis camp.

Each year I had known it would be a disaster.

My uncles always made it sound wonderful, reading aloud from the camp brochures about the "idyllic mountain setting, skilled counselors, and warm camaraderie with fellow campers."

"Sounds exciting," they'd say. "Wish I were young enough to go off to camp and learn a new skill. You'll love it, Janet."

What I learned, in order by year, was that I was tone-deaf, horses have miserable ridges in their spines, the weight of a backpack causes only slightly less pain than blistered heels, stage makeup produces instant acne, and last year, that sailboats, despite all the theories about deep keels, can be overturned. It is righting a sailboat that is impossible.

As for camaraderie, once the other girls discovered how untalented I was, they rushed to get themselves assigned to other groups.

So why did I do it? Why did I go on, year after year, letting my uncles sign me up for camp? Because my uncles are probably the two sweetest men in the whole world. They would sacrifice anything for me. But that's only half of the reason. The second half is — and it hurts to admit it — I have never been able to stand up to anybody about anything. Somebody once told me that people who act like rugs get walked on. That's me, Janet the Rug.

As the train pulled out of the station in a series of lurches, I closed my eyes and concentrated on what I would say to my uncles. It really was time to take a stand. I mean, here I was, almost sixteen years old, and it was time for me to make a few decisions of my own. "Uncle Jerry," I'd say, "I am almost sixteen, and I am long past old enough to choose my own activities. For starters, I don't want to take dancing classes after school. And after that, I don't want to go to any more summer camps."

And Jerry would say in his nice, friendly voice, "What is it you want to do, honey?"

And what would I answer? I chewed on my lip and tried to think of something, while my mind pulled down its shade and went blank. I wished I were like my friend Gale, who always knew exactly what she wanted to do. But the truth was I let people boss me because I wasn't ever really sure what I wanted to do, or if I did have an idea, I suspected that it was a dumb idea. I mean, it wasn't as though I had a marvelous track record of successes to give me confidence.

The train settled into a steady rhythm of sways and lurches. My thoughts drifted with the motion, fading in and out and finally away.

Much later I felt a hand on my shoulder, shaking me. I shuddered and tried to open my eyes.

"I'm sorry," someone — a boy — said, "but all the other seats are taken. Mind if I put your gear overhead?"

Mumbling, "Sure, go ahead," I managed to unglue my eyelids enough to watch him through my lashes. He looked about ten feet tall with his arms up and head back, as he shoved my suitcase into the storage rack. Without bending or stretching or even wincing at the weight, he swung my tennis satchel up beside it. Then he lowered himself into the aisle seat and folded his long legs into the narrow space. The train lurched into motion again.

"Where are we?" I asked.

"Bakertown," he said and turned to smile at me.

I blinked and ran my fingers through my snarled hair. My face was flushed, both from sunburn and sleep, and my tennis-camp T-shirt was twisted in deep wrinkles. I couldn't have looked a worse mess if I'd tried.

"Don't I know you?" we both said at the same time, then laughed.

"Sure, you go to Roosevelt High, too, don't you?" I said.

"That's it, I knew I'd seen you before. I'm Eric Russell."

Right away, I knew who he was. He'd be a junior this year, a year ahead of me, and though I'd never talked to him, I'd seen him occasionally in the halls at school. He was one of those tall, thin boys who show up in a crowd. Up close, his face was even nicer than at a distance, with eyes that sparkled and a wide smile.

I said, "I'm Janet Dwyer."

"Been on vacation?"

"Tennis camp."

He squinted at my T-shirt with its slogan *I survived Ikahwah Valley Tennis Camp*, which the camp hands out to every departing camper, and he laughed.

"For most people, that's a joke," I said. "For me, it's a fervent hope."

"Rough?" he asked.

"Ever been attacked by an automatic ball server?" I said.

"That bad?"

"That was one of the nicer things. I ache so much, even my eyeballs hurt."

"You must love tennis to go through all that."

I started to say, "No, I love my uncles," but changed my mind. That would be too hard to explain. Instead I said, "I guess I didn't realize how grueling it would be when I signed up. Where have you been this summer?"

"Visiting my grandparents. They have a farm outside Bakertown."

"That's right, that's what you said the last stop was. I fell asleep right after I got on the train. There was hardly anyone in this coach." Lifting myself upon my arms so that I could see over the seatbacks, I discovered that the car was full.

"You must have slept through two stops," Eric said. "I'm sorry about waking you up. But I got on three cars back, and they're full up, too."

"I didn't mean to take two seats. It's just that when I got on, most of the seats were empty, and I had had such a hard time getting my bags on the train, I didn't think I could lift them up to the rack."

"Not with aching eyeballs," he said, and we both laughed.

After that, we ran out of things to say. I mean, there I was, sore and tired, wondering whether it would look dumber to straighten my T-shirt, which had twisted sideways around me, or to leave it alone as though I always wore my T-shirts that way. And if I straightened the T-shirt, could I then pull out a comb and do something with my hair? Or would that make me look like one of those girls who is always fussing with her looks? I leaned forward, pretending to stare at the passing scenery, but really trying to glimpse my reflection in the window. All I could make out on the dusty glass was the outline of my head, no details. My hair was definitely rumpled.

Of course, I knew that I could say "Excuse me," and Eric would stand up, and I could climb out of my seat and go to the washroom where I could do my combing and straightening. But when I returned, wouldn't he wonder why I'd done all that combing? Would he think I was trying to impress him?

My whole trouble, I decided, as I stared at telephone poles flashing by the window, was that I wasn't used to being alone with a boy. I'd never been out on a date. And Eric was so nice-looking, anyone would know that he probably had dated lots. So no matter what I said, it might be the wrong thing, and I wouldn't know it was wrong and he would.

Beside me, he said, "You've got a good tan."

"Oh! Uh, well, tennis, you know."

"I don't tan at all," he said. "All I do is burn and peel."

I gave him a careful look and saw that it was true. A light line of red extended across his forehead and down his nose. It was one of those nice, arched noses, not too long or wide, covered with a pale pattern of freckles.

"Do you have freckles all the time or only in the summer?" I asked.

"Only in the summer," he said.

I started to say, *that's nice*, decided that sounded dumb, and returned my gaze to the window. Now that he'd mentioned my tan, I remembered one more consolation. Besides having a good tan, my hair was so sun-streaked that it was almost a true blond on top. No matter how messy it was, at least it was a good color.

After that we talked some about the scenery, with a few remarks thrown in about school. As we were in different grades, we didn't have any mutual friends, though we each ran through a list of names, saying, "Do you know so-and-so?" to which the other would say, "I know *who* that is, but I don't really know her."

We continued our pattern of fifteen-minute silences and two-minute conversations all the way home. As the train approached our stop,

I tried to squint through the dirt-streaked windows, to spot Jerry and Max in the crowd waiting on the platform, without actually getting my face against the glass. If I met them with a sooty face, they'd be sure I had been in some horrible accident. That's the way they were. I mean, I was in the third grade before they finally quit paying a neighborhood teenager to walk me to the bus stop and decided that I was old enough to cross a street alone. Everyone else I knew had been walking to the bus stop alone since their second day in kindergarten.

The train screeched to a stop, throwing me into the back of the next seat. Its covering was rough wool and smelled of smoke.

Eric caught my elbow. "You okay, Janet?"

I slid back into my seat and said, "Sure, I'm fine."

Eric's hand dropped from my arm. Reaching up, he caught the edge of the rack and swung out of his seat. I liked the slow, graceful way he moved. Probably he could sing, ride, hike, act, sail, or do anything else anyone tried to teach him, though all he'd mentioned to me was the summer farm work and a soccer league.

After he'd set my gear in the aisle, he lifted down an enormous backpack and shrugged into it, then reached up and dragged out a canvas laundry bag that was almost as tall as me and filled to bulging.

"You must have taken everything you own," I blurted out.

"I was there all summer. Uh, you need help with your suitcase?"

As he had both arms wrapped around his laundry bag, I couldn't imagine how he could help me, but it was polite of him to offer.

I said, "No, thanks, I can manage."

"Nice to meet you," he said. "See you at school."

"Yes, sure," I said, as I bent over to get a better grip on my dumb satchel. No matter how I held it, the handles of my racquets dug into my ribs. Why had Jerry insisted that I needed two racquets? I wondered for the thousandth time. He was right that some of the campers did bring two racquets, but they were the girls in the senior advanced group who, as far as I could tell when I watched them, probably had to switch racquets every so often to let the strings cool down. I mean, they had the kind of killer instinct that would make them professionals, for which I envied them. I didn't envy their ability to play tennis, as I didn't much like tennis, but I envied them the fact that they so obviously knew exactly what it was they wanted to do with their lives.

10

By the time I straightened up, Eric had worked his way through the crowd to the far end of the car. I took one more glance out the window, spotted Jerry's blond head, then stumbled between the seats dragging my gear. As I reached the outside exit, hands rose past the metal arch to catch my suitcase and satchel. Then Jerry was there, grabbing my arms to lift me from the train steps onto the platform. He gave me a big hug, swinging me around out of the crowd.

"Here she is! Look at her! Look at that tan!" he crowed.

I peered past his shoulder to my Uncle Max, who is as small and dark and quiet as Jerry is large and blond and noisy. Max waited patiently, my bags dragging down his arms with their weight. Our eyes met, and he gave me a quiet wink.

Jerry shouldered his way through the lobby of the train station, walking in long, fast strides, with me caught in the crook of his arm, while Max followed. The station echoed the sounds of the train and track from its tile floors and arched ceilings. Over the shouted greetings of the hundreds of milling people, the loudspeaker cracked announcements.

I tried to spot Eric. He had disappeared.

When we were finally settled into the car, headed home, with Jerry driving and Max in the seat beside him and me in back, Jerry shouted over his shoulder, "So how was tennis camp, honey?"

I thought of the careful speech I had planned. I would tell them that it was a great camp, and I appreciated the opportunity they had given me, but this was the last year that I would go away to camp. I would also say firmly that I was through with dancing classes.

Uncle Max turned to smile at me. "I bet you've got a terrific serve." His eyebrows drew together behind his glasses, in his worried look. "Was the food all right? You look as though you've lost weight, Janet."

Max looked pale. I knew he'd been working all summer, teaching summer session. He and Jerry couldn't afford to spend three weeks playing in the sun as I had, and what was worse, they didn't care. They were happy to work all summer to pay to send me off to an expensive tennis camp, because the truth was that providing the best for me was what mattered most to both of them.

After all they did for me, how could I tell them that I didn't appreciate it?

I said, "Camp was terrific, Max, really terrific. And the food was fine. I mean, it was nothing like your cooking, it was plain old camp food, but there was plenty of it, and it was fine."

Max's forehead relaxed. "You won't have to eat plain old camp food tonight. I'm cooking tonight, and it's a special surprise that I know you'll like."

"I'm sure I'll love it," I said.

Jerry shouted, "Max is fixing dinner but I'm doing the dessert! You're not going to believe it, Janet! You've never tasted anything like it."

"I'm sure I haven't," I said and laughed. I'd been through this same conversation at least a thousand times with my uncles. Now I really felt like I was home again.

Two

Life with two uncles is not a TV sitcom.

I know it sounds as though it might be, especially to people who have watched those shows featuring a handsome bachelor uncle in a plush, city apartment. There are always parades of glamorous girlfriends and a jewel of a housekeeper. The uncle makes cutesy mistakes, such as buying his niece high heels that she can't walk in, but she stumbles off to the party bravely, in order to avoid hurting his feelings. Then when disaster strikes, this time as a wrenched ankle that requires a rush to the hospital emergency room, uncle realizes his mistake, and he and niece have this heart-to-heart talk that smoothes out everything until the next episode.

Sounds like heaven.

What life with two uncles is really like is this.

My parents died when I was five. My mother's sister, my Aunt Eva, with whom I was staying while my parents were on the trip that ended in the accident that I still don't like to think about, kept me. She was in the middle of a divorce and her life was pretty messed up, but what else could she do with a five-year-old? She popped me into a variety of day nurseries while she was at work, then closed me in the back bedroom when her husband came over in the evenings to try to talk her into a reconciliation. His visits always ended in screaming fights.

I'm not quite sure what happened after that, as I was very young, but either Eva phoned my uncle or someone told him what was going on, because after I'd been living with her for about ten months, Uncle Max showed up. He was my father's older brother. I do remember him giving me a stuffed rabbit with a big ribbon around its neck and asking me if I would mind playing in the other room while he talked to my Aunt Eva. I remember that the rabbit was red plush, that Uncle Max's voice was so low I could barely hear it, and that occasionally Eva's voice rose to a whine.

While I was still playing with the rabbit, Eva packed all my clothes. Uncle Max sat on the floor beside me and asked me if I would like to go live with him for a while. I don't remember what I said, but I do remember that we drove all day in his car and that when we reached the house, I was too tired to walk. This big man with yellow hair came out of the house, scooped me up, and carried me in.

It's odd the way childhood memories run together. At that time I thought Jerry was a giant and very old. But of course, he wasn't either one. The actual situation was that Max taught math at the community college, and Jerry was in his second year as a student. They lived in a small house set on an acre of land at the edge of town. Max had spent two years caring for his dying father and then had taken over the responsibility of his youngest brother, and he really couldn't afford to add me to his household, but it wasn't until years later that I realized that. Max always acted as though he was glad to have me. I'm not sure how glad he was, but I was sure, right from the beginning, that he loved me very much. Max has never been the type to go around hugging and kissing — that's Jerry's department — but he is always very kind.

So for the past ten years, I've had two uncles as my only family, with an occasional Christmas gift from Aunt Eva, who has been through two more divorces since I lived with her. We have never had a housekeeper. Jerry finished college, went through a series of jobs, and for the last three years has been a sales rep for a company that installs air-conditioning. As for girlfriends, glamorous or otherwise, Jerry has his share, but he never brings them home. And although neither of my uncles discusses it, I think that Max was very much in love once.

I've kind of picked up the story in bits and pieces, the way people do with family gossip, and as closely as I can figure out, the lady Max loved was also a teacher. She waited for him through his father's illness, but she wasn't sure about sharing her life with a college-age kid brother. And I suppose the addition of a six-year-old niece cinched it. Or maybe it wasn't like that at all. Maybe she never loved Max enough to marry him. I'm never sure about why adults do things. They seem to think differently.

If my uncles don't live up to the sitcom idea of swinging bachelors, they're nothing compared to the house. You might see its like on a TV special titled, "The Deterioration of

Middle America," but you'd never see it on a sitcom.

Jerry drove the car down the long drive, swerving to miss the potholes. I clutched at the seat edge to keep my balance.

Max said, "That's got to be our next project, filling those potholes."

Jerry said, "Right." That's one more conversation I'd heard a hundred times.

After climbing out of the car, I picked my way around the metal rods and odd-shaped bits of lumber stacked on the porch steps. My uncles spend their weekends rebuilding old cars. Their latest project was parked on cement blocks to one side of the porch at about the spot where most people have flower gardens. It was missing its hood, tires, and two fenders.

Jerry saw my glance, patted my shoulder, and said, "Isn't it a beauty, Jan?"

I said, "Right, sure! Yes, it is," and headed into the house. I didn't dare ask what make it was. If I had, I would have been in for a half-hour explanation of what it was, why it was valuable, where they'd acquired it, what they'd done to it so far, and what they planned to do to it.

Jerry followed me through the house, carrying my bags. I noticed that in three weeks they had found time to rip out and board up the window in the entry hall, but they had not replaced the frame around the front door, which they'd removed six months ago.

"What's with the window?" I asked.

Jerry said, "We decided we might as well replace it along with the door frame. Its sill had dry rot, and that glass is a real heat-loss. I'm going to get thermopane, but it'll need a new frame."

"Why did you tear it out before you had the new window ready to put in?" I asked. Sometimes I wonder at myself. Why do I keep asking, when I know I'll hate the answer?

"I had to take it out first to check the condition of the wall studs and figure out exactly what size window I could put in there."

I didn't bother asking about the door. I knew what he would say. He'd explain that when he realized the window had to be removed, he knew there was no point replacing the door frame, as they would want the frames to match and they couldn't buy the framing until they were sure what size window they would need.

How did I know the answer? I knew because I'm an expert on the subject. For ten years I have watched my uncles rip out and replace one section of the house after another. The problem is, their ripping out is always way ahead of their replacing. Last year they finally finished the kitchen, and it looks beautiful, with all its paint and wallpaper and new cabinets and thermopane windows. It looks like something out of a house-decorating magazine. But the rest of the house looks like the entry hall. The fireplace in the front room has been rebuilt, but the floor around it is covered with patches of linoleum because my uncles haven't had time to install the new carpeting. The new carpeting is rolled up and stored in the hall, so that we have to step over it to get through the bathroom door. There is a new bay window in the dining room, but no one can reach the seat to use it because the bricks from the old fireplace are still stacked in front of it. My uncles say every week that next weekend they will carry them outside. After that they will refinish the floor, which has holes in it where they pulled out some boards that were rotting. The new boards for the floor are in the entry hall, under the missing window.

In Jerry's room, there's a newly plastered ceiling above his torn walls. He steamed the paper off but hasn't found time to replace it. Max's room has a big, gaping hole in one end, where he tore out two small closets so that he could remodel them into one large closet. His clothes have been hanging on the shower curtain rod for the past year. However, that doesn't matter, because it is a second bathroom and they removed the fixtures, except for the tub, two years ago, and the water line to the tub is disconnected.

Their standard answer to my questions is, "You'll see, honey, it's going to be beautiful when we finish."

I live in dread that they'll rip the fixtures out of our one functioning bathroom before they rebuild the other one.

"Home again!" Jerry said as he dropped my bags on my bed. To my relief, they had not been in my room. Besides the kitchen, my bedroom is the one room that is livable. It's not fancy. It hasn't been remodeled. It's just a plain old room, but it has all its walls, ceiling, floor, and door and window frames.

Glancing around my room with that calculating look in his eyes, Jerry said, "We really ought to repaper this place. And I keep thinking, maybe we could add another closet for you, between the windows."

"I love it exactly the way it is," I said quickly and kind of pushed him around so that he was facing the hall. In ten years, I've learned to keep my uncles, with their passion for remodeling, out of my room.

"Come on, I'm starved and dinner smells wonderful," I added. It did, too. Whatever

Uncle Max had going in the oven, it was filling the house with fantastic aromas.

We were halfway to the kitchen when the phone rang. Thinking it would be my friend Gale, who lives next door and would have seen our car turn in our drive, I said, "I'll get it, it's probably Gale," and ran back to my room.

I have my own phone. It was my Christmas present last year. Falling across my bed, I grabbed the receiver off the hook. The phone sits on a low dresser on the far side of my bed, and I can reach it with a swan dive.

"Hello?" I said.

"Janet?"

The male voice caught me completely by surprise. I said, "This is Janet."

"Hi, this is Eric."

"Hi." I couldn't think of anything else to say. He must have thought that my silence meant that I didn't know who Eric was. Or maybe that I knew several Erics.

He said, "From the train. Today."

"Sure."

"I — uh — I called to see if you'd gotten home all right. After I got off the train, I wondered if you'd gotten your gear off. Or if you needed a ride. So I went back and looked around for you, but I didn't see you."

Kneeling on my bed, I peered at my reflection in the dresser mirror. Even in the shadows of my room, I could see that my hair was definitely bleached to a fairly decent shade of blond on the top. Maybe that sounds dumb, but knowing that I didn't look too bad gave me confidence. I said, "My uncles met me at the station."

"Oh. So you had a ride. Okay, then."

"It was nice of you to ask," I said quickly.

"As long as you had a ride."

"Uh-huh. I did."

"Because my folks picked me up. We could have given you a ride," he explained.

"Uh-huh." My phone conversations had always been with Gale or other girls. I don't know why that should make any difference, but for some reason I couldn't think of anything to say to Eric.

He said, "Well — uh — see you at school."

"Sure," I said and hung up.

Before I went out to the kitchen, I combed my hair. It definitely had some great streaks. I hoped that made me look older. I have one of those round faces that never seem to age. I mean, my school picture last year looked almost exactly like my school picture when I was in first grade, and last year I was a freshman in high school. When I showed the two pictures to Gale's mother and complained about it, she said I was wrong and that I looked much older and more sophisticated, but I knew she was only saying that to make me feel better. Gale's mother is very kind.

From the kitchen, Jerry called, "Hurry up, Jan, dinner's ready."

They were at the table when I entered, bent over pans from which they were carefully spooning their portions. The kitchen is the one finished room in the house, a spotless arrangement of wood and marble counter tops with rows of shining pots hung above them from ceiling hooks. Even the table is a wooden cutting slab, so that pans can be set right on it from the stove burners. My uncles don't fuss with things like tablecloths or fancy china. Our dishes are a dozen different colors, bought for their sizes but with no thought to their patterns. Most of them were picked up at garage sales. Stacked on open shelves within easy reach, their variety of colors were cheerful, and sometimes I liked to rearrange them to make color patterns. That was about all I ever did in the kitchen, as my uncles were always too busy to teach me to cook.

"Is that cabbage?" I asked as Max quietly lifted a greenish ball of something onto his plate.

"It is *sarmale-varza umpluta cu carne*."

"It looks like cabbage."

"It is cabbage wrapped around the most delicious beef and mushroom filling you will ever taste," Max said as he spooned a serving onto my plate. "It's Rumanian."

"The only thing better will be the Italian tortoni I made for dessert," Jerry said. "I'm not sure, Max. You may have a bit too much thyme in this."

They both looked expectantly at me. I tasted the cabbage. It was nice, but to tell the truth, to me it simply tasted like hamburger wrapped in cabbage. However, I said what I knew Max wanted to hear. "It's perfect. It really is delicious."

Max peered at me over his glasses. "Can't tell you how nice it is to have you home, Janet."

I knew what he meant. My uncles competed with each other in the kitchen. Each one always found some little flaw in the other's cooking. I, on the other hand, could be counted on to say everything was delicious, which it usually was.

Jerry said, "Your friend Gale has phoned three times this week to find out when you were due back. Was that her on the phone?"

"Gale? Oh. No. It wasn't. It was — it was a kid I know from school. I'll call Gale after supper." I don't know why, but for some reason I didn't think I should mention that I had met a boy on the train. I had a kind of funny feeling that my uncles wouldn't approve. But still, after I'd referred to Eric as "a kid from school," I felt guilty. If Jerry had asked me, "What kid?" I would have told him. I never meant to lie to him.

But he didn't ask. Instead he said, "Sure, you do that while we're clearing up the supper dishes. She can come over and help us eat the tortoni."

"What is a tortoni?"

"Food for the gods," Jerry said.

"Whipped cream with macaroons," Max said.

After supper I phoned Gale to invite her to help us with the tortoni. She let out a wail.

"Oh, Jan! I didn't know you were coming home tonight! I thought you wouldn't be home until tomorrow! If I'd known, I never would have told Mrs. Chambers I'd babysit tonight. But I did, and she's coming to pick me up in a few minutes!"

"It's not a disaster," I said, though I really was disappointed.

"Yes, it is!" she shouted. Gale did a lot of her talking at the top of her voice. "I'll bet your uncles have some fabulous dessert for this evening!"

26

"Tortoni. It's whipped cream with maca-roons."

"I could die! I could absolutely die! It sounds like heaven!"

"That's what Jerry said. He says it's food for the gods."

"I'm sure it is!" Gale dropped her voice and whispered into the phone. "Listen, I have got so much to talk to you about, but I can't phone from the Chambers's because Mrs. Chambers doesn't like me to use the phone, but, anyway, I can talk until she picks me up. You won't believe what's going on. Kristy spends all her time practically glued to this senior boy, and Nadine has a thing for David Overton, remember him? She follows him everywhere, but I don't think he even notices her. And Stephanie had a party, it was fabulous, with guys and dancing and stuff. Oh, I wish you'd been here!"

I wished I had, too. When I'd left for camp, all my friends had been sitting around moan-ing about what a boring summer it was going to be. None of them had any plans. And the few parties we'd had at each other's houses during our freshman year had been all girls.

"You make me feel as though I'd been away for years, instead of three weeks," I said.

"It's been terrific," Gale said. "Never mind, you'll catch up. Now that Stephanie has started this party thing, we'll have more. At least I hope we will, because there were some great guys at her party that I've seen at school but never met, and it was, umm, well, you'll see."

"Speaking of guys you've seen but never met, do you know Eric Russell?"

"Don't think so," she said.

"He's tall and kind of fair and nice-looking, and he's a year ahead of us."

"A junior? Umm, maybe, I sort of recognize the name. Why?" Gale asked.

"I met him on the train. Coming home from camp."

Gale snickered. "So the summer wasn't a total waste."

"I met him. That's all. But then he phoned a couple of hours ago, to be sure I'd gotten home all right."

"That must have been some train ride."

"What's that supposed to mean?"

"Nothing," Gale said, her voice going singsong to tease me. "I understand completely, dahling, strangers on the train, a brief encounter, passing in the night, all that sort of thing."

"None of that sort of thing, I don't think. I mean, it was afternoon, hot, sunny, in a crowded coach car that smelled of last year's cigars."

"Ah, across a crowded room, through the

smoke, their eyes met, their fates became entwined —"

"Gale!" I had to shout to make her hear me above her own rising voice.

"Ooops! I hear a car honking in the drive. Must be Mrs. Chambers. I've got to run. Talk to you later," Gale said rapidly and hung up the phone.

When I returned to the kitchen, I said, "Gale can't come over. She has a babysitting job tonight."

Max asked, "Did you tell her about tennis camp?"

"Umm, sure," I said and then remembered that tennis camp was the one thing we hadn't discussed.

Three

On that first day of my return, my uncles were
so pleased to have me home that they didn't
notice the T-shirt. Instead, they noticed it on
the first day of school.

Maybe it was kind of a crazy thing to wear,
a T-shirt emblazoned *I survived Ikahwah Valley Tennis Camp.* It wasn't as though I had
enjoyed the camp. A week later I was still a
walking ad for liniment cream. I mean, I
winced if I tried to walk too fast. But the thing
was, in return for all that pain I felt I deserved
a little notice, and my friends would notice
the T-shirt.

Unfortunately, my Uncle Max noticed it, too.

As I was standing in front of the refrigerator with its door open, eating grapes from a plate on the refrigerator shelf and holding a glass of milk in my other hand, which is how I always ate breakfast, he walked into the kitchen.

"Good morning, Janet," he said. "So it's back to school today. Did you remember to check the bus schedule?"

"Sure," I said, turning to face him. "Same old stop, same old time, same old bus and cranky driver."

Uncle Max started to lean past me to find something for his own breakfast. Only our dinners are gourmet. All the other meals are serve-yourself and eat-on-the-run. Jerry and Max have to leave the house before I do to make it to work on time.

He paused, his hand half-closed around the milk carton, his eyes riveted to my T-shirt.

"Where did you get *that*?"

"Get what?" I said, although I knew what he meant. I had this sinking feeling inside, and I needed to spar for time.

"That shirt. Where did you get that shirt?"

"They gave them to us at camp."

"Gave them to you?"

"Uh-huh. They handed them out."

"Oh." I think Uncle Max needed time, too, because he carried the milk carton to the counter and slowly filled a glass for himself. Then he said, "It — uh — you weren't — that is, I don't think it's quite right for school, Janet."

All the rest of the world wore slogan T-shirts to school, including, I felt sure, the students at the community college where Max taught. I also knew for sure that what the rest of the world did had nothing to do with what I was allowed to do.

I said, "Everybody wears T-shirts to school."

Max said softly, "Well, of course, it's for you to decide, dear. It's just — I don't really care to have you go to school dressed that way."

What sort of answer could I give to that? If my uncle would ever tell me flat out that I couldn't do something, maybe I could argue. It wasn't fair. Uncle Max was always so kind about everything. And in the end, I always did what he wanted me to do.

Then he added, "I'll bet you've outgrown a lot of your school clothes. Would you like to go shopping Saturday and get some new things?"

What could I say? Uncle Max meant it. He would give me his charge card, and I could buy as much as I wanted. He wouldn't say a word about the cost, even though he and Jerry worked hard to keep up with the bills. But he or Jerry would go with me and somehow, no matter what I tried on, I'd come home with clothes *they* liked rather than what *I* liked.

I said, "Sure, that'd be great. Well — if you don't think this is right for school — I guess I'll go change."

Max looked so relieved that I lost any desire to rebel.

In the hallway I almost ran into Jerry, who was heading for the kitchen.

"Morning, honey," he said. "First day of school, huh?"

"Right."

"Had breakfast yet? You need a good breakfast before you face all those mean teachers."

Jerry liked to make jokes about mean teachers because Uncle Max was a teacher and probably the least mean person either of us knew.

I laughed and said, "Yeah, I'm all set."

Then Jerry noticed my T-shirt, stopped, blinked, and said, "That — uh — that a new shirt?"

Somehow that surprised tone from Jerry was too much. I had at least hoped that Jerry would like my shirt. I wailed, "Everybody wears T-shirts to school! How come I can't?"

"Can't you?"

"Max asked me to change it." I tried to sound pathetic. Sometimes if I sounded sad enough, Jerry would take my side.

This time he said, "T-shirts are okay for weekends."

So much for getting sympathy from Jerry. I mean, Jerry is only thirteen years older than me, not twenty-five years older like Max, so I had hoped he would understand.

Glaring at myself in my mirror, I pulled off my T-shirt and buttoned on a plaid blouse with a lace edge on its collar. It made me look about five years old. All of my clothes made me look five years old, which, it seemed, was the way my uncles preferred me to look.

Last Christmas, during my freshman year in high school, my Aunt Eva had sent me a makeup kit with eyeliner, blusher, lipstick, and mascara. I'd been delighted, but Max had said, "I shouldn't think those things would be good for your skin."

When I'd turned to Jerry for support, he'd said, "Eva must be out of her mind."

So I'd written a polite thank-you note to my aunt and put the makeup kit away, unused, in my closet. I'd thought about pointing out to my uncles that I was in high school and lots of my friends wore makeup, but in the end I'd decided that I didn't really care enough about makeup to say something that would make Max and Jerry unhappy.

After my uncles left for work, I gathered up my notebook and tote bag and headed for the bus, wearing my stupid, baby blouse tucked neatly into my jeans.

Gale met me at the bus stop. Uncle Max would have had a stroke if he'd seen her. She was wearing a red tank top, showing off the terrific tan on her shoulders, not to mention her very nice figure.

She said, "I'm scared to death of the new Spanish teacher."

"Have you seen the new teacher?"

We stood at the edge of a crowd of about a dozen neighborhood kids, all sporting new T-shirts and jeans. It was one of those hot September days that always hit as soon as school opened, so that by afternoon all the teachers would be rushing around pulling down the shades, and all the students would be poking each other to keep from falling asleep.

Gale said, "No, of course I haven't seen the new teacher, but the only reason I passed Spanish last year was because Miss Marcus liked me, so what will I do if this one hates me?"

"Why should this one hate you?"

"Because I am really rotten at Spanish," Gale moaned, rolling her eyes the way she does. Gale had one of those expressive, thin faces, surrounded by curly, dark hair, and somehow she could always manage to look both funny and foxy at the same time.

Our bus stop was at the corner of the road. As all of the houses in the neighborhood were forty or fifty years old and set back on acre plots, it was rather like being in the country, with no sidewalks and only a weed-filled storm ditch to edge the blacktop road. I could hear insects buzzing in the hedges that overhung the fences in front of the houses.

When the bus pulled up, Gale and I pushed our way to the back until we found a seat together. I looked out the bus window at the half-dozen dogs who had followed their kids to the bus stop. They stared back, sad-eyed, and let their wagging tails go limp as the bus pulled away.

Gale said, "Maybe you'll see him today."

"See who?" I asked, still thinking about the dogs.

"That boy you met on the train. That — Eric, wasn't it?"

"He's a junior. He won't be in my classes."

"Maybe you'll see him in the hall."

"Maybe." I hoped I would, but I didn't want to say too much to Gale. Gale was one of those bubbly people, with a loud laugh and the kind of voice that carries. I was afraid she might stage-whisper his name in her big voice and point at him if we passed in the hall, and he'd be sure to hear her and know that I had told her about him. It wasn't as though he had ever phoned me again, because he hadn't, not after that one call to ask if I had arrived home.

Gale said, "I looked him up in last year's yearbook. I know I've seen him. He's really good-looking."

"So are a lot of guys."

"Isn't that the truth? And know what? Bet I can absolutely guarantee that none of them will sit next to me in any of my classes." Gale's voice rose to a wail. "I'll be surrounded by turkeys, wait and see!"

A boy on the seat in front of us turned around and said, "Gobble, gobble."

Gale sputtered, "Oh, cute! Real cute!" but then she let her eyes slide sideways in a kind of flirting way she has, which made the boy laugh.

When he turned away, I whispered, "Do you know him?"

She whispered back, "No, but he's not a turkey, is he?"

"Maybe you'll get lucky. Maybe you'll get someone like that sitting next to you."

"Don't count on it."

"Okay, then, maybe you'll get a smart turkey who knows Spanish."

Gale gave me a "drop dead!" look, wrinkling her nose.

"So why did you sign up for Spanish again, if you're so worried about it?"

She said, "How did I know Miss Marcus was leaving? Besides, my dad says I absolutely have to take two years of Spanish, or some language, to get into college, and everyone says Spanish is easier than French or German. Listen, did I tell you? Stephanie phoned last night. There's going to be a dance at school Friday night. Everybody's going. Can you go?"

As Gale and I had never gone to any dances during our freshman year, I was surprised when she suggested it.

She said, "We're not freshmen now. It's time we went. And it's also time you wore something besides those little-girl blouses. You want to borrow one of my T-shirts for Friday? You could change at my house and not tell your uncles."

"I wouldn't lie to my uncles!" I blurted out.

"I didn't mean — oh, forget I suggested it."

"And, anyhow, I'm not good at dancing," I protested.

"Who is? Come on, Jan, it'll be fun," Gale said.

"Don't we need dates?"

"No, it's one of those record dances. They'll have the sound system blaring, and everybody wanders in and out. I'm going with Stephanie and Barb and some other girls, but it'd be a lot more fun if you came, too."

"I'm not sure. I'll have to ask Max."

"Why should he mind?"

"I don't know, but I've never gone to a dance before, so I'll have to ask."

"Tell him it's a school party and you're going with me. My mom'll drive us."

"Will she? Then I think it'll be okay. What are you going to wear?"

"My jeans and my A-shirt. I got a couple of new ones this summer. They're terrific."

An A-shirt, I knew, was a sleeveless T-shirt, with the straps set close to the neck to make a person's shoulders look wider. Really foxy. If I wore one, Max and Jerry would probably lock me in my room and throw away the key.

When we reached school, Gale and I headed for our homerooms to get our locker assignments and then spent our lunch hour trying to find our lockers. Naturally, our numbers were down different halls, about a thousand miles apart.

This year I had freshmen in the lockers on either side of mine. Neither of them could make their combinations work.

"They must have given me the wrong number!" one exclaimed, and then the kid on the other side of me shouted the same thing.

"What's the matter?" I asked them.

"I do the number exactly the way it's written, but the door won't open."

"Yeah," said the other one.

So I wasted more time showing them how to hit the locker door with a book right above the handle, explaining, "It's the only way they open. Timing is everything. You hit it *after* you've reached the last number but *before* you lift the handle."

I was explaining this for the third time when Gale found me. She dashed up, shouting, "How did you get a locker clear out here? Nobody has a locker out here!"

By nobody, she meant none of our friends.

After slamming my locker shut, I raced after Gale until we found Stephanie, Barb, and the others. Stephanie was by far the tallest, one of those bony people with long arms and legs and no extra weight, the kind clothes manufacturers design jeans for so that the rest of us have to cut off five inches from each pant leg and then try to figure out how to hem the fraying denim. She had new gold-framed glasses that reached from above her eyebrows to below her nose, with the lenses tinted gray. Barb was wearing so much eyeliner and mascara that I hardly recognized her. I mean, last year she had small, pale eyes in the middle of a round, pale face. And Kristy and Nadine had new haircuts. Everybody looked fabulous, especially Gale, who hadn't done anything different except wear that red tank top, but then, Gale always looked fabulous, with her curly hair and thin face and terrific shape.

The only thing different about me was a tan and my sun-streaks, which I had at the beginning of every school year. Otherwise I was exactly the same as always, with the same round, scrubbed-clean face above a blouse that made me look ten years younger, which is some trick at almost sixteen.

"How was tennis camp?" Kristy asked.

"I'm almost recovered," I said and wished I could have worn my tennis camp T-shirt to school.

"Meet any cute guys?" Barb asked.

"You kidding? This was a girls camp. Even the instructors were female."

"You ought to go to a coed camp next summer," she said.

I didn't bother answering. Barb didn't know my uncles. The only reason I attended a coed school, I suspected, was because that was what all public schools were. All of my after-school tutors had been women. Once I'd mentioned to Jerry that I had a friend who took guitar lessons from a really nice man and Jerry had said something about, "Yeah, but you're with us all the time, Jan," so I knew that my uncles thought of my tutors as substitute mothers.

It was as though Jerry and Max considered me a hobby-project, labeled "Remodeling Required to Change a Child into a Polished Woman." They sent me to tutors and camps the way they ripped out door frames and bought building materials, but they never quite completed the job. They never checked to see if I had learned anything. I'd barely get started failing at one skill when they'd pick out another skill and sign me up for lessons in that.

Stephanie peered at me through her enormous glasses and asked, "Are you going to the dance, Jan?"

"Sure, I guess so," I said. "I might as well. Gale's mom is going to drive us."

Barb said, "I've never been to any of the dances."

"Me, either," I said.

"I don't really know how to dance very well."

I laughed at that. "You're probably a lot better than I am. The only kind of dancing I've ever done is in this awful ballet class I take."

"You take ballet?"

"Once a week. With a bunch of other no-talents. We look like a room full of elephants with stubbed toes."

"Still, it's dancing. I've never danced at all. Maybe I shouldn't go," Barb said.

I said, "As for that, what difference will it make if we can dance or not? I mean, I don't know anybody who'd ask me to dance, anyway."

It turned out that I was wrong about that.

F _our_

The dance was in the school gym. Gale and I walked out of the lighted corridor into the weird, haunted house atmosphere. All the gym lights were out, but stage lights were set up around the gym with turning, colored filters in front of the bulbs, so that patches of blue, red, green, and purple light kept moving across the crowd. The music was turned so high we couldn't hear each other, even when we shouted.

Gale grabbed my hand and led me around the edge of the floor until we found Stephanie and Nadine. They were leaning against a wall, watching the dancers, and some of the odd-colored lights reflected on Stephanie's big glasses.

When they saw us, Nadine pointed at Gale's A-shirt and shouted something that I couldn't hear, but the look on her face made it clear that she liked it. She was wearing a T-shirt with a cartoon picture on the front, but in the darkness I couldn't see quite what it was. For the first time, I felt a little better about the puff-sleeved blouse I was wearing. In this light, even if people could see what a baby style it was, at least they couldn't see that it was pink-checked. Max had picked it out for me, naturally.

Finding a bare space of wall next to Stephanie, Gale and I leaned back against it so that we could watch the dancers and yet not look as though we were eager to join them. They thrashed their arms, swung their hips, and tossed their heads without taking up too much space, as though they were individually contained in invisible cages. If people moved beyond their space, they bumped into someone else.

A steady crowd of onlookers walked by us, circling the dance floor, their heads swiveling as they checked to see who was standing against the wall and who was dancing. As Barb went past, carried along by the crowd and looking very confused, Nadine leaned forward and grabbed her arm, pulling her out of the stream of onlookers.

"There you are!" Barb cried. I could see the words on her mouth even though I couldn't hear them. She slid into place against the wall, between Nadine and Stephanie.

As I leaned against the wall, my legs began to ache. It occurred to me that I had livelier times at home watching TV. Then the music stopped.

Nadine shouted, "I love that shirt, Gale!"

And Stephanie shouted, "Wow, I'll say! Where did you get it?"

We shouted at each other over the crowd noises for about two minutes, until the music blared out again. Then we resumed our stances against the wall, trying to look nonchalant. At least, I was trying to look nonchalant. I wondered if the others were as bored as I was. What with the lights and the noise and the moving chain of bodies in front of my vision, I drifted into a trancelike state, kind of sleeping while standing up. *Still*, I thought, *everyone has to attend one of these things once*. If I'd stayed home, knowing all my friends were at the dance, I would have been sure I'd been missing something fabulous. Next time, if I stayed home at least I'd know that what I was missing wasn't that terrific.

A hand touched my arm. I practically fell over from shock.

Looking up, I saw Eric standing next to me. He was saying something but I couldn't hear him.

I shrugged and lifted my hands, palms up, next to my shoulders so that he'd know I couldn't hear.

He smiled, nodded his head toward the dance floor, and made a beckoning motion.

I smiled back. Fantastic conversation.

Catching my hand in his, he led me through the onlookers onto the floor, where we kind of edged our way between the other dancers until we found a spot wide enough for the two of us.

"I'm not much good at this," I said.

He grinned, and I knew he couldn't hear me. He started waving his arms and twisting his body, but in the shadows and moving lights, I couldn't really see what he was doing. For a second I panicked. What was I doing out on the dance floor with a boy who obviously knew how to dance when I wasn't at all sure *I* did? About the only dancing I had done, besides my dreadful ballet lessons, was in front of the TV, watching the bandstand shows and imitating the dancers. Which would be worse, to stand like a statue or to try to disappear in the crowd and find my way back to my friends?

Still, if I couldn't see *him* very well, then he couldn't see *me* any more clearly. And besides, I didn't want to run away. I mean, Eric was nice and I liked him, and if I did something stupid now, he probably would never bother talking to me again.

Catching my lower lip between my teeth, which always helps me concentrate, I tried to imitate his motions. At first I felt really dumb and conspicuous. I kept wondering if my shirt was pulling out of my jeans. Was my hair all messed up and sticking out? Would somebody point at me and start laughing? Was I moving my hips too much? Would *everybody* point and laugh?

Then the music kind of took over, helping me move, and I saw Eric smiling and I relaxed and started to enjoy dancing. About the time I felt at home on the dance floor, the music stopped. That sent me right back into panic.

What was I supposed to do *now*? Should I wait for Eric to lead me back to my friends? Should I turn and walk off by myself? Was there something I was supposed to say to him?

The colored lights continued to slide across his face and shoulders. His smiling expression changed from orange to purple to green. Wondering what color my face was, I tried to smile back.

He said, "All the aches and pains gone from tennis?" at the same time that I said, "Are you glad to be home from the farm?"

We stopped, laughed, and said in unison, "Sorry, what did you say?" and laughed again.

He leaned down to repeat his question. I hadn't remembered that he had such long eyelashes. "Are you still playing tennis?" he asked.

"I think I've had enough tennis for this year," I said, thinking to myself that I'd had enough tennis for a lifetime.

"Yeah, it's hard to keep up with stuff like that, once school starts."

"How about you? Do you miss your grandparents' farm?"

"I think I chased enough chickens for this year."

"What do you mean, chased chickens?"

He started to answer. The music blared out. He shrugged, smiled, and started dancing again. Since I had no idea what else I should do, I danced, too.

When the music stopped, I said, "I guess I'd better go find Gale."

"Okay," Eric said and, to my surprise, followed me through the crowd.

Gale was still leaning against the same spot of wall, looking bored. When she saw me, she smiled. "I wondered where you'd disappeared to."

Although Gale knew perfectly well who Eric was, as we had discussed him, I didn't want him to know that I had mentioned him to her. I said, "Gale, this is Eric. We met on the train ride back from camp."

Gale slid her eyes sideways, glancing at him from under half-closed lids, which is this very flirtatious thing Gale does and I can't copy, though I've tried to do it in front of the mirror. She said in a tone of surprise, "Oh, were you at camp, Eric?"

"Huh-uh. I was visiting my grandparents. They have a farm up that direction."

I added, "He was chasing chickens. I never found out why."

Eric leaned down to say something, but the blare of the music drowned out his words. Gale and I both shrugged at the same time. Eric shouted, "Let's go!"

As it was impossible to discuss where it was he wanted to go, Gale and I followed him out of the gym. We blinked in the glaring lights of the corridor. Pointing down the hall, Eric said, "They've got Cokes and stuff in the east wing. Let's get something."

He walked to the end of the hallway and turned into the east wing at what was probably a normal pace for him, but I practically had to run to keep up. Gale, who is a couple of inches taller than me, didn't seem to have any trouble, though.

Around the corner we found a long table, manned by parents, that had paper cups, napkins, and plates of cookies, chips, and dip. Buckets on the floor were filled with ice and canned soft drinks. The food was free, but we had to pay for the Cokes. Before Gale and I had a chance to see what he was doing, Eric had pulled money from his pocket and paid for all of us.

"We'll pay you back," Gale said.

"That's okay," he said.

She said, "Gee, if you're going to be so generous, we should have brought our other three friends."

"In that case, you can pay next time," Eric said, and Gale laughed really loudly, as though he had said something very funny.

It was at about that moment that I wished desperately that I was wearing my T-shirt and not my dumb, ruffled, pink-checked, baby-style blouse. I mean, Gale looked so sophisticated in her A-shirt, with her shoulders showing. And she knew how to tilt her head and glance at a boy in that foxy way. It wasn't that she was making a play for Eric. I knew she wasn't. That was just the way Gale talked to everyone, including her father and my uncles.

She asked, "Did you say something about chickens?"

"Not me," Eric said.

"You started to," I said. "Only there was too much noise in the gym."

A mother who was standing near us, arranging cookies on the table, turned and said, "I don't know how you can stand it! I should think it would break your eardrums. That's why we decided to put the refreshment table this far away from the dance."

"It's awful, isn't it?" Gale agreed.

The mother said, "Last year we had the table right by the gym door, and after the first party, we couldn't get any more parents to volunteer to help. They were afraid they'd go deaf."

We wandered back down the hall toward the gym, waving at friends who were headed for the refreshments. As we entered the darkness, with its swinging circles of colored light, a boy in our class came up to Gale and shouted something in her ear.

Gale gave me a quick look before following him onto the dance floor. I wasn't quite sure what the look meant. She kind of raised her eyebrows and tucked her chin in, as though to say, *What did I do to deserve this?* Whether that meant that she was glad he'd asked because she wanted to dance with him, or sorry he'd asked because she didn't want to, I couldn't guess.

Eric leaned down and shouted, "Want to try again?"

We worked our way onto the floor. I was beginning to feel as though I belonged at the dance, and not like part of an audience.

During a break in the music, Gale found us. She said, "Maybe I should go phone Mom and tell her when we want her to pick us up."

Eric said, "Your mom is picking you up?"

"Uh-huh," Gale answered.

"If you want, I can give you a ride. I've got a car here."

Gale looked questioningly at me.

I wasn't sure what he meant. Was he asking to take Gale home, or did he mean both of us? As though she read my mind, Gale said, "I live next door to Janet. But we don't want to take you out of your way."

"That's okay," he said, which later I realized was one of Eric's favorite answers to practically any question. I mean, Eric was forever saying *that's okay* the way I'm forever saying *I mean*.

The music started up again, but this time it was a slow number, and I wasn't sure I could dance to that at all. Gale disappeared into the crowd, leaving me to wonder what to do next.

I mouthed at Eric, "I don't know how."

He mouthed back, "Me, either. Want to try?"

He put his arm around my waist, and we stood in one spot, shifting our weight from foot to foot. There wasn't space to do much else. All around us, couples were glued together, their arms wrapped around each other, which made me feel sort of odd as there was definitely a space between me and Eric. Looking straight ahead, I stared at his striped T-shirt. I tried once to look up at his face, the way I'd seen girls do on TV shows. I bent my neck as far back as I could and discovered that all I could see was the bottom of his chin, so to save my neck, I settled for turning my head slightly and staring out at the crowd.

Gale danced by with a boy who had his arms wound so tightly around her that her face was pressed into his shoulder. As he turned, she looked past him, only her eyes showing as she peered over his arm. She lifted her lids and rolled her eyes in one of her funny expressions. He wasn't the boy that I had seen her with earlier.

Eric leaned down toward me. "How do you like the lights?"

There was something about the lights that had been bothering me all evening, but until he asked, I hadn't realized what it was. "There's something wrong with the grouping. The gold one should be in that other corner."

"What?"

Realizing that I couldn't explain anything so complicated over the music, I said, "They're great," and continued watching the crowd. I have this compulsive thing about arranging articles and colors so that they form designs, but whenever I've tried to explain it to anyone they look at me as though I'm crazy, so I usually don't bother talking about it.

Stephanie danced by with Willard, this boy who is maybe an inch or so shorter than she is, but really likeable. He was in my freshman English class. When I smiled at him, he didn't even see me, he was that busy gazing into Stephanie's glasses.

The slow dance was the school's way of announcing that it was time to go home. As soon as the music stopped, all the overhead gym lights came on. Around us, startled couples separated, blinking at their partners as though they had been wakened suddenly in the middle of a dream.

We found Gale at the far end of the gym, talking to Barb and Nadine. "There you are," she said.

Eric said, "Does anyone else need a ride?" which I thought was very kind of him.

Nadine said, "No, thanks, my dad's picking me up. We'll take Barb home, too."

Barb said, "What about Stephanie?"

"She's riding with Willard."

So that took care of that. I had this vision of Eric driving all night all over town, taking each of us home.

As he led the way through the dark parking lot, Gale fell behind a step and touched my arm. I dropped back.

"Did you see Kristy?" she whispered.

"No."

"She was with that Mike — he's a senior. She dated him all August while you were up at camp. They were only at the dance for half an hour or so, and then they left."

"Who were you dancing with?" I asked her.

"You mean that last dance? Ugh, he's really a creep. Wanted to take me home, but I told him I had a ride."

"And that other boy? The one you danced with earlier?"

Eric had stopped a few feet in front of us by a car. We could see his dark silhouette bent over unlocking the door.

Gale said, "Oh, him. That's Rog. He's so-so, I guess, but he's so young. Listen, you don't mind if I ride with you, do you? I could have called Mom."

"What for?"

"If you'd wanted to be alone with Eric."

"Don't be dumb," I said quickly to hush her up, because her voice had started to rise and I was afraid that Eric would hear her.

Eric straightened up, opened the door, and waited for us. When we reached him, Gale asked, "Is this your car?"

Eric laughed. Even I, who knew nothing about cars, knew that this wasn't Eric's car. It was a nice car, not more than a couple of years old, with all the original fenders and seat covers. I wished that just once Jerry and Max would buy a car, even if it was used, that was less than ten years old and still in good condition. They always drove cars that looked like the machine-age answer to the patchwork quilt.

Eric said, "It's my folks' car."

"Do they let you drive it to school?" Gale asked.

"No way. I ride the bus like everyone else," he said, as he walked around to the driver's side.

Gale held open the door so that I could slide in first. I must have hesitated, because she put her hand firmly in the small of my back and pushed. It wasn't that I didn't want to sit in the middle, next to Eric, it was more that I wasn't completely sure that it was me he wanted to take home. Maybe now that he'd met Gale, he was more interested in her. I could see why he would be. She knew how to act around boys. Also, I'd never had a boy interested in me before, unless I counted that creepy Mickey person, who used to sit in back of me in freshman history and was forever following me around in the halls, asking me if I'd like to go to the movies with him.

Mickey was one of those boys who cut school every few days, and when he was there, he spent half the day sneaking around the locker room with a cigarette in his hand, trying to avoid the hall monitor.

About the time I thought he was going to drive me crazy, Gale had told her mother about him, and her mother had told me what to do.

It worked like magic.

The next time he asked me out, I'd said, "I'm sorry, I am not allowed to date."

And sure enough, he'd left me alone and started following another girl.

So when I climbed into Eric's car and sat next to him, I wondered if he'd rather have Gale in the middle. Of course, he hadn't asked her to dance, but then, maybe he'd asked me because he'd seen Gale with me. Maybe he'd thought he could meet her that way and ask her out when he knew her better.

About the time I'd convinced myself that that was the way it was, Eric said, "Tell me where to turn so we can drop Gale off on the way to your house."

If he'd been interested in Gale, wouldn't he have dropped me off first? I thought so.

His car's headlights swept an arc of light across Gale's driveway, displaying the neatly trimmed hedges, the flower beds, and the wide lawn that framed her freshly painted house. A planter box of trailing geraniums sat like a sentry under the carriage lamp by the front door. Everything was exactly where it should be, as though the house and garden had been readied for a magazine layout.

Maybe I should have suggested that Eric leave me at Gale's house. I could have walked home from there later.

But I didn't. Gale thanked Eric for the ride, hopped out of the car, ran to the front door, and waved good-bye to us. As soon as she was inside, Eric backed down the driveway.

"Next door?" he asked.

I pointed out our drive to him, a break in the tall hedge.

His nice car hit every pothole in our dreadful driveway. His lights pointed out the tangle of weeds that didn't conceal the three half-dismantled cars in the front yard. Jerry's clunker was parked by the porch, but not close enough to hide the stack of old boards that Jerry had ripped out of the entry wall. The door frame was still missing, but at least from our angle Eric couldn't see the boarded-up window.

"It's kind of dark. You sure your family's home?"

"My Uncle Max is always home, and that's Jerry's car, but they're probably in the back in the kitchen."

"Wait a minute. I'll leave my lights on and walk up to the door with you."

"Don't do that. You could break your neck. There're so many holes in the walk, I mean." How could I explain that our entry was a booby trap of stacked boards and bricks? I was grateful that Uncle Max had only been able to find a twenty-watt bulb the last time he'd replaced the porch light. It made a dot of light toward which to walk, without showing that the paint had been scraped from the wall a year ago and not yet reapplied.

"All right, but I'll wait until you get inside."

"Thanks, Eric. Thanks for the ride," I said, hurrying out of the car so that he wouldn't have time to change his mind and walk up to the door with me.

Five

Saturday morning I lay in bed watching the sun make patterns on my window shade, my mind only half-awake. I could still hear the music from the dance and see the moving lights, orange and green and purple, swinging across the dance floor. Slowly the colors faded to light and shadow, and the shapes picked up the leaf patterns of the tree outside my window. When the music turned into a steady, metallic banging, I slid out of my dreamworld.

On the far side of the house, Jerry and Max were working on one of their cars. It could have been worse. Instead of clanging metal in the distance, there could have been the sound of a wall in the next room being ripped out. I gave up any hope of more sleep, got up, pulled on my jeans and sweat shirt, and headed for the kitchen. Halfway through the living room, I came to a dead halt. What I saw was beyond belief.

Up to that moment, I really thought I had seen everything horrible that two men could do to a house. But I had been wrong. Here was a new shock.

Vaguely remembering that there had been two large, cardboard cartons in the front room for the past week, I wondered why I hadn't checked their contents before. Then I remembered why. Over the years, I had learned to shut my mind and eyes to the junk that littered our house. I'd learned that if I asked questions, I received half-hour explanations of how that particular item fit into the latest remodeling plan.

This time I should have asked. Had I known what the cartons contained, perhaps I could have talked my uncles into storing them in one of their bedrooms. Instead, they had removed the cartons and left their contents standing in a corner of the living room. What they'd contained were a new sink and toilet for the bathroom my uncles had started to remodel two years ago. If they kept to their usual schedule, the sink and toilet would stand in the living room for another two years.

Gale is never going to believe this, I thought. I caught my lower lip firmly between my teeth, which is a good way to prevent screaming, and marched into the kitchen.

Standing in front of the open refrigerator, I found a piece of bread, wrapped it around a slice of bologna, and stood eating my breakfast, with my bread in one hand and a milk carton in the other. I was too upset to bother pouring the milk into a glass. Not that it mattered. We all drank from the carton when we were in a hurry, a habit that I'd heard Gale's mother complain about in reference to Gale's brother. I'd never told her that we did that at my house. Gale's mother is a very sweet and very proper lady. She insists that everyone sit at the table for all meals. Her table is always neatly set, with a tablecloth, napkins, and correctly arranged silverware.

Uncle Max came in the back door, rubbing his hands together. "Cold out this morning! Hi, Jan, how was the party last night?"

"Very nice," I said. He had asked me the same question when I'd come into the house the night before, but he had also been watching a late movie on the TV and hadn't really heard my answer.

"Much of a crowd?"

"Oh, gosh. Yes. I mean, a person could hardly move."

He looked at me a bit more directly than usual, or at least that's the impression I got, and asked, "What did you do?"

"Oh, uh, stood around talking and listening to the music and stuff. And some parents had brought soft drinks and cookies and stuff."

Max turned on the burner under the coffee pot.

"Glad you had a good time."

"Uh, Max, what — what's that stuff in the front room?"

"What stuff?"

"The sink and the — uh — commode. What are they doing in the front room?"

"They're for the second bathroom," he said over his shoulder as he reached up to lift his coffee mug from its peg above the stove.

"And when are you going to put them in the bathroom?"

"When? Well, pretty soon. Just as soon as we can get the new water lines installed."

I spoke slowly, trying hard to keep my voice from rising. When I get upset, my voice goes squeaky. If that happened, Max would want to know why I was upset, and then I would have to give him a long explanation of why people do not leave toilets in their living rooms, and I wasn't sure I could explain why. At least, not in a way that Max would understand. I knew that as far as he and Jerry were concerned, those two porcelain pieces were merely building supplies, and that's the way they would think of them until they had them installed.

I said, "If you're not ready to use them yet, why did you unwrap them?"

"To be sure they weren't chipped. We got them wholesale, so we thought we'd better check them."

"Well, then," I said even more slowly, "why didn't you carry them on into the bathroom, out of the way?"

Max poured himself a mug of coffee, then wrapped his fingers around it. "Ah, that feels good. My hands get so cold working on the car. Don't you like those fixtures, Janet? Maybe we should have looked for colored ones, but then they wouldn't have matched the tub, and we didn't want to replace the tub."

"White is fine," I said through the very narrow slit between my teeth. "But why didn't you put them out of the way in the bathroom?"

"They'd be *in* the way, there. We've still got to rip out that one wall to replace the pipes. They're safer in the front room, where they won't get knocked over."

I bit down hard on my bread-wrapped bologna.

Max said, "Is that all you're having for breakfast? Better have a banana," and wandered back outside, carrying his coffee mug.

I headed for the bedroom to phone Gale and do a little shoulder-sobbing. As I sprawled across my bed and reached for the phone, it rang.

In answer to Gale's hello, I said, "You're psychic. I was going to call you this very minute."

"Did you have a nice time last night?"

"What do you mean, did I have a nice time? You were with me."

"Afterwards," she said. "After you dropped me off. When Eric took you home."

"I should have got out of his car at your house. Sometimes I forget what a mess this place is."

"Oh, did he go into the house with you?"

"You think I'm crazy? Of course not. I didn't even let him get out of the car. The front yard is enough of a mess, without letting him get closer to the house."

"So what did he say?" Gale asked.

"Say?"

"Didn't you talk at all after you left me?"

"Well, sure, I mean, I told him where our driveway was and I told him good night and I thanked him for the ride, I guess. I mean, I don't remember every word we said."

Gale said, "That's all?" She sounded disappointed.

"What did you expect?"

"Oh, I thought maybe he asked you out. Like to a movie. Or maybe to the next dance."

"Why should he do that?" Not that I wouldn't have liked it if he had, but no boy had ever asked me out except that weird kid who followed me last year. I didn't expect boys to shower me with invitations.

"He danced all night with you."

"He didn't!"

"Well, practically all night. I never saw him dance with anyone else. He must like you."

"Maybe I was the only girl at the dance that he knew." It would have been nice to believe Gale's theory that he danced with me because he liked me more than other girls, but after all, I had danced with him because no one else had asked me. Not that I didn't enjoy Eric's company. I did. But the fact was, we probably danced together because neither of us had anyone else to dance with.

Gale made this kind of sighing moan that

she does when she rolls her eyes. I could imagine her facial expression. "You're impossible," she said. "A darling boy like that, he could have asked any girl to dance with him."

"You think so?"

"Honestly, Jan! You're a sophomore in high school and you don't know anything! Eric came looking for you last night. And when he found you, he stuck with you. He didn't say thanks and walk off after one dance. And he made a big point of going out to the refreshment table with us and of asking if we wanted a ride home."

"Maybe it's you he wanted to take home."

"Don't be dumb! You are really dumb! Did he ask me to dance? He could have, you know, after we came back in from the hall. Or he could have suggested switching partners when I was dancing with The Creep. If he'd done that, I'd have been his grateful slave forever."

"Thanks a lot, friend."

"So, he didn't, did he? He stayed with you. Which is what guys do when they *especially* like you. Which Eric does you."

"You're crazy," I said.

"Uh-huh. We'll wait and see, okay? I'll bet you anything that Eric phones you next week."

She was half right and half wrong. Eric didn't phone. But he did ask me out. He asked me on Tuesday. I was running down the hall, hoping that I could get to my locker to grab my math book, which I had forgotten to take with me, and still get back to math class before the final bell rang. The hall was its usual over-crowded, horror-show scene, with everybody either standing around in groups, blocking traffic, or shoving through groups, using their bodies as guided missiles to make pathways. I had almost made it to my locker when Eric shouted my name.

Glancing around, I saw him halfway across the hall. He waved, pushed past a few people, and fell into step beside me.

"I'm late, and I've got to get all the way back to the west wing after I get my book from my locker," I gasped.

"That's okay," he said and jogged after me. While I frantically spun my locker combina-tion, hit the door, popped it open, and rum-maged through the pile of papers, notebooks, sweaters, and books for my math book, he stood over me. I slammed the locker shut.

"Find it?" he asked.

"Yup." I headed back toward math class. The bell rang. Miraculously, the hall emptied. I kept running.

Eric jogged, his long stride easily carrying him at the speed of my fastest dash. "What's your last class?" he asked.

"Lit," I managed to say. I was really out of

breath by the time I reached my classroom door.

"With Neufeld?"

I nodded, pulled open the door, ducked into the room, and tried to turn invisible as I hurried down the row to my desk. Maybe Eric didn't mind being late, but I did. As I slipped into my place, I wondered what his next class was and if it was even in this end of the building.

My math teacher said, "Forget your book again, Janet?"

I nodded without looking up. I knew the whole class was looking at me, and I felt about three inches tall.

"That's the second time this week, and this is only Tuesday," she said, and the rest of the class laughed. Maybe their laughter put her in a good mood, because she started talking about something else. It took me another five minutes to get myself calmed down enough to look up at the blackboard and follow the problem she was explaining. Even then, I had trouble concentrating. As though it wasn't enough to be late two days in a row, this would be the day Eric followed me down the hall. I tried to push him out of my mind, but the thought of him kept returning. What did he want? Why had he followed me to my locker and then to class? Why did he want to know what my last class was?

I stood automatically when the bell rang, gathered my books, and headed for my Lit class in Mr. Neufeld's room. After carefully arranging my notebook, bag, and books on my desk, I tried to do a quick review of the short story that had been our homework assignment. Although I'd read it carefully, I didn't understand it. I mean, I understood that the main character robbed a bank, was caught by the police, and went to jail, but I also knew that that wasn't all there was to the story. I knew it had some hidden meaning that I had missed, because all our reading assignments had hidden meanings.

The boy who sat in the desk in front of me rushed in just as the bell rang and knocked all my books to the floor. We both bent to pick them up, almost bumped heads, backed away, and muttered apologies to each other.

Mr. Neufeld said, "Janet and Albert, whenever you're done visiting, may we start class?"

I thought about putting my head down on my hastily piled books and remaining there, motionless, until school ended. I didn't need two put-downs in one day.

Mr. Neufeld said, "Janet, would you explain the character flaw in the protagonist that led him into a life of crime?"

There it was, the hidden meaning that I had missed. The message of the story had been about a character flaw. I knew what the term meant, but think as I might, I could not decide what the flaw had been in the man in the story.

In my smallest voice, I said, "He was — uh — he was a thief?"

"He became a thief, yes. But why did he become a thief? That's what we must decide. There's a clue in the first paragraph, and the author refers to it in at least three other places."

I shook my head. Saying, "I don't know," was more than I could manage. It wasn't that I was afraid of Mr. Neufeld. I mean, I knew he wouldn't yell at me or anything like that. But when a teacher stares at me, as he was doing, my mind goes blank. Probably he thought I hadn't even read the story.

He turned away and asked someone else the question. As soon as that student gave the answer, I knew it was right. And it wasn't that hard to figure out. Why hadn't I been able to do it?

After class I rushed into the hall and turned toward my locker. Eric fell into step beside me. He must have been waiting beside my classroom door. As we hurried, I kept swinging sideways to slip between students coming from the other direction. So did Eric. Halfway down the hall and past a crowd of guys who were shoving each other around and laughing, I found myself facing Eric. Not face to face, but more face to shirt.

He said, "I was wondering, that is, I think there's another dance Friday, isn't there?"

"Is there?" I said, trying to find an opening in the next crowd.

Eric stepped in front of me, pushing his way through. I followed. Over his shoulder, he said, "Yeah, there is."

While I tossed the books I didn't want into my locker and pulled out the ones I did want, he stood next to me, his arms stretched out at shoulder height, his hand resting on the top of my locker door. I could almost have walked under his arm without ducking.

Following me back down the corridor toward the outside door, he said, "Are you going?"

I had to throw most of my weight against the door to open it. Eric followed me out and right to the bus stop. I wasn't ignoring him, not at all. I was aware every minute that he was beside me, but I didn't know what to say.

"Are you?" he asked again.

I said, "I'm not sure," as I peered around the other kids, looking for my bus and for Gale. It was one of those days when schools should cancel classes, thereby improving the health of young America. The sky was so blue I had to squint to look at it, without so much as a small, fluffy cloud, while a light breeze stirred the trees along the curb, making their leaves rustle.

Eric said, "We could go together. I could pick you up. If you'd want me to."

I peered up at him. Maybe it was a silly thought, but I've always liked colors, and I couldn't help noticing that his hair was almost the same shade as tree bark and that his eyes, under those long lashes, nearly matched the sky.

I said, "I'm not sure. I mean, I'd have to ask. To ask my uncles, that is."

"What if they say it's okay?"

My bus pulled up to the stop. I said quickly, "Then I guess, sure, I'd like to."

The loading students caught me in the line, half-carrying me onto the bus. I shouldered my way down the aisle until I found Gale. As the bus headed toward our neighborhood, I wondered if I had said the right thing. Maybe I just should have told Eric that I would definitely go to the dance with him. Probably I could have asked Gale and she would have known, but I didn't feel ready to tell her. In the first place, I was worried about what my uncles would say. And in the second place, this was the first time a boy had asked me for a date. I wanted to think about it a while to sort of get used to the idea before I talked about it with Gale.

When we left the bus at our corner, Gale asked, "Want to come over to my house for a while?"

Sitting next to her on the bus, keeping Eric's invitation a secret, had been hard enough. I knew I couldn't spend the afternoon with her and not mention it. I said, "I've got to go right home today."

"Okay, I'll phone you later."

After waving good-bye, I hurried up the road and turned into my drive, losing myself behind the tall hedge. When I'd been much younger, back in third grade, I'd read stories about castles and moats and princesses. In those days I'd loved the hedge, pretending it was the castle wall, separating my castle from all the world. I'd even pretended that the broken-down cars in the front yard were the alligators who defended the moat. I, of course, was the princess.

Now I didn't feel anything like a princess. For that matter, I didn't want to be a princess. I only wanted to be a normal teenage girl, living in a neat house with a neat front lawn. Letting myself into the empty house, my glance immediately fell on the bathroom fixtures in the front room, and I quickly added another want to my list. I wanted my uncles to keep their hobby projects out of sight.

Clearing a place at the kitchen table, I spread out my schoolbooks and began to work on my assignments for my classes the next day. My mind didn't want to concentrate on history. Instead, it wandered through the corridors at school, remembering Eric. One part of me wished he hadn't asked me to go to the dance with him. That was the part that was nervous about telling my uncles. The rest of me was glad he had asked.

Perhaps I needed to approach my problem the way I would work out a school assignment. I mean, when the English or history teachers assigned research papers, they gave us our choice of topics. With that sort of assignment, I made a list of ideas, read over the list, considered how I would handle each subject, and then picked the idea that I would use.

On a clean sheet of paper I jotted down: 1. Tell my uncles at supper that I am going on a date. 2. Ask my uncles if I may go on a date. 3. Tell them that a boy asked me out and see what they say. 4. Ask Max first. 5. Ask Jerry first, definitely. Cross out four.

While I was still thinking over my list, Jerry and Max came in the back door. I sort of slid my arm across my notebook and gave them a big smile.

Max said, "That's what I like to see, a student busy studying. I wish all my students were like you, Jan."

Jerry said, "You should turn on the light. You'll ruin your eyes."

Right at that moment, which was probably the worst possible timing that ever happened to anyone, the phone rang. Jerry picked up the kitchen extension. After he said hello, his eyebrows rose. He held out the phone to me.

"For you, Jan."

I didn't even think to tell him that I would take it in my room. My dumb brain hadn't picked up any signal from his raised eyebrows. Assuming it was Gale, I took the receiver from his hand and said, "Hello."

"Hi, Janet. Eric here. Did you find out if you could go to the dance?"

I glanced at my uncles. Max was busy at the stove.

Jerry remained two feet away from me, watching me.

"Uh, no, I haven't," I said to Eric.

"Oh. You want to ask now while I wait?"

"No."

There was this long pause while Eric thought his own thoughts, probably something along the line of wondering if I was crazy, and then he said, "Did I call at a bad time?"

I said, "Yes."

"I'm sorry. Should I call back later?"

It must not have occurred to Jerry that it might be rude to stand and stare at me while I was talking on the phone, because he stayed right there. I said, "Uh, I'll see you at school tomorrow."

"Oh. Well." Another pause. Then Eric said, "Yeah, that's okay."

After I hung up, Jerry said, "Who was that?"

"A boy from school."

Max turned from the stove, coffee pot in hand, to look at me.

Jerry said, "What did he want?"

Forgetting my list, I blurted out, "He wants me to go to a dance with him next week."

Jerry said, "Go with him alone? On a date?"

I stared at the floor. In a small voice, I said, "I guess so." From the tone of Jerry's voice, I knew that none of the ideas on my list would have been any help.

While I tried to think of a way to explain that I was almost sixteen, a sophomore, and lots of my friends went on dates, Jerry said, "Is this boy in one of your classes?"

I shook my head.

"He's just somebody you've seen at school? Do you know where he lives? Do you know his family?"

As I couldn't answer all his questions at once, I didn't try to answer any of them. Without looking up, I shrugged.

"You don't even know him, and he wants you to go out with him?"

Max made a throat-clearing noise and said, "It isn't Janet's fault if she receives a phone call from a boy she doesn't know."

"I do know him. I mean, his locker is near mine, and I've talked to him — a couple of times —" My brain trailed off with my voice.

Maybe I should have explained about meeting Eric on the train and seeing him at the party, but I couldn't get the words out. Besides, I was afraid that Jerry would find something terrible about all that. Then, too, my throat was tightening up, so I knew that if I said another word, I would start crying. Grabbing my notebook from the table, I ran to my room and slammed the door behind me.

What was the matter with my uncles, I wondered, as I sat on the edge of my bed chewing on my lip to hold back the sobs that kept trying to push up into my throat. Why couldn't they see that I wasn't five years old anymore? Tomorrow I would have to tell Eric that I couldn't go to the dance with him, and then he would think I'd said no because I didn't want to go, and he would forget about me and find another girl to ask out. I didn't want him to ask anyone else out. I remembered how good I'd felt, as though I belonged on the dance floor with him, when the music beat its rhythm and Eric smiled.

There was a small tap on the door. I thought it was Jerry, and I didn't want to talk to him. I glared at the door but didn't answer.

Max said softly, "Jan, are you all right?"

I walked to the door and pulled it open. Max peered at me over his glasses rims. He said, "Supper will be ready in about half an hour."

"I don't want supper," I said, looking away from him.

"Janet, Jerry didn't mean — that is, I am sure this boy who called you is a very nice boy. And it was nice of him to ask you out. He probably doesn't realize that you aren't old enough yet."

I forced myself to ask, "Old enough for what?" and it took a lot of courage because I wasn't used to demanding explanations from Max. He was usually so kind that I seldom had any reason to question him, let alone argue with him. The things I did want to argue about were things that were easier to put off because they were difficult to explain, such as his taste in clothes for me. Or the condition of the house. With those things, it was easier to tell myself that I'd talk to him about it another time.

Max said patiently in his teacher voice, "You aren't old enough to be going out on dates."

"What if — I mean, could I go out if there were another couple? Or some other kids? Or something?" I could barely hear myself, I was talking so softly. It was as though my voice was afraid to say my thoughts.

"Let's think about that. Why don't you wash up for supper? After we've all had something to eat, we'll talk about it," Max said, so I knew that he wanted to go back to the kitchen and find out what Jerry thought of that idea. He added, "How was ballet class?"

"That was yesterday," I reminded him. "It was okay."

It had not been okay, it had been awful. It was held in a huge room that had once been a grocery store and taught by a teacher who was interested in collecting as many fees as possible, but not at all interested in discovering the next Pavlova, or she would certainly never have allowed my uncles to enroll me in the class. I can fall over my own shoelaces even when they're neatly tied. Still, groaning and prancing flat-footed around a huge room filled with other equally clumsy people wasn't as bad as having to practice guitar or having to pronounce French into a tape recorder for an hour each day, as I had had to do for my previous tutors. All the ballet teacher expected of us was that we show up for a two-hour session every Monday afternoon.

"It's supposed to be excellent exercise. I'm sure you'll do well," Max said and hurried off to the kitchen. A few minutes later, I wandered in after him. Right away I could tell, by the tightness around Max's eyes, that I was not going to be allowed to go out with Eric, even accompanied by a brass band and half of the police force.

While Jerry served the *coq au vin*, which was chicken in wine sauce that I would have liked better without the wine, and Max ladled out *champignons provençale*, which I could plainly see were mushrooms, no matter what Max called them, I waited for them to stop comparing recipes and start discussing me.

That happened over the *cafe noire* and *fromages assortis*, which was very strong coffee in small cups served with cheese slices, a combination that replaced dessert when Jerry decided he was putting on weight or Max had been to the dentist. In either case, their resolutions to give up sugar never lasted more than three days.

As Max passed me the cheese, he said, "Jan, Jerry and I don't think that you know this boy who phoned you very well. It's not as though he were the brother of one of your friends."

As all of my friends' brothers were either in grade school or college, I hoped that wasn't going to be the only category of boy my uncles would consider suitable for me. I didn't want to wait for Barb's twelve-year-old brother to grow up before I was allowed to date.

"We really wouldn't feel comfortable about letting you go out alone with a boy," Max said. "But, still, we don't want to be unfair."

Jerry scowled at his coffee. Obviously, he was willing to be unfair, but Max had asked him to say nothing more.

"So what I thought," Max continued, "was this. If you really do want to go out with this boy, why don't you invite him over to dinner, and then we could all go to the movies together?"

My voice died somewhere in the back of my throat, practically choking me. I couldn't answer. There was no answer. How could I possibly tell Eric that I could go out with him if my uncles could come along with us?

As both of them were staring at me, waiting, I finally managed to mumble, "I'll think about it."

The lines around Max's eyes relaxed. He

leaned back in his chair and said, "Now tell me the truth, Janet. Should the marinade for the mushrooms have had a touch more garlic?"

And I knew that as far as my uncles were concerned, the subject of dating-for-Janet was closed.

Six

The next day was another warm one, with shimmering skies and a sort of soft, lazy breeze that drifted through the classroom windows. I sat very straight in my seat, trying to listen to my teacher while on both sides of me boys nodded off to sleep. One slid slowly down until his neck was pressed against his chair back and his eyes were a narrow slit. The other boy gave up completely, resting his face on his folded arms on his desk.

At noon I got my lunch, found Gale, and hurried outside to claim a spot on the front steps.

"I fell asleep in math," Gale moaned as she

dug into her brown paper bag for her sandwich. "I almost fell out of my chair. Now why do you suppose my mother always tosses my banana *on top* of my sandwich? Look at that!"

She held up her mangled sandwich in its plastic bag.

I tried to sound very nonchalant. "Uh, are you planning to go to the dance again this Friday?"

"Sure, why not?" she said as she smoothed her sandwich out by laying it on her leg and pressing it flat with her palms.

"You're mashing the peanut butter out the sides."

"I am? Oh, darn."

I continued, in the same offhand voice, I hoped. "Is, that is, can your mother drive us?"

Looking away, I gazed at the solid mass of bodies that lined the steps and lawn.

"Sure, she will. Look at that, I've got peanut butter on my shirt! And you know what she'll say?"

"Who?" I asked.

"Mom! She'll say, 'How did you get peanut butter on your shirt?' and I'll say, 'Trying to flatten my sandwich,' and she'll say, 'Now, Gale, don't be silly. You're so sloppy.' And she'll really believe it's all my fault!"

I laughed. "Gale, I love your mother. And

everything she says is true. So you must be sloppy."

"Thanks a lot. Hey." She jabbed me in the ribs with her elbow and lowered her voice. "Don't look up but your boyfriend is heading this way. So get your smile ready and prepare your casual, offhand hello."

I almost shrieked, "What!" but bit it back in time. From somewhere above me I heard Eric say, "Hi."

"Hi, Eric," Gale said, and I could practically hear her eyes batting in her tone of voice. "Sit down, we've got inches to spare."

When I looked up and smiled, he said, "That's okay, I can stand." What else could he say? The space between Gale and the person on her other side was maybe six inches wide. He couldn't possibly sit down unless he sat on Gale's lap.

Jumping up, Gale said, "Here, sit here, listen, I just remembered I've got to get some stuff from my locker. See you later!" And before I could ask, "What stuff?" she was gone. If that was Gale's idea of subtle matchmaking, I wasn't too impressed.

Eric took her place on the step. I smiled at him again, unable to think of anything to say, and he smiled back. He had the nicest smile. But he didn't say anything.

As I'm not much good at silences, I said, "Want part of my sandwich?"

"No, thanks, I've finished lunch. I just wondered, I — that is, did you find out about Friday? If you could go?"

"Oh, yes, well," I said, and concentrated on breaking a small piece off of my sandwich so that I wouldn't have to look at him. I never planned to lie to Eric or to my uncles or to anyone. I really never did. And it didn't start out as a lie. I mean, the words I said were true. They were just not quite complete. I knew I was evading something I didn't want to face, but I never meant to let it turn into an out-and-out lie.

I swallowed the bite of sandwich and said, "Uh, I'm planning to go Friday, I mean, I can, but I'm not sure what time so — Gale's mother can drive us there so maybe it would be better if I went with Gale."

Eric didn't say anything. I realized that I sounded as though I didn't want to go with him and was making excuses. That wasn't what I wanted him to think at all, which was why I quickly added, "I mean, can I meet you there? At the dance? Would that be all right?"

Eric said, "I guess so. That is, I sort of wanted — look, I could pick you up any time. I don't mind waiting."

My thoughts spun. I had to say something to make him know that I really did like him, but at the same time make him understand that he couldn't pick me up and that if he wanted to see me at the dance, he'd have to meet me there. I said, "I might be at Gale's house. We — we have some things to do, and Gale sort of expects me to go with her."

"We can give Gale a ride." I liked the way he said *we*, as though he and I had some sort of connection and could be grouped together.

"It's not — I mean, would you mind if I met you at the dance? This time?"

"No, that's okay." He still sounded puzzled.

"We won't be very late," I said, unable to think of what else to say but wanting to keep the conversation going so that he wouldn't think I was trying to get rid of him. What I needed, I thought, a lot more than a math class, was a class in what to say to boys.

Eric said, "After the dance, can I drive you home? And Gale, too, if she wants a ride."

What could I say except, "That would be fine."

Telling Eric not quite the truth wasn't the same thing as telling my uncles a lie, which is what I did next. I'd never done that before, unless I counted the times I'd told them I had loved summer camp or a new frilly outfit or the ballet lessons that they paid too much for because they thought these were things I needed. That sort of lie is not the kind of lie I told them next.

When I mentioned the dance at supper Friday night, I didn't even say that it was a dance because I knew they would wonder if I was planning to meet "that boy." Instead I said that I was going to a school party with Gale and that her parents would drive us there and back.

Jerry said, "I can do that. Or maybe Gale's parents would like it if I picked you up afterward. Then they wouldn't have to go out late at night."

With scarcely a pause for breath, so that I wouldn't have time to change my mind, I said, "I think Gale's parents are going to a movie or something, and they'll pick us up on their way home."

It's a good thing the lighting above the table was poor, because I could feel the blood rising to my face. I knew what I'd done. It was one thing to call the dance a party, so that Jerry wouldn't think to ask about whether Eric would be there, but it was another to make up a complete lie about Gale's parents. I didn't know what their plans for the evening were, but I certainly knew that they would not be picking us up.

Max said, "Aren't you going to wear something fancier for a party?"

Glancing down at my checked flannel shirt, I said, "This is fine. Nobody dresses up, and sometimes it's kind of cold in the gym."

As I hurried from the kitchen, someone banged on the front door. My heart stopped. Surely Eric wouldn't come to my house after I'd told him so definitely that I wanted to meet him at school. But what if he decided to stop by to see if I'd changed my mind and would like a ride after all? He couldn't possibly guess why I wouldn't let him come to the house, so he just might do that. He had some definite, old-fashioned idea that he should pick me up at my house, probably something his parents told him, and it probably reflected good manners, but I wished he were a little less well-behaved.

Shouting, "I'll get it," I rushed to the door.

It was Gale. She peered in. "You ready? We are."

I could see her parents in their car in our drive.

"Wait, I have to brush my teeth."

After calling, "Be right out," to her parents, Gale followed me into the bathroom. While I brushed, she gave me a good staring at, looking me up and down.

"What's the matter?"

"That shirt," she said. "It's awful. It's flannel."

"It hasn't got a ruffled collar."

"No, but it's got long sleeves. You're gonna pass out from the heat once you start dancing."

Leading the way back to my room, I said, "I don't care, I'm not going in ruffles or pink checks, and this is the only other thing I've got."

"Eric going to be there?"

"He's — he's driving us home, if that's okay."

"He won't want to when he sees you looking like that."

"Oh, honestly!" I exclaimed and swung to face her.

"Come on, what about that tennis T-shirt that you brought home from camp? Why don't you wear that?"

"My uncles won't let me out of the house in it."

"Oh." That shut Gale up, but only for a few seconds. She scowled, rolled her eyes, then said, "Tell you what, it just might be cold in the gym. You'd better put on that T-shirt under your flannel shirt."

"Are you crazy?"

"Hurry up, do it, my folks are in a hurry."

Not for one second did I fool myself. I knew

perfectly well what Gale had in mind, and it was something I hadn't had the nerve to do alone, but now that she'd said it and stood over me waiting, I did it. I knew that if I stopped to think about what I was doing, I wouldn't do it, so I stopped thinking and slipped off my shirt, dug out my tennis T-shirt, pulled it on, and tucked it into my jeans. Then I buttoned my flannel shirt over it.

Grabbing my bag, I raced through the house, poked my head in at the kitchen doorway, shouted, "I'm off. See you later!" and ran out the front door toward the car, with Gale at my heels.

After her parents had dropped us off at school, we headed down the long walk toward the lighted doors. The hallways echoed with people-noises.

Gale said, "Stephanie and Barb should be here by now. I wonder if The Creep will ask me to dance again?"

"Maybe he won't be here."

"Maybe it will snow before midnight."

"Yeah."

Gale gave me her sideways look, smiled slowly, and said, "Know what? I was wrong. It's very warm in here, and if you keep on that flannel shirt you will get overheated and catch a serious cold that could then turn into pneumonia. In the interest of your health, you should leave that flannel shirt in your locker."

"Oh, I don't know —" I mumbled, but I really did know. I'd known from the moment I'd pulled on my T-shirt that I would not go into the gym in my flannel shirt.

"Suit yourself," Gale said.

That really set me back. I'd wanted Gale to talk me into taking off my shirt, so that I could somehow blame it on her that I was doing something that was dishonest. But she was right, it had to be my own decision. Leading the way, I went to my locker, pulled off the flannel shirt, and tossed it inside.

Eric was waiting for me by the gym door. He leaned against the open door casually, his shoulders kind of pulled up toward his ears, his thumbs hooked in the back pockets of his jeans, as though he wasn't waiting for anyone and was simply watching people go by. But as soon as he saw me, he straightened up and smiled, so I knew that he had been watching for me.

Gale said, "Hi, Eric. See you later, Jan," and hurried past us into the gym before Eric had a chance to say a word.

I smiled back at him, wishing I were like Gale and could always think of something to say. Eric nodded toward the gym. I followed

94

him inside, through the crowd of warm bodies, my bare arms brushing against other people's arms. Because I was used to wearing flannel shirts or frilly blouses or sweaters at school, I felt undressed in my T-shirt, even though everyone else wore T-shirts, too. And quite a few wore the A-shirts, with their bare shoulders catching the changing light patterns.

When we found an open space big enough to accommodate the two of us, we stopped, faced each other, and began to move to the music. This time I felt much more sure of myself. I knew that whatever I'd done at the last dance, it must have been all right, or Eric wouldn't have asked me to go to this one with him.

During a break in the music, Eric leaned over so that his face was close to my ear and said, "You were wearing that shirt on the train, weren't you?"

"Uh-huh."

"Played much tennis since then?"

"About as much as you've chased chickens."

He laughed and touched my hand. I think right then, at that moment, we both knew that there was something special between us. I mean, it's hard to explain because I don't understand it myself, but I knew that Eric was no longer someone I'd wave to in the hall and then walk by, and I knew he felt the same way about me.

The tennis and the chickens ended up being a standing joke between us, something private that we shared.

After the dance, we dropped Gale off at her house. As Eric backed out of her driveway, he said, "You want to go straight home or would you like to go get a milkshake?"

"A milkshake would be nice," I said.

Eric drove to the Ice Palace, which I'd always thought sounded more like a skating rink than a restaurant. It was one of those round, glass buildings with a counter, a dozen booths inside, and a take-out window. The parking area was filling up as we pulled into a space.

"You want to go inside or eat in the car?" Eric asked.

I almost started to go inside, but then I had this awful mental picture of myself walking in and sitting down in a booth looking across to the next booth, and seeing my Uncle Jerry. As far as I knew, Jerry wasn't dating anyone just now. Jerry never talked about his girlfriends, but he'd been home every evening since I'd returned from camp a month ago, so I guessed that he was between girlfriends. But I could be wrong. And if he had gone out tonight, he was as apt to end up at the Ice Palace as anywhere, because in a town our size, there were only a few places to choose from after ten PM.

"The car's fine," I said.

Eric said, "Yeah, it looks like it's crowded inside. I'll pick up our shakes at the window. What flavor do you want?"

"Chocolate, if that's all right."

Eric's eyebrows shot up. "That's a very unusual flavor. I'll have to check and see if they have any."

I had to laugh at myself. My answer had been so dumb, as though I were asking Eric's permission to choose chocolate. While Eric went off to get our shakes, I glanced around at the other cars, half-expecting to see one of my uncles. What was the matter with me? I hated all this guilty stuff I was going through, as though I'd done something wrong. Was that why I even asked permission to pick a milk-shake flavor? Was I so used to letting Jerry and Max make my decisions that I couldn't make a decision for myself?

Eric leaned through the car window and handed me two shakes. I held them while he opened his door and got back into the car. "They gave me chocolate when I explained that it was for a tennis player. Only tennis players get chocolate."

"What do chicken chasers get?" I asked.

"I told them I wanted two chocolate shakes for the tennis player because tennis makes you very thirsty."

"Didn't they think that was strange? Playing tennis at night, I mean?"

"Now that you mention it, she did look at me as though she wasn't sure she should serve me," he said.

"I'm surprised she didn't slam the window shut," I said.

Eric said firmly, "Next time we go out, I won't ask you what you want. I'll decide for you."

"That sounds like my uncles."

Eric turned sideways in the seat and looked down at me over his milkshake container. In the parking area's overhead lights, the interior of the car was mostly in shadow, so that Eric was a silhouette against the windshield.

He said, "You mentioned your uncles before. Do they live with you or are they here on a visit?"

"*I* live with *them*."

"Uh — what about your parents?"

"I don't have parents. I mean, they died a long time ago."

Eric mumbled, "I'm sorry, I didn't mean —"

I was used to that reaction from people who asked about my parents and then were worried that they had touched an old wound. "It was a long time ago, and I don't really remember them. I've lived with my two uncles since I was six. They're my father's brothers. Max is the oldest and Jerry is the youngest and my father was in the middle."

"Aren't either of your uncles married?"

"Nope. They're a couple of old bachelors. That's what they call themselves, a couple of old bachelors. Not that Jerry is all that old."

"That must be kind of hard for you. Not having an aunt or mother or anyone."

"Well, you see," I explained, "I have an Honorary Mother. Gale's family has always lived next door, and so I have Gale's mother. She always says I'm her Honorary Daughter."

Eric's arm was stretched along the back of the seat, casually, as though he weren't aware of it. Maybe he wasn't. He was turned facing me, with his left elbow propped on the steering wheel, his left hand holding his milkshake. Maybe he wasn't thinking about his right hand, the fingers only inches from my shoulder. But I was. Without moving my eyes, I could see the dim outline of his hand in the shadows. Worse, I could feel it *not* touching me. I mean, that sounds crazy, but that's how it was.

He said, "Seems odd, two bachelors raising a girl."

"You think they should have put me in an orphanage?" I said, trying to make a joke. The reason I was working at a joke was that I wondered if he *would* touch me, or maybe put his arm around me. If he did, I didn't know what I should do.

"No, of course not," he said perfectly seriously. "I didn't mean that, I only meant that I never heard of men raising children. It's — uh — don't you have a housekeeper or something?"

"What for? We all take care of the house together, and my uncles are terrific cooks."

"Your uncles cook?" Eric's eyebrows flew up.

"Sure. Fancy stuff. Gourmet."

"Oh, I see," he said, but he didn't sound as though he really understood at all.

His fingers brushed my shoulder. I could feel them through the light material of my T-shirt.

My mind came to a screaming halt. I mean, like I really panicked. Not because of Eric. All of a sudden I wasn't the least bit worried about Eric. I didn't have time to be. I had a much bigger worry. Staring down at my shirt, I remembered that I had left my plaid shirt in my locker at school.

I felt embarrassed asking, but I blurted it

out anyway. "Eric, could we possibly go back to school for a minute?"

"What for?"

"I — I hate to ask — I know it's a big bother — only the thing is, I left something in my locker. A shirt. I have to have it."

"It's not any bother, and I wouldn't mind driving you back, Janet, but the school will be locked up now. You won't be able to get to your locker."

Even in the shadows he saw my dismay, because he added, "Is it so important?"

I couldn't explain to him. He'd think I was terrible, lying to my uncles about what I wore to the dance.

I said, "No. No, it isn't, it's just that I was going to wear it tomorrow, but I can wear something else. It's — it's okay." And I tried to force an *it's okay* smile as I handed him my empty milkshake container.

After Eric took the containers to the trash can, he asked me what time I was supposed to be home. As I wasn't sure what time it was, because as usual I'd forgotten my watch, I said, "I guess I'd better go home now."

I didn't really want to go home at all. What if Max and Jerry were in the front hall, ripping out the ceiling or something? How would I ever explain to them why I had left the house in a plaid shirt and returned in a T-shirt? Maybe I could ask Eric to take me to Gale's house and then phone my uncles and tell them I was spending the night at Gale's. I did that sometimes.

No, I couldn't do that. Even if her family hadn't gone to bed, her parents would think it very strange if I showed up a half hour later than Gale, without my overnight bag, and said I was staying the night. And I certainly wasn't going to start lying to Gale's mother. She'd see right through me.

All the way home, I didn't say a word, and worse, I didn't realize how unfriendly that must have seemed to Eric. I was so busy trying to figure out what to do, I couldn't think of anything else. I felt like the whole inside of my chest was squeezing together until I could hardly breathe, I was that scared.

Eric stopped in the drive, his car lights picking up the bushes and casting their ragged shadows against the house wall. When he started to open his door, I woke out of my worries.

"No, don't get out. I can walk myself to the door. There're so many potholes! Thanks a lot! Thanks for the milkshake, I had such a nice time," I said quickly, keeping my voice low as I opened the door on my side and hurried out of the car.

"Is something wrong?"

"Wrong? Oh, no, it's only — sometimes my Uncle Max goes to bed early, and his window is right there and I don't want to wake him, so I'll go up quietly," I said as I closed the door very softly and hoped that both my uncles were really asleep. "See you Monday."

I think Eric said, "Okay," or something, but later I couldn't remember, because as soon as I turned away from his car, I had a good, shaking case of fear. If there were some way to go around to the back of the house to peer in the windows to check where my uncles were, I would have done it. But there wasn't. Not with Eric sitting in the drive, his headlights shining on my front door, obviously waiting until I was safely inside. I knew at once that that was what he was doing, because that's what Gale's mother did when she brought me home at night.

I hurried to the door and waved good-bye to his headlights. They didn't move. I clenched my teeth, made a smile in his direction, and slowly turned the knob.

The entry was dark. No uncles. I slipped inside. The sound of Eric's car backing in our drive seemed like a roar. Surely it would bring my uncles running.

Not that they normally ran every time a car backed out of our drive. And not that they rushed out to check my clothing every time I returned home. They didn't. They weren't like that at all. But as I stood there, waiting for my heartbeat to slow down, I imagined all sorts of things that had no basis in anything that had ever happened to me.

Then I heard the TV. I peered around the entry archway. My uncles had forgotten to turn on the lights. In the reflected light from the TV I could see Max stretched out on the couch asleep, and Jerry slumped down in his chair, also asleep.

While my heart went into its overtime act, I tiptoed through the shadows to my bedroom, felt around in the dark for my jacket, pulled it on over my T-shirt, and returned to the living room. My only hope was that neither of them would have noticed that I had not taken my jacket with me.

In the entry I opened the door softly, then banged it shut.

Max remained stretched on the sofa, but Jerry jerked forward in his chair.

"That you, Jan?" Jerry called.

"Uh-huh. What're you watching?"

"Oh, umm, the TV," he said, and I knew he'd been sound asleep.

Max said, "Have a nice time at the party?"

"Uh-huh."

"Want something to eat?"

"No, thanks, they had a lot of cookies and stuff. I think I'll go on to bed."

"Sure, honey, see you in the morning," Jerry said.

I hurried to my room, closed my door, and leaned my back against it. I was shaking so hard I expected the door to rattle. Never in my whole life had I felt so rotten about anything, and I was determined that I'd never go through anything like that again. I would not lie to my uncles. Never again. Not about anything.

That night I really meant it.

But the next morning, when Jerry said, "I must have been asleep when you came home. I didn't hear Gale's car." I didn't tell him that I hadn't come home with Gale's parents. I didn't say anything. Which was still lying.

Seven

Maybe if Jerry hadn't started dating again, I would have had to make a choice between Eric and lying. But he did start dating, which meant that he was out later than I was on Friday nights. With his poor night vision, Uncle Max didn't like to drive at night, so both of my uncles were happy to assume that Gale's parents were providing our transportation. And I did nothing to give them any idea that it might be otherwise. I didn't lie, but I didn't tell the truth, either.

When I was ready to leave the next Friday night, I said, "I'm going over to Gale's now. I'll be home after the party."

Jerry and Max said, "Have a nice time, Jan."

And that was that.

As was becoming usual, Eric drove me home. When we pulled into the driveway, Jerry's car wasn't in sight. And when I entered the house, Max was asleep on the sofa. It never occurred to either of my uncles that I was deceiving them, as I had never done so before. They also assumed that if it wasn't convenient for Gale's parents to give us rides, I would have mentioned that Gale and I needed a ride.

And why shouldn't they assume that? In the past I had always asked for anything I needed, knowing that they would provide it. And a lot more. They constantly bought me books and records that I might have liked when I was ten. They even suggested, over Sunday breakfast, that I take piano lessons as well as ballet, then discussed with each other the cost of pianos. It would have been a terrible sacrifice, yet they insisted that they could afford one.

I suppose I should have said flatly, "I don't want to take piano lessons," but that would have required standing up for myself. Instead I slid down in my chair and let them go on discussing pianos, feeling more like Janet the Rug than ever.

When I told Gale about the piano, she said,

"That's crazy, Tin Ear, everybody knows you're the only kid in school who can't hum 'Chopsticks.' "

"Sure, but tell my uncles that."

"Listen, Jan, you can't let them put all that money into a piano. You've got to say something. Here, I've got an idea. Why not tell your Uncle Max that homework is taking up so much of your time, you wouldn't have time to practice?"

So all the way home from the school bus stop — which was only half a block's distance, but I stretched it by walking slowly — I practiced my little speech.

"Uncle Max, I don't want to take piano lessons because I have too much schoolwork. Uncle Max, I —"

While I wandered around the empty house, putting together a snack for myself, I kept repeating it. Anyone should be able to say one sentence firmly, according to Gale, and I was determined to do so, but when Max came through the kitchen door, I found myself gazing out the window and mumbling apologies.

"It's — uh — Uncle Max, I — you know about that piano —"

"Jer and I are going to town to look at pianos on Saturday." He said it with enthusiasm, as though he could hardly wait to throw away his money, as he puttered around the stove putting on the coffee.

"But — the thing is — I have friends who take lessons and — well, they practice for hours every day."

"That's no problem. Jer and I would enjoy listening to you practice."

Sure, I thought, he and Jerry could go outside and bang on their cars while I stayed inside and banged on my piano, and all the neighbors would be thankful that our houses were not very close together.

"Uncle Max, it's not that."

The fact that I was calling him "Uncle Max" and not just "Max," as I usually did, must have finally dawned on him, because he put down the coffee cannister and came over to the table. "Is something wrong?"

"Uh — no — it's only that — I really don't have time to do all that practicing. With school. And ballet class. And — we've started doing research papers in English class and everything takes more time —" My voice faded into a whisper. Why couldn't I come right out and say no? That's what Gale would have done.

Max said, "Would you rather not take piano lessons?"

"I — I would — I mean, it's terrific of you — only — I'm so busy now."

"You may be right, Jan. Look, why don't we forget about it until next summer, when you have more time?"

"Sure," I mumbled and waited for a miracle, which for once I got.

The phone rang. I said, "That's probably Gale," and ran to answer it in my bedroom. It was Eric.

"Janet? What are you doing?"

I stretched out on my bed and closed my eyes, trying to imagine him in his house, holding the phone. "Talking to you. Where are you?"

"At home."

"Yeah, I know, but where at home?"

"Huh?" He hesitated then said, "I'm sitting on the floor in the kitchen under the wall phone. Is that what you want to know?"

"Uh-huh." Now I could picture him, with his knees up under his chin, his face tilted down. I could even imagine the light dusting of freckles across the arch of his nose.

"Why does it matter?"

"I don't know. I wondered, that's all."

"Were you late getting home Friday?"

"No, why?"

"I wouldn't want to get you home too late. I wouldn't want your uncles mad at me."

"They wouldn't be."

"How do you know? They haven't even met me. Don't they worry about you going out with someone they haven't met?"

My throat tightened. I mumbled, "They haven't said so."

"Maybe I can meet them next Friday."

"The thing is — the house is kind of torn up right now so — they don't like people coming over. It's — we're remodeling."

After this long pause, Eric said, "Janet, are you ashamed to introduce me to your uncles?"

"Of course not! Why would you think that?"

"Oh, I don't know. I thought maybe — maybe I'm not the kind of person they want you to go out with."

"That's crazy!" I rolled over onto my stomach, clutching the receiver in my hands. "It's not that, at all! It's —" Catching my lip between my teeth, I tried desperately to think of a reason. The one that popped into my mind was so true that I was surprised at myself for being able to say it. "It's my house, Eric. It's so awful right now, with walls torn out and all. I'm ashamed to have anyone see it. Please don't be mad."

My voice had risen to a tight squeak. Eric must have thought I sounded odd because I was embarrassed to admit that I was ashamed of my home. Certainly he never guessed that

I was covering up the real reason for keeping him away from my uncles.

He said, "That's okay, I guess I shouldn't have asked. Only I thought maybe — well, if that's all — listen, are you going to the football game Friday?"

"Sure."

"With me?"

"Uh-huh. Do you mind if Gale goes with us?"

"That's fine."

"Could you pick us up at her house?"

By the end of the week, I'd almost forgotten that Eric was a secret from my uncles. It was easier that way. And I was having so much fun having a boyfriend. That's what Eric was, my boyfriend. Everyone in school said so. In gym class one day Nadine shouted, "Hey, I saw your boyfriend at the Ice Palace with some other guys last night."

That was the first time anyone had used that word to me about Eric. I was so surprised I stared at her with my mouth hanging open. But when I thought about it, I knew that she was right. Eric was my boyfriend.

He met me during lunch break every day, and sometimes when we had a few minutes between classes we'd stand together in the hall, talking. He phoned me every afternoon as soon as I got home from school, and we'd talk for at least an hour, until I heard Max's car in the drive. Sometimes Eric would call me again in the evening. Luckily I was always the one to answer the phone. My uncles never asked about my phone calls, assuming I was talking to Gale or Barb.

That Friday, after we'd dropped Gale off at her house, we sat in the car in my driveway and talked. Eric flipped off the car lights, so the only light was Max's twenty-watt bulb, which gave off about as much light as a distant planet.

"You want to go to the movies tomorrow night?" Eric asked.

"I can't!"

"Why not?"

"I — I'm only allowed to go out on Friday nights."

"How come?"

"I guess — well, I only started going out at night this year. Maybe later I can go out on Saturdays."

"Have you asked?"

"No, but — they think I go out too much now. I'm sorry."

"Okay, that's okay. I don't want your uncles to get mad at me."

I hadn't ever asked my uncles if I could go

out more than one night a week, but I had an idea that if I did say I was going out on Saturday, they would begin to wonder where I went at night. As they had accepted the idea that I went to school functions on Friday nights and had stopped asking questions, I was afraid to press them too far. Somehow, sometime in the near future, I had to make them understand that I was old enough to date, but I hadn't thought of a way to do it yet. And I didn't think they were ready yet.

"Maybe — I need to go to the library tomorrow afternoon. You want to meet me there?"

"I don't know if I can get the car in the afternoon."

"I always take the bus," I said. "It stops near my house."

"That's not the same."

"What's that mean?"

Eric turned away from me. He traced the pattern of the wheel with his fingers, concentrating on drawing a slow circle. "I don't know — only — I'd like to take you out, like to the movies or something."

His voice trailed off. I thought I knew what he meant, that he wanted a real date with me where he picked me up at my house and we went out alone, without Gale. At the moment,

I didn't know how we could arrange that. Would he soon tire of picking me up at Gale's or meeting me places? And then would he look around for another girlfriend?

I said, "I'd better go in now." Was he going to meet me at the library or wasn't he? I wasn't sure and didn't know how to ask him.

All he said was, "Good night, Janet."

So the next day, when I pushed open the heavy, brass-trimmed doors of the town library, I didn't know whether I would find Eric inside or not. We hadn't mentioned any time. I'd thought of that before I left home, considered phoning him, and then decided not to.

The library was one of those huge, echoing old square buildings made of stone blocks. Max once told me that it had been built with Carnegie money, whatever that was, and that its duplicates stretched across the country. Everything about the building, except the librarian, said, "Shh-h-h." She smiled and said a loud, cheery, "Hi."

I waved. Even though the librarian always talked in a normal tone, there was something about the high stone arches and the many-paned windows that soared up to the ceiling that made noise seem unacceptable. Wandering past the checkout desk, around a row of bookshelves, through the children's corner and the reference room, I stopped in the magazine room. An old woman sat in a corner by a window in one of the plastic armchairs, reading. My reason for coming to the library was a report due in my history class. After I'd shrugged out of my backpack and dropped it on a long table, I collected half a dozen news magazines and sat down to study them. What I needed was information on the last election.

Thumbing through them slowly, I tried to build up some interest in my subject. Maybe if I'd had a better understanding of politics, or if I were old enough to vote, I'd have been more interested. As it was, I sat there with the sun pouring in the window and warming my back, while the small print swam before my vision. I jerked my head and forced my eyes wide open. What I needed was a radio with some loud rock music to keep me awake. As I jotted down the names of a few political organizations, I noticed that of the six magazines I'd chosen, three had red covers, one had a cover that had a black edge and very dark photo-illustrated center in shades of brown, and the other two used bright blue as their main color. I wondered why. Were bright colors used to attract a buyer's eye to the news rack? Was the brown cover a trick contrast to the bright covers? Half-asleep, I arranged them in a pattern, two across, three down, with red in the alternating spots. The red-blue emphasis disturbed me. Standing up to stretch, I wandered past the shelves and picked off another dozen magazines, then began to spread them across the table to form a color design.

When I'm really bored and can think of nothing else to do, I draw small squares with crayons, making patterns. Now I made the same patterns with magazines that could be rearranged, a trick that was impossible with crayon. Fascinated by the variety of patterns I could form, I didn't notice anyone else walk into the room.

In my ear, Eric said, "That doesn't look like studying to me."

I jumped with shock and bumped into him. He caught my elbows, laughing. Turning to face him, I sputtered, "You scared me to death!"

"You look pretty lively."

"Oh! You know what I mean."

He grinned, his light eyes shining under those long lashes. "What are you doing, anyway?"

"I'm — uh — well —"

"You're not going to tell me that's your homework, covering a tabletop with magazines."

"No-o. No, it's not, only my homework is very boring, and so I started arranging the magazines, sort of."

He studied my arrangement, his head tilted to one side, then walked slowly around the table to consider it from all angles. With the sunlight from the high windows touching his hair, gray T-shirt, faded jeans, and white sneakers, he became a reverse silhouette, a pale outline against the dark background of the bookshelves.

"I don't get it," he said. "They're not alphabetical, and they're not arranged by size." Holding up a hand, he added, "Don't tell me! I'll figure it out."

"Not in a million years."

He made a face at me, curling his upper lip in a silent snarl. "Is it a code? Do the first letters of each magazine name stand for something?"

"Nope."

He bent over the table, peering at the smaller printing on the covers. "It can't be the dates, unless you don't know that July comes before August. Or is it the numbers of the days? Nope. Unless you don't know how to count. Hmmm. Is it something inside the magazines? Some order of information in the articles?"

"It's the covers," I said.

"Something on the covers? The names? The article titles?"

He had circled back to me and stood over me.

"Now you're trying to intimidate me. If you want me to tell you, all you have to do is ask."

"I am not intimidating you. How am I intimidating you?"

"You're standing over me looking down at me. That's very intimidating."

"What?" he exploded, and I swung around, remembering the woman who had been sitting by the window. She was gone. Eric stretched up on his toes. "I can't help it that you're short."

"I'm not short!"

"Then how come I can look straight ahead and not see you?" he asked, staring over my head.

"Because you're on your toes," I said and jabbed him in the ribs with my fingertips. He dropped back on his heels, bent toward me, and caught my wrists. I tried to wrench free. When he wouldn't let go, I turned my back on him, my arms twisting around my body, and tried to hook my foot behind his ankle. His hands slid away from my wrists and he wrapped his arms around me, pinning my arms to my sides. Then he tickled me.

I was giggling so much that I could hardly speak. "Stop that!"

"You started it!"

"I didn't! You did!"

"How do you figure?"

I wriggled my arms around until I could reach his ribs. "By being too tall!" I tickled his ribs again. We were laughing so hard, we both forgot that we were in the library. He swung me around, lifting my feet from the floor as he tried to catch my hands and hold on to me at the same time.

"You're just doing this because you can't solve the puzzle!" I whispered.

"What am I doing?" he whispered back as I managed to free one hand and tickle him again.

"Attacking me."

He turned me around to face him and firmly pinned down both my arms. "All I'm doing is defending myself."

"You'll get us both kicked out of the library," I said.

"Me! You started it!"

"No, you did!"

We were both laughing so hard we could hardly stand. We leaned against each other, shaking. In my ear, he gasped, "Want to call a truce?"

"Yes, all right," I gasped back.

"How do I know you'll honor a truce?"

"Don't you trust me?"

"You're a born truce-breaker, if I ever met one," he said.

I managed to pull my foot back enough to kick him lightly in the shins.

He winced, said, "I *knew* you weren't to be trusted," and tickled me until I was laughing so hard I could barely catch my breath. My sides ached.

Standing in his arms, my shoulders heaving as I tried to stop laughing, I heard myself making hiccuping sounds that were almost like crying.

"You okay?"

"No, I'm choking to death," I said and turned my face toward him.

He peered at me, looking worried, until I stopped gasping and breathed normally. Then he said softly, "Truce?"

Remembering that we were in the library, I whispered back, "Truce."

And then he kissed me. I'm not sure he meant to. He looked sort of surprised, but not as surprised as I felt. Stepping back, but with one arm still around my shoulder, he said, "Let's go somewhere. You want a milkshake?"

"Yes, sure, I guess so."

He grinned. "Is it that hard to decide?"

We spent the rest of the afternoon in a booth at a coffee shop that was two blocks from the library, staring at each other while our chocolate milkshakes turned warm. When it was time for me to go home, Eric walked with me to my bus stop.

During the evening, while Max watched TV and I pretended to watch, I thought about Eric. What was he doing right now? Was he out in his car, riding around town? Was he at the movies? Had he gone alone? Nadine said she had seen him at the Ice Palace once with some other boys, so maybe he'd gone to the movies with some friends and then on to the Ice Palace.

When the phone rang, Max said, "Hmmph?" and half opened his eyes. He was stretched out on the couch, his feet propped up on the arm.

I jumped out of my chair and ran to my room to grab the receiver off the hook.

"Janet?" Eric said. "I had to ask you something."

"Where are you?"

"How come you always ask where I am?"

"I guess it's not important."

"It must be, or you wouldn't ask."

"Well," I said slowly, "I sort of like to picture you. In my head."

"Okay, I'm on the upstairs extension. What kind of picture do you get?"

"Where is the upstairs extension?"

"In the hall at the top of the stairs."

"Are you sitting on the stairs?"

He laughed. "Hey, you want a complete picture, huh? Okay, I'm sitting on the stairs with my feet, hmmm, two steps lower than my, uh, seat, and I'm barefoot."

"What are you wearing?"

"What? Oh, the same shirt and jeans I had on this afternoon. Wow, I can see that I'll have to be careful what I wear when I phone you."

"I'm sorry," I said.

"That's okay. And now I get to ask you a question, and I want a direct answer and no smart remarks."

"Would I make a smart remark?"

"Uh-huh."

"So what's your question?"

"You never did tell me what you were doing with those magazines on the library table."

"Didn't I? That's right. Oh, I was arranging them in a color pattern."

"Why?"

"Because I like to make patterns."

"What kind of patterns?"

"It's hard to explain." I closed my eyes and imagined him on a staircase. As I had never been in his house, I had to make up the staircase. I made it curved, with a red carpet runner and white balustrades, and I imagined Eric's head resting against the balustrades, his long body and legs stretched across the stairs, and his bare feet digging into the carpet.

"Try," he said.

"I like to arrange things — objects, colors, anything. Sometimes I spend half an hour rearranging pencils and books and stuff on my desk."

"What for?"

"I don't know what for. I wish I did. It's just something I do. I move things around until they please me, and I can't even tell you what I mean by that. It's a feeling I get when I put colors or objects together and then have a balance that feels right. I guess that's dumb."

"I don't think so," he said, and he sounded as though he meant it.

After we'd said good-bye, I hung up the phone and lay back, staring at my ceiling. I could see the magazine covers in my mind, the three reds and two blues and a brown that I had started with, and the covers I had picked from the shelf because they were in shades of gold and orange and a hot pink that both clashed and blended with the red.

The phone rang again. It was Nadine, asking me to a party at her house on Saturday night.

"I'd like to," I said, "but I'm not sure if I can."

"Everybody'll be there. Gale and Barb and Stephanie and Willard, did you know about Stephanie and Willard? And Kristy and Mike, and do you know David Overton?"

"Sort of, but not really."

"Oh, darn, I was hoping you did so you could ask him for me. Well, never mind. Anyway, I'll ask Eric, too."

"I'll let you know Monday," I said and spent the rest of Saturday evening watching the TV and wondering how I should go about asking Max if I could go to a party at Nadine's house on the following Saturday. I finally decided to wait until Sunday dinner, when I could ask Max and Jerry at the same time, so that if they both objected, I'd only have to go through being turned down once.

"Saturday nights, too?" Max said when I told my uncles that Nadine was having a party.

Jerry said, "Who'll be at the party?"

I looked away from him, answering, "Um, Nadine and Gale and Barb and Stephanie, and I don't know who all."

Jerry said, "Sounds like fun. I guess it's okay if Nadine's parents will be home."

"Sure, they'll be there," I said, knowing that Jerry thought it was an all-girl party.

E^{ight}

On Saturday afternoon Gale's mother took us shopping, as she did every couple of months or so, and Max handed me two twenties, as he usually did when I went shopping with Gale's mother. I bought a bright red T-shirt.

When I came home, Max asked if I had a nice time and had I bought anything special, as he always did, and I gave him my usual answer.

"Sure, we stopped for hot dogs and shakes, and I bought some pajamas and stuff."

He said his usual, "That's nice, hon," and went back to the stack of papers he was grading.

That night I wore the red T-shirt under one

of my lace-edged blouses, but as soon as I reached Gale's house, I ducked into her room and took off the blouse and stuffed it into my bag. I'd made up my mind that I would not go to Nadine's party looking like a kindergarten child, and the odd thing was, I didn't feel as guilty this time as I had the first time I'd switched shirts.

"You're turning into a hardened criminal," Gale teased.

My confidence collapsed. I felt shaky inside. "You think I should put on my blouse?"

"Don't be dumb," she laughed. "You look terrific."

From the hallway, Gale's mother called, "Gale, Eric's here. Are you and Janet ready?"

She didn't know that Eric was my boyfriend. I mean, Gale's mom would have been the first person that I would have wanted to tell, because she was such a neat lady. She was forever showing me and Gale how to brush our hair to give it more body, or how to check clothing labels so that we wouldn't get stuck with stuff that wasn't colorfast. And Saturday, when we went shopping, she bought Gale some new records and helped us figure out which kind of dance steps went with which music.

I really would have liked to tell her that Eric was my boyfriend. Then I could have asked her anything I needed to know, like what to say when he said, "See ya."

I never knew whether to say, "Sure," or "When?"

And Gale's mother would have told me. Only I couldn't ask her those things, because that would mean telling her that Eric wasn't just our friend, that he was really my boyfriend. If she knew that, she would want to know why he didn't pick me up at my house, and no matter what I said, she would guess that I was going out with Eric on the sly. Despite the fact that she was probably the world's nicest mom, she would never be part of a lie. Also, she refused to do anything that would put her between me and my uncles. Once I had asked her if she could explain to my uncles that I didn't need ballet classes, and she had said, "I can't do that, Janet. I can't tell your uncles how to raise you."

I could understand her viewpoint. It wasn't as though she or Gale's father were close friends of my uncles. They were friendly, as neighbors are, waving as they passed, but nothing more, so she was probably right. My uncles might have resented it if she had started telling them what to do. Still, it would have been nice for me to have her argue on my side.

After giving my hair a last check in Gale's

mirror and noting with regret that my sun-streaks were fading, I followed Gale to the door to meet Eric. Gale looked fantastic in a new T-shirt that had gathered sleeves, and Eric just plain looked fantastic. I don't know why, but for some reason he seemed better-looking every time I saw him. It was a real shame that I couldn't tell Gale's mother about us, because she probably could have explained why I felt that way.

When we arrived at Nadine's house, it re-minded me of Gale's place, with neat hedges and a fancy doorstep light. Inside was a living room with matching furniture, the kind of place they show in magazine ads. The walls and drapes were the same pale blue, and there were matching lamps on the end tables. There were even a couple of huge ferns, one in a beautiful ceramic container on the glass coffee table in front of the couch, the other on top of a bookcase that was filled with neatly ar-ranged ornaments. How I wished our house could look like that.

When I took off my jacket in the guest room and returned to the front room, Eric moved up behind me so close that I could feel him, even though he didn't actually touch me. In my ear he said, "You look terrific in red."

I thought about saying that he looked terrific in anything, but instead I said, "Thanks."

We found a place on the floor by the coffee
table and sat down close to each other. Nadine
had some records playing on her stereo, all the
hit tunes that I heard on the radio. Four or
five kids gathered around her, digging through
her record collection and saying, "Wow!
You've got *that* one," and arguing over which
to play next. Everyone else sat around in
groups, looking at each other, and I think we
all wondered what we were supposed to do.
Anyway, I wondered.

When there were about twenty people in
the room, Nadine's mother poked her head
through the doorway and said, "Nadine! Nadine, dear! Why don't you bring your guests
into the kitchen?"

So we all stood up and filed into the kitchen,
thinking she wanted to feed us something and
didn't want it spilled on the rug. But the
kitchen turned out to be one of those family-
room things, with a big area beyond the table
that was sort of like a second living room,
except that the floor was linoleum. There was
a fireplace that didn't have a fire in it.

Her mother said, "If you boys want to push
back the furniture, you can use the floor for
dancing," and waved at the plaid couch.

While the boys pushed the couch, chairs, and end tables against the walls, Nadine went back to the front room to turn up the sound on the stereo.

After that, we all stood around for a few minutes more, staring at each other, no one wanting to be the first to dance in the middle of Nadine's family room with Nadine's mother watching.

But then her mother said, "Now, all of you help yourselves to the food. I'm going in the other room to read, so if you want anything, holler."

Gale, who usually knows what to say, said, "Thanks, Mrs. Casey."

Nadine's mother had put out a huge spread for us, with little cracker things that had been broiled and tasted like pizza, and plates of donuts, and cider and soft drinks.

Eric said, "Now I'm sorry I ate supper."

I said, "Does that mean I get your share?"

"No way," he said, reaching over my shoulder to pick up a Styrofoam cup of cider.

"You don't have to knock me down. I'll move," I said.

"That's okay. Girls first, boys most."

"What!" I shrieked.

And all of a sudden, I didn't seem to have any trouble figuring out what to do at Nadine's party. Eric and I kidded each other about who ate the most while we both ate more than our share. Then we listened to a guy named Kevin tell some riddles that nobody could guess. While we were still arguing over the answers, someone turned out half the lights, giving the room a kind of dim glow, which made it easier to dance. I mean, with the lights down, I didn't feel as though I was putting on some sort of exhibition.

"Dance?" Eric asked.

"Sure," I said.

"You think you can stay away from the food that long?"

"Who, me? You've eaten twice as much as I have."

"That's because I'm twice as big."

"Oh, you're not!"

"Okay, I'm not," he agreed. He caught my hand, and we started to dance. "But still, on a proportional basis, I get more."

"That doesn't make any sense at all," I argued. "If you reason this through, you will see that I obviously need more food than you do."

"How do you figure that?"

"Because," I said solemnly, "you are already as tall as you need to be. I, on the other hand, could use a couple more inches."

"Why do you want to be taller?" he asked.

"So I can see over the heads in front of me at the movies."

"Oh, I thought maybe you wanted a longer reach for tennis."

"If we're going to get back to that old argument," I said, "I shouldn't think you'd eat anything at all."

"How come?"

"If you were an analytical thinker, you would know that the shorter one remains, the closer one is to a chicken's height."

"Wow! What's with the big words?"

"You started it," I said.

The music had switched to a slow song, and I don't know quite how it happened, but somehow I'd moved into Eric's arms. We were dancing so close that I could feel his breath on my cheek. It made me a little nervous.

"I started it? How?" he asked.

"With some remark about a proportional basis, or something."

"I don't remember."

"Pretty convenient."

"But I do remember some kind of remark about chickens. Are you making fun of me again?"

I giggled, which is what I always ended up doing when we got into one of these silly conversations. Eric pressed his face against mine.

His skin felt warm. I felt like I was burning up.

The music stopped, and we moved apart, neither of us looking at each other. I know because I kind of looked at Eric out of the corner of my eye and he was looking the other way. Past his shoulder I saw Stephanie standing in the circle of Willard's arm, her hand on his shoulder, while with her other hand she pushed her glasses up on her nose. Mike and Kristy didn't even bother dancing. They sat in a shadowed corner, their arms around each other.

Although Eric and I spent the rest of the evening together, following each other around the room from the food to the dance area to conversation groups, we never touched again until after the party.

As always, Eric dropped off Gale at her house before driving me home. When he turned into my driveway, he flipped off his headlights. A dim glow shone through the windshield, a blending of moonlight and Max's twenty-watt bulb. It seemed to me that we sat there for hours, facing each other in the front seat, each knowing what the other one was thinking and neither of us able to think of what to say. I mean, I knew that Eric wanted to kiss me, and I suspect that he knew I knew. What he didn't know was whether I wanted him to, because I wasn't sure myself. It wasn't that I didn't want to be kissed, and definitely if anyone was going to kiss me, Eric was my first choice, but it was more that I wasn't sure how to react. It was different, here alone in the car, from in the library.

Eric said, "I could walk you to the door."

I said, "You'd break your neck. Finding my door is like going through one of those fields that — oh, like in war."

"You mean a field that's been mined?"

"Uh-huh." We'd been through this conversation before, but it helped fill the time. I was always surprised at how easily we could talk sometimes, and how at other times we had such difficulty.

I got out of the car on my side, saying, "I guess I'd better go inside now."

Eric opened the car door on his side. I was afraid to speak across that distance. My voice might carry into the house. All I could do was wait for him to walk around and join me.

"I don't think you should," I said, peering up into the darkness at him.

He put his arm around my shoulders and said, close to my ear, "I'm feeling brave tonight."

So that's the way we walked up to the front

door, with Eric's arm draped around my shoulders. I sidestepped one of those dumb holes in the driveway, catching at Eric's waist with my hand so that he wouldn't stumble. From somewhere out in the weed patch, crickets chirruped. Eric sniffed.

"The air smells so clean here," he said. "You really are in the country."

"Almost," I said, glad that it was dark and he couldn't see the torn-down junk cars in the weeds.

At my doorstep, Eric leaned over me, moving slowly, as though he half-expected me to move away. When I didn't, he kissed me.

I didn't have time to wonder about kissing him back.

Right then, Jerry's car swung into the drive, his headlights catching us.

Startled, Eric stared into the blinding lights. I shrank away from him. I don't think I'd ever been so terrified in my whole life. It wasn't that I had ever had any reason to be afraid of Jerry. It was more that I'd never been in such a situation, and I had no idea how to handle it.

The car door slammed. Then I could hear Jerry's footsteps, then see his silhouette in front of the headlights, then only hear him again as he walked around Eric's car. While

I waited, I could feel my heart pounding. It seemed like years before Jerry stepped into the dim glow of the house light.

Jerry's big, open face looked smaller, as though all his features were scrunched together in an effort at self-control. I'd never seen him like that.

Eric, who didn't know him and couldn't guess the meaning of that expression, said nervously, "Uh, good evening, sir. I, uh, I hope I didn't get Janet home too late."

There was this awful silence. When I couldn't stand it anymore, I said, "Jerry, this is my friend, Eric."

Eric said, "Nice to meet you, sir."

Jerry's voice came out small. "Where's Gale?"

Eric said, "We dropped her off first."

Jerry said, "Do you drop the girls off one by one and kiss them each goodnight?"

Eric stared at him, stunned, his eyes wide, his mouth open.

I gasped, "Jerry, that's not fair!"

Jerry said, "Fair? You said you were going to a party with your girl friends. You didn't say anything about boys. You also didn't leave here in that shirt."

And there I was, spotlighted by the car headlights, with Jerry and Eric both staring at me. It showed all over their faces that they knew I was a liar but they didn't want to believe it. There wasn't anything I could say that would make it right with either of them.

Eric said, "I guess I'd better be going."

Jerry said, "Right."

Eric said, "Uh, I have to get my car out."

Jerry glared at him. For an awful second, I thought he was going to sock Eric. But then he let his shoulders drop, turned, and walked back to his own car.

I said, "I'm sorry," to Eric's back as he walked away from me. He didn't answer, and I couldn't blame him. He had been treated like a boy who had talked a girl into sneaking out without permission. He knew that's what Jerry thought. And I hadn't even defended him, not that it would have done any good. But still, I should have said, "Jerry, don't blame Eric. He thought you knew I was with him."

Only who could say anything, with Jerry glaring like that? I fled into the house.

Slamming the door, I started for my room.

In the glow from the TV, I saw Max sit up on the couch and grope about for his glasses. "That you, Janet? How was the party?"

I found Max's glasses on a packing box that had been shoved next to the couch six months ago and had somehow evolved into a table. "It was okay," I mumbled.

Straightening his glasses on his nose, Max peered up at me. "Something wrong, Janet?"

Until he asked, I hadn't realized that I was shaking. I wasn't crying, just shaking, as though I were freezing or coming down with the flu. I tried to say no, but no sound came out. Max reached over and flipped a light switch. The indirect lighting that he had installed in the ceiling turned the room into daytime. He looked funny standing there under all those little pinpoints of light, his clothes rumpled, his hair sticking out in clumps. I made a sound somewhere between a giggle and a sob, which was the most I could manage. That really upset my uncle.

"You'd better sit down. You sound like you've had a terrible fright. Did someone frighten you?"

I whispered, "Yes, Jerry."

"Jerry! Where's Jerry?"

"He's — oh, he's gonna kill me!" I burst out and then I really did start crying. I hadn't sobbed like that in years, big, wracking sobs that caught in my throat until I thought I'd choke on them. I felt Max's hand on my shoulder, guiding me to a chair. I huddled in it, covering my face with my hands.

The door slammed again. Max said, "What did you do to Janet?" in that soft, polite voice he always uses.

"What did *I* do? You mean, what did *she* do!" Jerry shouted.

Max said, "You've frightened the child."

"Did she tell you what she was doing?"

"No, but I'm sure there's no need to shout."

Jerry went right on shouting. "She was standing in the driveway necking with some strange boy!"

There was this long, awful silence. I wanted to say that first, Eric wasn't a stranger, and second, he only kissed me goodnight and we were *not* necking, and third, Jerry had ruined my whole life because how was I ever going to be able to go back to school where I would have to face Eric? But I couldn't say anything. None of my arguments made any difference. What mattered to my uncles was that I had lied to them. I felt so rotten, all I could do was sob.

Max spoke first. His voice always stayed calm, I suppose from years of practice as a teacher. He said, "Janet. Honey. Maybe you'd better go on to bed. It's late."

Without looking at either of them, I ran out of the room. As I reached my door, I heard Jerry shout, "Is that all you've got to say!"

Max said, "I don't think it will happen again."

"You bet it won't!"

Closing my door behind me, I threw myself across my bed. What was Jerry going to do, lock me up and bar the windows? Not that he had to. If Eric ever told anyone how my uncle had shouted at him, no boy would dare come near me again. Not that I wanted any other boy. Eric was the only boy who mattered to me.

Sunday morning I didn't leave my room until after I heard Jerry's car back out of the driveway. It was almost noon. When I entered the kitchen, wearing my jeans and plaid shirt and a very frozen face that wasn't going to betray me by frowning or crying, Max stood at the stove. Autumn sunlight streamed through the window, making leafy patterns on the bare wood table top.

Max said, "Good morning."

I helped myself to milk from the refrig, grabbed a banana from the bunch on the counter, and retreated to the far side of the table where I could stare out the window. Behind the house stretched an old orchard of gnarled pear trees that no one bothered harvesting anymore. Their leaves were beginning to turn. The tall grass between the dark trunks moved softly in the morning breeze, a golden ripple of reflected sunlight.

"Janet, Jerry and I have been talking."

I was sure they had. I wasn't sure I wanted to hear what they had to say.

Max went on softly, "We would like to meet your friends. Why don't you have a party here?"

Inside, my mind screamed the answer. I could just see my friends coming into this house, stumbling over a pile of lumber in the front yard, edging their way around the rolls of carpeting in the hall, and then stopping, speechless, to stare at my uncles' idea of interior decorating in the living room. I was probably the only teenager in the whole world who had a toilet in the living room.

I shook my head.

Max said, "Well, think about it, will you? And, Janet, we were talking about something else, too. We've agreed that maybe we were wrong. Maybe you are old enough to go out on a date occasionally. But, uh, we really would like to know the boy before you go out with him."

All I could do with that suggestion was shudder. In the first place, Eric would never come back to my house to meet my uncles. In all likelihood, he would never speak to me again, so I wouldn't have the opportunity to ask him, anyway. And in the second place, there was no way I could think of to say to a boy that my uncles wanted to get to know him before I was allowed out the door with him.

Max said, "Janet, Jerry knows a nice young man. He's the younger brother of a friend of Jerry's. He thought that perhaps you might like to go out with him some evening."

Why did I suddenly feel as though I were living in one of those foreign nations where parents prearranged marriages for their infant daughters? This time I managed to answer. I said, "I don't think so, Max. But thanks, anyway."

Leaving my banana and glass of milk untouched on the table, I walked out the back door and cut across the yard and through the hedge to Gale's house.

Gale was washing her hair, so I stood in the bathroom talking to her over the sound of running water behind the shower curtain. I loved Gale's bathroom. Everything matched, from the curtains to the carpet to the wallpaper and towels. There were even small bars of seashell-shaped guest soap in glass jars above the dressing-table sink. While we talked, I rearranged the jars into a pleasing pattern of sizes.

After I'd told Gale my whole awful tale, she called, "So why not have a party?"

"You're joking, I hope. Can you imagine the kind of party my uncles would give? They'd probably hand out paper hats and expect everyone to bob for apples."

The water stopped running. Gale poked her head around the curtain. "Your uncles aren't that bad. They wouldn't do that."

"That's what you think. And can you imagine what would happen about the time one of the boys *breathed* on a girl? My Uncle Jerry would rush in screaming, 'Rape!' and throw them all out."

Gale laughed. "I think you're overdoing it. Your Uncle Jerry is really very sweet."

"He used to be sweet. Recently he's turned into a monster."

Gale disappeared behind the shower curtain, then reappeared wrapped in a towel. She stepped out of the shower and walked to her room, trailing wet footprints. I followed her. While she rummaged around in her closet, deciding what to wear, I stretched out on her bed.

She said, "I've been thinking about that. You know what I think is the trouble with your uncles?" She stopped, held up three T-shirts one at a time, tossed two back into her closet, and then continued both talking and dressing. "I think your uncles can't face the fact that you're not a little girl anymore."

"You're telling me?"

"Thing is, you're going to have to prove to them that you are practically an adult."

"How do I do that?"

Gale stared at her reflection in the mirror. "I hate my stupid hair."

"Gale, what should I do?"

"You aren't going to like my suggestion."

"Tell me, anyway."

Turning from the mirror, she waved her brush at me to emphasize her words. "If I were you, I'd go ahead and go out on a date with that friend of Jerry's."

"I don't want to go out with someone I don't know!"

"Why not? He must be a very shy, quiet, proper person or Jerry wouldn't suggest it. So all you have to do is put up with one boring evening at the movies with him."

"And what will that prove?"

"It will prove that you are old enough to date. The next time someone that you like asks you out, your uncles won't be able to say that you aren't old enough."

As much as I hated the idea, I could accept Gale's reasoning.

Jerry mentioned his friend's brother to me again when we were eating dinner, saying, "Doyle really would like to meet you, Jan."

I couldn't look at Jerry yet. Instead, I stared at my plate, not answering.

Jerry said, "Jan, I'm sorry I shouted at Eric. Do you want me to phone him and apologize?"

As Jerry was a very proud person who did not like to admit when he was wrong, I knew that he must feel very guilty to make that offer. And, too, I couldn't go on not speaking to him forever. We had to live in the same house.

I said, "No, it doesn't matter."

Jerry must have thought that my answer meant that I was no longer interested in Eric, because he said, "Then what about it? Would you like to go out with Doyle?"

Despite all my doubts and best instincts, I remembered Gale's advice and said, "Sure, I guess so."

Actually, it seemed pointless to bother now. As I had told Gale, it no longer mattered whether my uncles considered me old enough to date. No one wanted to date me. At least, no one I wanted.

I spent the next miserable week at school being ignored by Eric. He passed me in the halls twice a day. The first couple of times, I said, "Hi," and forced a smile.

He nodded.

By Wednesday I was too intimidated to even open my mouth. And so when I'd see him approaching down the long hallway, I'd duck sideways and walk close to the lockers on the far wall.

When I knew he was past me, I'd turn and stand still, watching him walk away. Once I thought he swung around just as I turned, as though he had turned to watch me and then saw me stop and so had quickly continued on his way, but I wasn't sure. If that was what caring for a boy was like, I decided I'd rather forget boys. They weren't worth the misery. Unfortunately, although I reasoned all that out and knew I was right, I still missed Eric terribly.

Nine

I went out on my first real picked-up-at-home date with Jerry's friend's younger brother. Before he arrived, I managed to scatter the pages of the evening paper over the toilet, concealing it fairly well. If he thought it odd that we had a bathroom sink and a mountain of newspaper in our front room, he never mentioned it to me.

As soon as I met Doyle Boynton, I knew I had never seen him before in school, which was just as well because I definitely never wanted to see him again. The reason I hadn't seen him was that he attended a private school for super-intellectuals, or at least, that was what Jerry told me.

Doyle was dressed in a suit and tie to take me to a movie. I was dressed in a ruffled pink blouse, a full skirt, panty hose, and flat-heeled pumps, all uncle-approved. We looked like something out of the Victorian era.

"Doyle, this is my niece, Janet," Jerry boomed in his Jolly Giant voice.

"It's my pleasure to meet you, Janet," Doyle said in this teacher's pet, sticky sweet voice.

Jolly Giant walked us to the door, exclaiming, "You two have a nice time!"

It wasn't easy, but I managed a sickly smile.

I will say in Doyle's defense that he was average-looking, and maybe a little on the above average side, with clear skin and clean fingernails. I noticed those things because there was nothing nice to notice about Doyle except his looks. We went to the movies in his parents' car, which he drove with an abandon that made me quickly buckle on my seat belt.

As the car turned out of town, I asked, "Where are we going?"

"Over to Allenton," he said. "There's a great show at the Paramount."

"That's fifteen miles," I said. "I thought we were going uptown."

"Nothing on uptown," he said. "You'll like this show, baby."

No one had ever called me "baby," and I hated it. But still, so far all I had against Doyle was the way he drove, so I said, "What kind of show is it?"

"If I told you ahead of time, you wouldn't be surprised."

Right then, I should have insisted that he turn the car around, but I'd never been able to tell other people what to do. We sped down the highway, probably setting a record for the time required to reach Allenton. Doyle parked in a lot behind the theater. As we walked along the dark sidewalk, he put his hand on my waist, as though he were guiding me. I moved faster, away from him, to the lighted walk in front of the theater. In the back of my mind a suspicion about the show had been growing, and when I saw the marquee, I found I was right. It was one of those stupid horror shows. I know horror movies are popular, but they give me nightmares.

Probably I should have asked Doyle about the movie when he first picked me up, but I hadn't thought to ask him anything. I'd let Jerry do the talking, giving a cheery little speech about where I went to school and where Doyle went to school and how he had known

Doyle's sister for years. Now it was too late to object to the movie. There wasn't any other theater in Allenton, and I certainly didn't want to drive to the next town.

We stood in the lobby, waiting to reach the popcorn counter.

Doyle said, "See that girl over by the water fountain?"

I looked through the crowd. The Allenton theater was one of those old ones, built in the thirties, with arched doorways, stuccoed walls, and heavy velvet curtains. Underfoot was a heavily patterned carpet in a dull orange-brown that might originally have been red but had faded. Overhead were crystal chandeliers that were so dusty they gave off very little light. I could barely see the girl by the fountain.

"Used to date her last year," Doyle said.

She was very pretty, but I thought it odd that he should tell me about who he dated. I mean, why should I care?

Doyle said, "She's one of those beautiful but dumb dolls. After the first couple dates, a real bore. See that girl just walking in the door? That's Annette Something, never can remember last names, anyway, I went with her my freshman year, but she was a real baby. She's turned out okay, though. Guess I ought to call her again. Say, what year did you say you were?"

"Sophomore," I said. "What year are you?"

"Junior," he said. "I could graduate this year if I wanted to. I really should be a senior because the school counselor said I was way too smart to take the regular program. She wanted me in the accelerated class. I'd have finished up a year sooner. But the way I look at it is that who wants to wind up on a college campus at sixteen, right? I probably could do it, because I'm tall for my age and everyone thinks I'm older. I've dated lots of college girls and they always think I'm a college man, but still, why rush it, huh?"

We reached the counter. Doyle bought popcorn for both of us. Then he put his hand on my shoulder and steered me toward one of the archways. As we passed a group of girls, he called, "Hi, Andrea!"

A girl looked up, gave a small smile, and looked away.

Doyle said, "She's in my math class. Dates a friend of mine."

As the lights lowered, Doyle spotted two seats. He led the way into the row, pushing past people's knees. We sat down, and the theater went dark.

Doyle passed me the popcorn and said,

"That Andrea is only a sophomore, but she looks a lot older, don't you think? She's got a lot of class. I like a girl with class."

Someone behind us said, "Shhh."

Doyle shrugged, slid down in his seat, and munched popcorn all the way through the selected short subjects and the coming attractions. When the main feature started, he sat up and moved about. I could hear him, but I couldn't figure out what he was doing until I felt his hand touch my far shoulder. He had his arm around me. I leaned forward. The tilt of the seats made that uncomfortable. There was no way I could sit away from the seat back for the whole picture.

"Look who's in this," Doyle said. "She's a knockout."

In the light from the screen I saw his profile. He stared at the credits for the main feature as though he was unaware that he had his arm around me. As the movie began, his hand tightened on my shoulder. I tried to move away from him, leaning against the far armrest. Doyle leaned over the armrest between us to whisper close to my face.

"I'm sure glad we got here in time. I hate getting to a movie late. Some girls are never ready when you pick them up, and then you always miss the first part of the show."

If I edged any further away, I'd be up over the armrest and into the lap of the man in the next seat. Ten minutes later I hadn't heard a word of the movie. Or even seen any of it. Instead I'd been sitting rigid, watching Doyle's free hand move across the armrest toward my hands. Even though I'd moved away from him, he'd kept his arm on my shoulders. To my horror, his other hand closed over my hand.

I sat motionless for another five minutes. Then I found the nerve to pull my hand free. I pretended that my bag had slipped off my lap, which also gave me a chance to lean forward, away from his arm.

As soon as I sat back, he put his arm around me again and edged closer. This time he practically had his head on my shoulder. He started to run his other hand up and down my arm.

I stood up, almost knocking him out of his seat.

"What'cha doing?" he whispered.

Leaning toward him, I whispered, "I'll be right back," and then edged away from him, climbing past knees, until I reached the aisle. I hurried up it to the lobby. At the archway, I paused to look back. Doyle hadn't followed me. He probably thought I'd gone to use the restroom. Instead I went looking for someplace to be alone and think. The first place I spotted was a phone booth in a shadowed niche at the far end of the lobby. I sat down on the little seat inside it, leaving the door ajar so that the overhead light wouldn't come on.

What was I supposed to do now? If I couldn't get Doyle to keep his hands off me in a crowded theater, what was I going to do alone with him in his car?

And how had I got into this mess, anyway? Why was I fifteen miles from home with an octopus? Because of Jerry, that's why. Because Jerry thought he knew better than me how to judge a boy. Because Jerry thought I wasn't old enough to pick my own friends. I had a mind to phone Jerry and let him drive over to Allenton to pick me up.

But as I rummaged in my bag for change, I realized that it would take Jerry twenty minutes, at least, to get here. I wasn't going to sit in a phone booth for twenty minutes. In another five minutes Doyle would probably come out to the lobby to look for me, and what would I do? I wasn't about to explain to that creep why I had phoned my uncle to come get me.

Above the phone in the booth was an advertisement card with names and addresses of some restaurants and two taxi companies.

Why not? I dialed the phone. When a voice answered, I said, "How long would it be before

I could get a cab? I'm at the Paramount."

The voice said, "About two minutes. I've got a car cruising near there now."

"All right, I'll be out front," I said and hung up. I knew that I didn't have enough money to pay a cab and that a fifteen-mile drive wouldn't be cheap, but I was so angry with Jerry that it seemed to me the least he deserved.

As I pushed open the heavy glass door and stepped out into the clean night air, a cab pulled up to the curb. I climbed into the back-seat. I'll admit that I was kind of relieved to see that the driver was a woman. I was thoroughly sick of males at that moment.

"Nice night," she said.

I agreed and gave her my address. As she drove off, she said, "What's that movie like?"

"I don't know. I didn't stay to see it."

"Uh-huh. Pretty rotten, huh?"

"I, uh, I got this terrible headache." I knew she didn't expect me to explain to her why I'd left the movie early, but I felt as though I had to say something. She had her car radio turned to a rock station, so after that I sat back and neither of us spoke.

When she turned into the drive, I said, "Could you wait a minute? I've got to go get some money from my uncle. How much do I need?"

She said, "Twelve bucks, even."

My heart stuck in my throat. I knew Jerry deserved to pay a lot more, but knowing it and telling it to Jerry weren't the same things.

I hurried up to the house, walked into the living room, took a deep breath, and then in a very small voice said, "Jerry, there's a taxi outside that I owe twelve dollars. And a tip, too, I suppose."

Max and Jerry were in front of the TV, as usual. Jerry looked up, surprised. Something in my face must have told him that I wasn't joking, because he gave me a puzzled look and headed out to the driveway. Max got up slowly from the couch and switched off the TV. He said softly, "Are you all right?"

I nodded. Max didn't say anything more until Jerry returned.

As soon as Jerry closed the door behind himself, he said, "Now what's all that about?"

In my mind I had framed a neat speech. I'd had that ride home in the dark backseat of the cab, and I'd worked it all out. I was going to say politely, "Your friend the creep couldn't keep his hands off me, and I do not remain with such people," and then walk out of the room, my head high.

But instead I blurted, "It's all your fault, Jerry! All I can say for your friends is that they're a bunch of creeps, and from now on I'll thank you to stay out of my life because I am almost sixteen years old and I am very well capable of picking my own friends and that goes for everything else, too. Including my clothes and my hobbies and my summers and just plain everything! Have you got that?"

By the end of that speech, I was screaming. It was the first time in my life I had ever screamed at either of my uncles.

Jerry shouted back, "What were you doing in Allenton?"

And I shouted, "That's where that creepy Doyle took me, to see some rotten horror film, and then he spent the whole time pawing at me, and let me tell you something, I *know* why that boy goes to private school, he goes to private school because his parents don't want the public to know they have such a rotten kid, that's why!"

Somewhere in the middle of that tirade, Max said, "He did *what*?"

I shouted, "He had about fifteen arms that he kept trying to put around me, and he kept feeling my arms with his creepy hands, and if that's your idea of a *nice* boy —"

Max said, "Good Lord!"

But I wasn't done. I don't know what happened to me, but once started, I was unleashed.

I glanced down at myself, saw my stupid clothes, and said, "And that's not all! I was the only girl in that movie theater in a ruffled blouse, and from now on I am going to pick out my own clothes so that I look like everyone else, and I am going to quit taking ballet lessons that I hate, and — and —" I pointed a shaking finger at Jerry. "And you are going to move that ugly, awful toilet out of the middle of the front room and put it in the bathroom where it belongs, so that I don't have to be ashamed to ask my friends over!"

And with that, I did march out and up to my room, slamming the door behind me.

Things were strained around our house for the next few days. I could definitely see that Max and Jerry had had an argument. They didn't joke about the menus at supper. Worse, they didn't talk at all. We had some dreadfully silent meals. And all day Sunday, while Max pounded on a car outside, Jerry ripped pipes out of the bathroom. I'd never before seen them work on different projects at the same time. They always worked together.

When I went off to school in a T-shirt on Monday, both of them saw me leave the house, and neither of them said anything other than, "Have a nice day."

Ten

The late autumn warm spell lingered, shimmering on the sidewalks and sweetening the air. At noon we lunched outside on the steps. I was halfway through telling Gale about my disastrous date when she tilted her head, narrowed her eyes, and hissed at me from between smiling lips, "Guess who is coming over here."

Then she jumped up, said loudly, "I forgot, I have to check some books out of the library," and dashed off.

I was still staring stupidly after her when Eric eased down into the vacant spot she had left. He said, "Hi."

I said, "Hi."

"How you been?"

"Fine. And you?"

Probably it set some sort of record for trite conversation. I wished I could think of something friendly and casual to say, but after a long silence during which both of us did a lot of staring at our hands, all I could think of was, "I'm sorry about the other night."

Eric didn't answer.

I took a deep breath and made myself go on talking. "I mean, I really am. So is my Uncle Jerry. He offered to phone you to apologize."

Eric said, "Why?"

"I told him that you thought he knew that I was with you. That it wasn't your fault. He thought you knew I'd been lying. That's what he was mad about. The lying."

"Why did you lie?"

"My uncles said I was too young to go on dates."

"I wish you'd told me that."

"I should have."

Eric said, "I could have maybe gone over and met your uncles. Like on a Saturday afternoon. They might not have minded that."

"I know that's what I should have done," I said. "I know that now. But I didn't think of it then. Would — would you like to come over this Saturday?"

Eric turned his head away to stare out across the school lawn toward the row of trees that lined the walkway. Students lounged in the shade, bright dots of color in the moving leaf shadows. He said softly, "I don't think so."

I bit my lip to keep back the tears that threatened to fill my eyes. "Aren't we friends anymore?"

He said, "We're still friends." But he said it quickly as he stood up. Without looking at me, he walked away. So I knew what he meant. He meant he wasn't angry with me anymore, and he also meant that he wasn't interested in dating me anymore.

By blinking very hard, I managed to keep the tears from falling. As it turned out, I might as well have let them fall. I didn't see anything else that happened that afternoon, anyway. My classes began and ended, bells rang, people answered questions, teachers gave assignments, locker doors slammed, and finally, my bus pulled away from school with me on it. Gale sat beside me, peering into my face. She didn't ask me what Eric had said to me. All she had to do was look at me and she knew.

When we got off the bus, she invited me to her house. I shook my head. Gale said, "Hey, there're other guys besides Eric."

I managed to mumble, "Yeah, Doyle."

Gale giggled, said, "I'm sorry," and clapped her hand over her mouth. I had to giggle, too. It hurt. Giggling and crying at the same time is very uncomfortable.

Gale tilted her head, narrowed her eyes, and did that slow smile thing that she does. "Think of all you can learn from Doyle," she teased. "Such an enriching experience!"

I stopped crying and made a face at her. "You mean like how to go to a movie with an octopus?"

"No! You can learn about every girl in the county. Sounded like he dated them all."

I said slowly, "That was odd, wasn't it? I wonder why he kept pointing out girls to me?"

Gale, who probably thought more about boys than I did, said, "I've heard of guys like that before. They're usually creeps. So they try to make girls think that other girls are crazy about them by constantly talking about other girls they've dated."

"I never thought of that."

"What you should have done," Gale said, "was point out other boys and say things like, 'That's Sam over there. When he takes me out we go to expensive restaurants.' Things like that."

"But I didn't see anyone I knew, and I've never gone out with anyone but Eric!"

"So what makes you think Doyle had gone out with those girls he talked about? He probably even made up half the names."

"I guess so," I said. "See you tomorrow." There wasn't any reason for me to hurry home. The sun was shining, the insects were buzzing in the hedges, and the air smelled of a leaf fire somewhere in the neighborhood. We could have stood talking for as long as we wanted, if only I hadn't felt the lump returning to my throat. I couldn't talk about Doyle or anything else when my mind was full of Eric. And I wasn't ready to talk about Eric, not to Gale, not to anyone. I had to be by myself to think over what he had said to me and to get used to the idea that he was not my boyfriend anymore and never would be again. Waving goodbye to Gale, I headed home.

As I walked through the front room to drop my books on the kitchen table, I had a feeling that something was missing, but I couldn't think what it was. Opening the refrigerator, I peered in, tried to decide what I wanted, realized that it didn't matter at all as long as I tossed something in my empty stomach, and ended up pouring myself a glass of milk. Glass in hand, I wandered back out to the front room. What

I was really thinking about was Eric, the way the corners of his mouth turned up before he spoke, the way his hand felt holding mine, things like that.

Going out on a date with dumb Doyle had been a waste of my effort and Jerry's money. I had done it to convince my uncles that I was old enough to date. But it didn't matter whether they thought I was old enough or not. I might as well spend the rest of my life in ruffle-collared, pink-checked blouses. There wasn't even any point in going to the Friday dances anymore. Even if someone else asked me to dance, I wouldn't want to because if I danced with another boy it would only remind me of the times I had danced with Eric, and I would probably start crying right there in the middle of the dance floor.

All the rest of my life was going to be as drab as our front room, with its old brown couch and easy chair that had belonged to my grandparents, and the packing-box end table, and the bare floor.

As I studied it, I realized that the room itself wasn't bad. The rebuilt fireplace was really very pretty, except that its mantle was empty and the couch was pulled in front of it so that Max could watch the TV from the angle he liked best. The fireplace remained unused and ignored, one more project that my uncles had started with great enthusiasm and then abandoned.

Why did they do that, I wondered. They had completed the fireplace, and done a neat job of it, but then they had left the floor around it a patchwork of worn linoleum, not bothering to lay the new carpet they had bought. It was still rolled up in the hallway where we had to keep stepping over it. And then they had enthusiastically replastered and painted the walls a very pleasant cream color that I had picked out to blend with the gold carpet, and which caught the sunlight that streamed through the wide south window. But they had never bothered replacing the moldings that had been removed during the painting. And as for the window, with its peaceful view of the old orchard, they had temporarily moved a bookcase in front of it while they painted and then never removed it, so that the view was almost completely blocked.

Maybe the problem with my uncles was that they enjoyed their projects — whether they were laying bricks or papering or rebuilding a staircase — in much the same way that they enjoyed rebuilding old cars, but they didn't really know how a house should be decorated.

They didn't study room arrangements of furniture in magazine ads the way I did.

The back door slammed. Max called, "Hi, Janet."

"I'm in here," I said.

He wandered into the living room. "Nice day."

"Max," I said as I continued to stare at the room, "why does the couch have to be like that?"

"Like what?"

"Like in front of the fireplace. Wouldn't it be nicer if we moved it over here, so that when we sat on it we could look out the window, and then maybe the bookcase could go over there by the corner, and see, we could put the other chair there and —"

Max said, "Sure, if you want."

I closed my mouth and stared at him. He meant it. He didn't care a bit where I put the furniture. He and Jerry had pushed it around to make room for their projects and simply left it all in the last spot each piece had reached. The way they'd unwrapped the sink and toilet and left them in the front room.

And then I knew what was missing. "What happened to the bathroom fixtures?"

"Jerry put them in his room. He didn't know you didn't like them out here until you said so."

"What do you mean, *I* didn't like them? You mean that you and Jerry did like them in the front room?"

Max said, "No-o-o, it's just — I guess neither of us ever noticed them again, once we'd unpacked them."

"You didn't notice?"

"No, but if it matters to you, then we want you to say so, Jan. We don't want you to be ashamed of your home. We want to have it look however you think it should look, only I don't think either Jerry or I is much good at that sort of thing. What do you think?"

Maybe I would never have told him if he hadn't asked, but he had asked. I said, "I think that the first thing that needs doing around here is putting the carpet in the living room, and then the furniture should be arranged right. And honestly, that couch and chair are awfully worn-out, but maybe if I took an upholstery class I could fix them up, if you don't mind."

Max looked really surprised. "You want to take an upholstery class?"

"They have them at night at the park department, Max. And let's face it, I'm not graceful or athletic or musical, so all the ballet and piano and singing and riding lessons in the world aren't going to do me much good, but I really do like to see the way people do rooms. I mean, I think I might like to do that, like to learn how to re-cover furniture and decorate rooms."

"I never thought of that," he said.

"I'm almost sixteen. I'm old enough to think of what I want to do."

Max grinned and put his hand on my shoulder. "I guess you're right, Janet. And you're right about this room. As soon as that brother of mine gets home, we'll start unrolling the carpet."

Wednesday night Gale came over to see our front room. As I had talked of practically nothing else for two days, she was very curious. When she walked in the front door, she stopped, threw up her hands, let her mouth drop, and went through this big, overacted routine of astonishment, delight, and surprise.

Max glanced up from his usual place on the couch. The couch, however, was not in its usual place. And the room really did look like somebody's else's house, with the gold carpet installed, the baseboards replaced, the furniture arranged to take advantage of the view and fireplace, and with a few touches of my own, such as a tablecloth to hide the packing box and a vase filled with dried flowers on the mantel.

Jerry hurried out of the hall toward the front door, saying, "Hi, Gale! Like the room?"

She clapped her hands together. "It's fantastic! You know, Mr. Dwyer, this is going to be a gorgeous house when you get it all finished. It's so homey. It has that country feeling, really relaxed. It'd be perfect for a party."

Although Jerry was on his way to pick up his date, he stopped at the front door and turned back. "Yeah, it is nice," he said slowly, as though he were seeing the room for the first time and weren't the one who had built the fireplace, plastered the walls, unrolled the carpet, and moved the furniture.

Gale persisted as only Gale could. "I remember that Janet said something about you offering to give a party for our friends, and now that the house looks so — so — I can't believe it, it's so beautiful I'd love to have everyone see it!"

I would have kicked her if I'd thought that would shut her up, but I knew it wouldn't.

Max said, "Janet was the one who originally picked out the colors for the paint and carpet, Gale."

"I know, she told me."

Jerry said, "About that party. What do you think, Max?"

Max said, "Would you like that, Jan?"

And then they were off, planning my life as usual with Jerry saying, "Jan could invite some of her friends, and we could serve *kalfkychling* or *stroganoff* —" and Max saying, "Or maybe her friends would like Cantonese —" and Jerry interrupting, "Or Mexican, or remember that Austrian dish we did one time —"

I gritted my teeth and waited, trying to think of a way to say no without hurting their feelings, because there was no way that I could imagine the gang from Nadine's party at my house. I couldn't ask the girls without the boys. They wouldn't be interested. And I couldn't ask the boys. My uncles would expect them to eat all their foreign dishes and then play some sort of kiddie games before going home at nine o'clock.

Before I could say anything, Gale said, "That would be fantastic! Could we really? I could help Janet plan the party, and we could ask the people who were at Nadine's place. There were about twenty of us, if that's not too many, and as long as you don't have the carpet or furniture in the dining room yet, we could use that for dancing."

"That's an awful lot of people," I mumbled.

I couldn't read the expressions on my uncles' faces. Both of them looked blank, which meant they were trying hard not to let their thoughts show. Max said, "That's not too many. We can cook for a couple dozen, can't we, Jer?"

Gale said, "Nadine and David and Mike would help. They're good at cooking. And we'd all clean up, so you wouldn't have to do that. And Willard can bring his stereo, and everybody's got records —" She tilted her head and glanced up at Jerry from the sides of her eyes, the way she did, and I knew that Gale was purposely mentioning all the boys so that my uncles would understand that this was not to be any little-girls-in-pink-dresses party.

Jerry knew exactly what Gale was doing. I could tell by the way his mouth twitched, and then he grinned. "Yeah, sure."

"And, uh, Janet could ask Eric to bring his records," Gale added.

"By all means, ask Eric," Jerry said in an odd kind of flat tone, then added, "Hey, I'm late. See you all later," and left.

Max looked from Gale to me and back again, his eyebrows drawn together in a puzzled expression, as though he was pleased that we were going to have a party but wasn't sure how it had all come about.

It was one thing for Gale to cheerily suggest that I invite Eric, quite another for me to do it. We asked everyone else at school the next day, but I couldn't walk up to Eric in the hall and invite him to a party. When Gale asked if I would like her to invite him, I almost said yes, then changed my mind. It wouldn't be right. He would think that I was using Gale to try to get back together with him. He might feel embarrassed about saying no to her invitation, or at least think he had to give her an explanation.

On Thursday night I phoned him. Maybe it would have been nicer if I had had the courage to go up to him and ask him face to face, but I didn't have that much courage. Neither could I give the job to Gale. And so I compromised.

His voice over the phone brought back the memories of all the times we'd talked, chatting about nothing for hours. I rolled over on my back and stared at my ceiling.

"I'm having a party at my house on Saturday," I said. My voice came out hurried, as though I had to give him a long message in a few seconds. I didn't know how to control it. "Gale's helping me. My uncles — we're having a supper. And dancing. Like at Nadine's. And I guess about the same people."

I stopped, out of breath. Eric didn't answer.

I said, "You're invited, too." He still didn't say anything. Should I tell him that I especially wanted him to be at the party, I wondered, or would that sound like I was begging him? Finally, I said, "My Uncle Jerry said I should be sure to ask you," which was sort of the truth.

"Did he?" Eric sounded as though he doubted me.

I blurted out, "Are you still mad at me?"

"No."

"I've told you I'm sorry. Don't you believe me?"

"I believe you."

So that was that. I knew there was no point talking to Eric any longer or trying to apologize to him further. From the shortness of his answers, I knew that he was trying to be polite and at the same time make it clear to me that he was not interested in me any longer. As far as he was concerned, whatever there had been between us was over.

"I'm sorry I bothered you by phoning you," I said.

"That's okay." For a moment, he sounded like the old Eric.

" 'Bye."

"Janet?"

"What?"

"Uh — thanks for asking me. I — I have something else I have to do Saturday. But thanks, anyway."

"Sure," I said and waited, in case he wanted to say more. I didn't really think he did. I knew he didn't have anything else planned for Saturday. He only said that because he wasn't the sort of person to be intentionally rude.

He said, " 'Bye," and hung up.

Eleven

Without Eric, the party wouldn't be fun for me, but by Friday my uncles were having a marvelous time comparing recipes. It was as though they'd found a whole new hobby for themselves, called Entertaining Janet's Little Friends. They were going at it with their usual rush of enthusiasm. My only consolation was the thought that if the party turned out to be a total disaster, with the kids hating the gourmet food and my uncles glaring at any boy who came within ten feet of a girl, at least Eric wouldn't be there to witness my social demise.

I wore a dark blue T-shirt that was about the same shade as my jeans and, I hoped, made my hair look lighter. Gale and I had spent the afternoon lugging cushions over from her house to toss around on the dining-room floor, so that people who weren't dancing could sit along the wall and listen to music. As I hurried from my room to the kitchen, I paused to re-arrange a few of the cushions. That was as much as I'd been allowed to do, arrange the cushions. No one had asked me what I thought we should serve. If they had, I would have sug-gested pizza or hot dogs.

But what did it matter? Even if I had, they would have found a recipe for marinated pizza and then drowned the hot dogs in wine sauce.

Max looked up from where he was bent over the maple cutting-block, pulverizing a pile of ingredients with a tool that looked like a small hatchet.

He saw the T-shirt, all right, but all he said was, "I don't think we have enough room at the table for everyone to sit down."

"Could we sort of put the food out on the counter and let people help themselves?" I asked. "We could carry our plates into the dining room and sit on the floor."

Jerry gave Max a look, and I knew what they were both thinking. They'd said it to me enough times. If a dish wasn't served and eaten at exactly the right moment and temperature, it's flavor was lost.

Max forced a smile, saying, "Sounds fine, Jan. However you think it should be."

"That's what we did at Nadine's."

"Then that's what we'll do here."

Jerry turned the water on higher, I think to drown out our words and his own thoughts on the subject of serving food.

Gale arrived first, dressed in an orange A-shirt and skintight jeans. She wandered through the kitchen making sniffing noises. "Fantastic! Everything smells marvelous!"

My uncles grinned, and Jerry managed to say, "You sure you've got room to eat in that outfit?"

If I'd been wearing jeans that were that tight, I think he would have told me to go find a pair that hadn't shrunk. I wondered if regular parents were like that, nicer to other people's kids than to their own.

Kristy and Mike and Nadine and Stephanie and Willard arrived together, but Kristy and Mike wandered off to the far side of the fireplace and sat on the floor in the shadowed corner, while the rest of them followed me into the kitchen. Stephanie peered through her big glasses at the mushrooms that Jerry was preparing. She stood by Willard, leaning lightly against him, her arm around his back and her hand resting on his shoulder. I introduced them to my uncles.

Willard asked, "Is that a gourmet recipe?"

If Jerry noticed Stephanie's arm, and I think he did, he didn't let his thoughts show. He smiled and said, "I guess you could call it that. It's an Italian recipe."

Willard said, "Gale told us that you were gourmet cooks."

Nadine said, "That sure looks good. I love mushrooms. Could you show me how to make it?"

"Gourmet cooks do *not* let amateurs mess up their recipes," Gale said, knowing that my uncles never let me cook.

Jerry said, "I guess I — sure, here, Nadine, I'll show you how to make bread crumbs while Willard grates the cheese."

"First, you'd better show me how to grate cheese," Willard said.

"I thought bread crumbs came out of a tall, thin can," Nadine said.

Gale said, "Bite your tongue!"

The doorbell rang. I shouted, "I'll get it," but everyone was too busy watching Jerry demonstrate cheese-grating to care. I hurried through the dining room and front room, noticed that Kristy and Mike had blended into one outline in the corner, and ran past to open the door. Barb came in, followed by two boys and a girl named Susan who I didn't know very well. For the party, Barb had used her whole eye-makeup kit, shading her lids in stripes of pastel tones above her stiffly painted lashes. She looked at the boarded-up window in the entry.

"Looks like my house. My folks are always remodeling."

"Are they really?" I asked.

"Move on in," a boy behind her said. "You're blocking the way, and I can smell food."

"Come on into the kitchen," I said.

Barb said, "There's another car right behind us."

"Okay, I'll wait. Go on through."

They laughed and pushed past me, heading for the kitchen. Although most of my guests wore T-shirts and jeans, Susan had on a flowered gypsy-style skirt and a blouse with long, full sleeves. I heard her whisper the name Kristy, and the rest of them laughed. Two more carloads of kids walked up the drive, after leaving their cars on the road. It wasn't dark out yet, but the sun had almost set, so that the autumn sky glowed lavender. The aroma of leaf fires hung over the neighborhood.

"Hi," people shouted to each other. "Hey, yeah, this is the right house. There's Janet! Hi, Janet!"

David Overton, who hadn't been at Nadine's party, was in the crowd. Gale must have invited him. Although I knew that she didn't know him well, I also knew that if Nadine had hinted that she would like David at the party, Gale wouldn't hesitate to phone him.

"What a neat place! You're really out in the country!"

"What kind of car is that?"

"Hey, look, there's another one. Are those antique cars?" a boy asked.

"Ask my uncles and you'll learn more about cars than you may want to know," I said.

"Are your uncles here?" David asked as he walked by me into the living room.

"They're in the kitchen with everyone else. Go on in," I said, pointing out the direction.

David smiled, and I understood why Nadine was interested in him. He was one of those boys who looked plain until he smiled. Then his whole face lit up.

Before closing the door, I took one more look outside. I didn't see anyone else. The weeds that stood three feet tall between the old cars looked almost pretty in the late daylight, reflecting the sunset off of their swaying, gold-brown leaves. Beyond the hedge, I heard a car door slam, and I waited.

Whoever it was must be going to another house, I decided when several minutes passed and no one appeared. With a last glance at the fading sky, I stepped back inside and started to close the door.

Then I saw Eric at the edge of the drive near the hedge, looking at me. In the dusk he was a shadow shape, motionless. I thought about saying his name but decided not to. He would have to make up his own mind about whether or not he wanted to come to the party.

Finally he waved. I waved back and waited. He walked slowly up the driveway, skirting the potholes, turning to look at everything: the old cars, the hedge, the weeds, the house itself. Tilting his head back, he squinted into the fading shimmer of the sky to look up at the roof.

"I've never been here in the day," he said.

"Now you can see why I kept warning you about the driveway."

"It's neat. It really is. You've got a lot of privacy."

"Maybe out here. Wait until you see the crowd inside. I think Gale asked everyone she bumped into, all last week."

"How come Gale? Isn't this your party?"

"Yes, but Gale did most of the asking."

He stopped at the bottom of the steps and looked up at me, as though he was unsure of what he wanted to do next. I felt the same way. Had Eric decided to show up at my party because he knew all our friends would be there and he wanted to remain part of the group? Or had he come to see me?

"Everybody's in the kitchen," I said.

"Everybody is always where the food is."

"My Uncle Jerry is giving a demonstration on how to grate cheese."

"How come?"

"Because somebody wanted to help him make the mushrooms parmesan. Willard, I think. And Jerry said that he could grate the cheese, and Willard didn't know how to grate cheese. So Jerry's teaching him."

Eric nodded but didn't say anything.

"You want to come inside and watch?"

With a sort of "I don't care" shrug, he turned away from me to stare at the old cars in the weeds. But his profile had a tight look, with his mouth and eyes pinched, and I thought that he probably was so busy thinking that he didn't see anything.

"Are you going to stand outside all night?" I demanded. When he didn't answer, I added, "Are you afraid to meet my uncles?"

He said, "I don't think so."

"Then what's the matter?"

"I don't know."

For some dumb reason, my heart felt as though it were pounding in my throat. I made myself go down the stairs anyway, to stand beside him. Looking up at him, I said, "Are you still mad at me?"

"I told you I wasn't."

"Then why won't you come in the house?"

"It's — I'd sort of like to settle something with you first."

"All right," I said.

"Because otherwise you're going to keep asking if I'm mad, and I'm going to keep saying no, and you're going to keep on not believing me."

"Uh-huh." I didn't know what he was talking about, but as long as he stayed there, talking, it was all right by me.

"See, at first I was mad because you lied. But then I got to thinking. You must have wanted to go out with me an awful lot to lie to your uncles. That is, I sort of don't think you usually lie to them."

"I've never had any reason to," I admitted. "They don't usually say no to me. At least, not until this year. So when they said I couldn't go out on dates — I mean, you're the first boy

I've ever —" My voice quit on me, sticking somewhere in my throat with my pounding heart. I hadn't meant to tell Eric that he was the first boy I'd ever dated.

"Yeah, I know. I figured that out, finally. I haven't gone out with any other girls, either. I guess I don't know much about girls."

"What's that mean?"

"Oh, only that when I ask my folks for the car, I don't have to tell them I'm going on a date. Boys don't. But I guess girls do — have to tell their folks, I mean — and so then if they say no . . . Anyway, I can see it's harder for you."

"I should have told you they'd said no. But I was afraid you wouldn't ask me out again," I admitted.

"Do you want me to ask you out again?" He still wouldn't look at me. He gazed over my head at something in the distance.

"Do you want to?" I asked.

"That's not fair. I asked first."

I wasn't going to say, yes, I wanted him to ask me out. Then what if he didn't? Instead, I said, "I invited you to my party, didn't I?"

He looked down at me and smiled. "Yeah, that's right."

"So are you going to come inside with me

or are you going to stay out here all night by yourself?"

"If you put it that way, I'll go inside."

I ran up the steps in front of him. As we cut through the living room, I nodded at Kristy and Mike, who were wrapped in each other's arms in the corner. Close to my ear, Eric whispered, "Uh-huh. Same crowd."

In the kitchen under the row of gleaming copper pans that hung from the ceiling hooks, Max was surrounded by David and Nadine and several others, all chopping and mixing under Max's supervision. At the sink counter Jerry closely watched Willard grate cheese on the steel grater.

"Not too hard. Don't press down," Jerry muttered.

Concentrating, Willard worked with his tongue caught between his teeth.

Barb shouted, "Hi, Eric!"

Jerry looked up, hesitated, then smiled. "How are you at grating cheese, Eric?"

"Never tried it."

Willard said, "Hey, Mr. Dwyer, don't give him my job."

"All right, I'll start him separating the whites from the yolks for the merinque."

Eric whispered to me, "How do I do that?"

Jerry pulled open the refrigerator and began to unload it, stacking egg cartons and bottles and boxes on the nearest counter. As Jerry worked, he shouted instructions to Willard and Gale, who had taken over Nadine's job. Beyond him, Max's voice droned softly, explaining a recipe to his crowd. From the dining room, Willard's stereo and Mike's record collection kept the sound level at a steady high.

I felt as though Eric and I were an island in a sea of confusion. I whispered back, "An old chicken-chaser like you ought to know how to separate eggs."

"Thanks a lot. I suppose that means you won't help me."

Giggling, I admitted, "I can't. I don't know how."

"You're kidding."

"No, but if my uncle can teach Willard, he can teach us."

For a second I thought that Eric was going to turn around and run out of the house. He said slowly, "Us? We're going to learn to cook together?"

"Sure. I may as well learn, too. I mean, unless you really don't want to. You don't have to, you know."

Eric grinned. "That's okay," he said, "as long as we're in this deal together."

— FEAR STREET® —

R·L·STINE

Sunburn

AN ARCHWAY PAPERBACK
Published by POCKET BOOKS
New York   London   Toronto   Sydney   Tokyo   Singapore

AN ARCHWAY PAPERBACK *Original*

An Archway Paperback published by
POCKET BOOKS, a division of Simon & Schuster Inc.
1230 Avenue of the Americas, New York, NY 10020

Copyright © 1993 by Parachute Press, Inc.

ISBN: 0-671-73868-2

First Archway Paperback printing June 1993

10 9 8   7   6

FEAR STREET is a registered trademark of
Parachute Press, Inc.

AN ARCHWAY PAPERBACK and colophon are
registered trademarks of Simon & Schuster Inc.

Cover art by Bill Schmidt

Printed in the U.S.A.

IL 7+

chapter

1

Buried Alive

Claudia Walker surfaced slowly from a deep sleep. She felt something cool and damp covering her chest and legs. She could smell the salt air of the sea.

In the distance she heard waves breaking on the shore. She wanted to drift back into sleep but couldn't. Her face was burning.

She tried to open her eyes, but they seemed to be swollen shut. She struggled to sit up. But something—a thick, heavy weight—pressed down on her.

Her eyes opened a crack and she saw flies buzzing around a mound of dried seaweed near her head. A sand fly skittered across the sand. The fly buzzed toward her, its green eyes twitching. A thin, hairy leg touched her chin.

Moving steadily, the fly walked across her lips.

Claudia tried to brush it away, but couldn't raise her hands. She struggled to move as the fly made its way across her cheek toward her swollen eye.

The harsh afternoon sun beat down. Claudia licked her lips. They were blistered and cracking. Her throat was parched, and it hurt to swallow.

Why can't I move?

What is holding me down?

Finally Claudia forced her eyes open all the way. A mountain of sand was piled over her. Her entire body lay buried beneath it.

I've been buried—buried alive! she realized, a tremor of panic rising in her chest.

With great effort she raised her head high enough to see ocean waves lapping closer. The tide was coming in, Claudia realized.

I've got to get up. Got to get out.

Or I'll drown!

She tilted her head back against the hot sand and uttered a cry for help. Her voice cracked. Her dry throat ached.

There was no reply.

"Is anyone here?" Claudia screamed. "Can anyone help me?"

A gull winged high overhead, its cries mocking her.

The cruel sun blazed down on her.

Claudia struggled to pull even one arm free. But the heat had drained her strength.

How long have I been sleeping here?

How long have I been buried?

Where are my friends?

Her temples began to throb. Raising her eyes to the bright, cloudless sky, she felt dizzy.

2

SUNBURN

She struggled to lift her arms and legs from under the weight of the sand. But it was no use.

Her heart thudded heavily in her chest. Sweat poured down her forehead. She called out again.

No answer. Only the crash of the waves and the shrill cries of the gulls overhead.

"Can't *anybody* hear me?"

She knew that if her friends had returned to the house, they'd never hear her. Craning her neck, she could see the steep wooden stairway leading up to the house, up the face of the sixty-foot cliff.

The house itself had thick stone walls, like those of a castle. No one would hear her from up there. No one would come.

She screamed anyway.

chapter

2

The Shadow of Death

Dear Claudia,

How the heck are you?

I know this is short notice, but I'm inviting you to the first annual reunion of Bunk 12 from Camp Full Moon.

The four of us had such a short time together last summer that I got to thinking it would be great to see one another and catch up. (None of us has been too terrific in the letter-writing department, especially me.)

My parents will be away the first week in August. They told me to invite some friends to stay at our summer house on the beach so I won't get lonely.

So how about it, Claud? Can you come? It'll be just the four of us from Bunk 12— you, me, Sophie, and Joy.

SUNBURN

I hope you're having a really boring summer in Shadyside, so you'll say yes. I promise it won't be boring here!

Please come!

Marla

That letter was how Claudia came to be on this lonely beach. Although surprised by Marla's invitation, Claudia had accepted at once.

She'd been having a dreadful summer. She had broken up with Steve, her boyfriend of two years, after a silly argument on the Fourth of July. A week later she lost her summer waitressing job when the restaurant had closed.

It will be great to see the girls again, Claudia thought as she stood on her porch on Fear Street, reading and rereading Marla's invitation.

They had spent three weeks together the previous summer and had become such good friends. They'd shared so many good times, so many laughs—until the accident. . . .

Still gripping the invitation tightly in her hand, Claudia rushed into the house, told her mother about it, and hurried up to her room to call Marla. "I'm dying to see you!" she exclaimed. "And your summer house. I remember you describing it as a real mansion!"

"It's a quaint little shack," Marla joked. "I think you'll find it comfortable."

Two weeks later Claudia was on the train to Summerhaven. She had brought a book to read on the long trip. But instead she just stared out the window,

5

thinking about Marla and the other girls and their brief time together at camp.

Four and a half hours later Claudia stepped onto the wooden platform at Summerhaven, squinted into the bright sunlight, and saw Joy and Sophie parked next to a small pile of suitcases.

Joy carried one sleek, designer bag. Sophie had four mismatched pieces, each one bulging. Claudia had to laugh. It was so much like camp, when Sophie had arrived with two trunks full of clothes and an entire duffel bag of cosmetics. She had explained that she could never decide what *not* to pack.

As Claudia waved and started toward them, a sleek silver Mercedes glided up to the station. Marla leapt out from the driver's side, leaving the door open, and ran to hug Joy and Sophie.

From across the long platform, Claudia admired Marla's new look. She seemed taller and even more slender. Her strawberry-blond hair had grown long, and she looked very preppy in a turquoise designer top over white tennis shorts.

Joy was as exotic-looking as ever. She had slightly slanted green eyes, olive skin, dark, full lips, and straight black hair, which fell loosely down her back nearly to her waist.

Sophie hadn't changed either, Claudia saw. She was still the shortest of the four, with frizzy, light brown hair, bobbing on top of her round face. She wore wire-rimmed glasses to make her look older and more sophisticated, but Sophie still came across as about twelve.

Joy was the first to see Claudia. "Claud!" she

shrieked, loudly enough to make everyone at the station turn to stare at her.

Before Claudia could reply, Joy had run up and thrown her arms around her. She was hugging her as if they were long-lost sisters.

Sophie approached and gave Claudia a short hug. Her greeting was polite and cool, and somehow more honest.

Marla gave Claudia a quick hug and said, "Let's go. I'm not allowed to park here."

A few seconds later they were rolling through the small beach town of Summerhaven, leaning back against buttery-soft leather seats and staring out from the air-conditioned coolness of the Mercedes.

Marla drove past the boardwalk and tiny beach shops selling surfing and fishing gear, then past blocks of summer bungalows. The bungalows gave way to larger houses and then to no houses at all.

"Marla," Sophie said, "I thought your family lived in Summerhaven."

"No," Marla replied, her eyes on the narrow road. "The house is out on the Point, about fifteen miles from town. We just use the Summerhaven post office."

The road curved through high, grass-covered sand dunes. Beyond the dunes, Claudia could hear the steady, soft roar of the ocean.

"This part of the beach is all protected land," Marla explained. "It's a bird sanctuary."

They drove through miles of sanctuary. Once out of it, the road narrowed even more, becoming a gravel path wide enough for only one car.

Claudia gasped out loud as the Drexell mansion

suddenly rose up in front of them. Marla had shown her snapshots of it at camp, but they didn't come close to portraying the size or beauty of the enormous house.

Marla opened a metal gate and pulled the car through a space in the tall, perfectly trimmed hedge that bordered the property. It had been planted to disguise the metal fencing. The gray stone house was completely visible now, set back on a wide, manicured lawn like a fairy-tale castle.

The driveway led around to the side of the house. Claudia could see a conservatory with a stained-glass dome. In back, a wide terrace led to tennis courts, a colorful gazebo, gardens, an enormous swimming pool, and several smaller buildings.

Marla ticked them off carelessly, "Oh, that's the boat house, and that's the equipment shed, a cabana, in case you don't want to change in the house, the gardener's shed, woodshed . . . That larger building behind the house is the guest house."

"Hey, Marla, do you have a map?" Joy joked. "It'll take me all week to figure out how not to get lost!"

"Don't worry," Marla replied, pulling the car into the four-car garage. "We'll stick together. I'm so glad you all came. I won't let you out of my sight."

"We'll stick together. . . ."

Now, buried in the sand, with the waves slipping closer to her, Claudia remembered Marla's words.

"We'll stick together. . . ."

But where was Marla now? Where was Joy? Where was Sophie?

8

How could they have left her buried under the burning sun?

Claudia closed her eyes. Her throat ached. Her face was burning. The back of her neck itched, but she couldn't scratch it.

Water rolled over the sand, making it suddenly heavier on her chest.

The waves are getting closer.

I'm going to drown, Claudia realized.

She opened her eyes to find herself in shadow.

The shadow of death.

It's getting darker. Darker.

Death is closing in.

As Claudia made one last frantic struggle to free herself, the shadow rolled silently over her.

chapter

3

First "Accident"

*I*t took Claudia a long while to realize that the shadow was that of a guy standing over her. She saw his bare legs first, dripping with water, sand clinging to his ankles.

Gazing up into his face, she uttered a soft cry of surprise.

His dark eyes stared down at her. His short black hair was wet, matted to his forehead. He had muscular arms, crossed in front of his chest. He wore long, baggy, orange swim trunks.

"Do you need help?" he asked softly.

"Yes," Claudia replied quickly, struggling to nod her head. "I-I'm stuck."

A wave crashed against the shore. Frothy, white water washed up nearly to Claudia's face.

The boy started shoveling away the heavy, wet sand

with both hands. "Can you move? Are you hurt?" he asked. "I was walking back from a swim. I heard you scream. Are you all alone?" He gazed up and down the beach.

Claudia struggled to answer him, but her parched throat closed up. She nodded.

He scooped away most of the sand, working quickly, his dark, handsome face set with concentration. He took her hand and tugged it. "Can you stand up?"

"I—I think so," Claudia stammered. "I am a little dizzy, though."

"You've got a bad burn," the boy told her, frowning.

"I fell asleep, I guess," Claudia said shakily, allowing him to pull her to her feet. "My friends left me. I don't know where they went. I—"

She stood unsteadily, holding on to his hands, and squinted against the sun. The sand was a dazzling white in the bright daylight, nearly as white as the Drexells' newly painted dock down the beach.

"If you hadn't come by . . ." Her voice trailed off. She shook her head, trying to shake some of the wet sand from her straight, auburn hair. "Even my hair hurts!" she exclaimed.

The damp, sticky sand clung to her skin. Her entire body was covered. She itched all over. She tried brushing it off her legs.

"I've got to take a shower," she groaned.

"Are you staying up there? At the Drexells'?" He pointed up the side of the cliff.

"Yeah." Claudia nodded.

"I'll help you," he said quietly. "Put your arm around my shoulders."

11

She obediently followed his instructions. His skin felt surprisingly cold; from the ocean, she realized. She leaned heavily against him. He was so cool against her burning skin.

He's really great-looking, Claudia couldn't help but think. And really strong. She loved his dark eyes. "I'm Claudia," she told him. "Claudia Walker. I'm visiting Marla Drexell."

Her arm around his shoulders, she allowed him to lead her to the steep steps that led up the cliff to the Drexells' estate. She waited for him to tell her his name.

"You'd better get something on that sunburn right away," he said. He held on to her waist, helping her up the narrow, wooden steps.

"What's *your* name?" she asked.

He hesitated. "Daniel," he answered finally.

"Do you live nearby?" Claudia asked.

"Not really," he told her, a strange smile on his face.

Is he laughing at me? she wondered, feeling some regret. She realized she wanted Daniel to like her.

But he just thinks I'm ridiculous, buried up to my head, my face burned red as a lobster!

At the top of the stairway stood a chain-metal gate. Claudia grabbed the gate and pulled. It clanked but didn't move.

"It's always locked," Daniel told her. "The Drexells keep their property very well secured. They also have a guard dog." He bent over and searched the low shrubs until he found a black metal box. He pulled the lid up to reveal an electronic keypad. Claudia watched him tap out a number code on the keypad. The gate clicked, then swung open.

"How do you know the code?" she asked, stepping unsteadily onto the grass.

He flashed her a mysterious grin. "I know a lot of things."

Feeling stronger, Claudia made her way quickly across the grounds, past the tennis courts and pool, toward the back terrace of the house. As she neared the terrace, she saw Marla behind a sliding glass door, a startled expression on her face.

The door slid open and Marla came running out, dressed in her tennis whites, followed by Joy and Sophie. "Claudia—what are you doing out here?" Marla cried. "We thought you were upstairs."

"Huh?" Claudia managed to gasp. "You—you left me down there to fry!"

"No!" Joy cried. "After we buried you, we went for a walk. When we came out, Marla said you'd gone back to the house. So we came in too!"

"I can't believe you left me buried in the sand, asleep!" Claudia cried angrily.

"We honestly didn't see you!" Sophie protested.

"Ow. Look at her face," Joy said, tsk-tsking.

"We didn't know you were still there. How did you get back in here on your own?" Marla asked.

"Daniel helped me," Claudia told her.

"Who?"

"If it hadn't been for Daniel—" Claudia started and turned to introduce him.

There was no one behind her.

He had vanished.

* * *

13

Claudia's being left in the sun was the first "accident" of the week. The next "accident" wouldn't occur until the following morning.

It would take the girls even longer than that to realize that something strange was going on at the Drexell mansion.

Now, all Claudia could think of was treating her badly burned face. She showered and changed into a loose-fitting blue and yellow sundress. Marla appeared in Claudia's room with a bottle of aloe lotion and a jar of soothing skin cream. She made Claudia drink an entire bottle of water.

"I'm so sorry. Really," Marla kept repeating. "I'll never forgive myself. When we got back from our walk, we took the other path up from the dunes. I just assumed——"

"I don't even remember falling asleep," Claudia said, frowning unhappily as she studied her scarlet face in the dresser mirror. "It must have been that new antihistamine my allergy doctor gave me." She groaned. "This is going to blister. Then it's going to peel like crazy. I'm going to look like a monster!"

"I think you look great," Marla said unconvincingly. "I like your hair. You're letting it grow?"

"Yeah." Claudia pulled her auburn hair back. Then she rubbed more cream onto her face. "I'm never going in the sun again," she muttered.

Dinner was served in the large, formal dining room with the four girls huddled at one end of the long, marble-topped table. An enormous crystal chandelier hovered low over a centerpiece of white and yellow flowers.

"This is a little fancy for me," Sophie confessed, gazing uneasily about the room. "You're going to have to tell me which fork to use."

"I don't think so," Marla replied dryly. "We're having cheeseburgers and french fries for dinner."

They all laughed. It seemed funny to eat cheeseburgers and french fries in the midst of all that splendor.

"Alfred is barbecuing the hamburgers out on the terrace," Marla told us. "At least, I hope they're hamburgers. Alfred is very nearsighted. He could be barbecuing the dog and wouldn't know it!"

Sophie and Claudia laughed, but Joy groaned and pretended to gag.

The three girls had met Alfred when they arrived. He was a jolly, plump, middle-aged man with a pink bald head and a tiny gray mustache perched under a bulbous nose. He was the only servant on duty for the whole week, Marla had explained. The others had been given the time off by her parents.

He entered the room now, carrying a large silver salad bowl in both hands.

"I'll serve the salad, Alfred," Marla told him.

"The hamburgers are almost done," he informed her, setting the bowl down beside her on the table. His shoes squeaked as he left the room.

Marla stood up and began filling the china salad plates with salad. "We've got so much catching up to do," she said enthusiastically. "I've missed you guys, I really have. I apologize for not writing more."

After passing out the plates, Marla sank back into her chair.

All four girls lifted their salad forks and began to eat.

"Well, who wants to go first?" Marla asked, smiling. "Who wants to tell what's new and exciting in her life?"

There was a brief silence.

"Don't everybody answer at once," Marla joked, rolling her eyes.

Claudia chewed on a cucumber slice, thinking hard. What was there to tell? It hadn't been a very exciting year for her.

She glanced around at the other girls.

To her surprise, she saw that Joy's expression was contorted; by what, she didn't know.

"Joy—" Claudia started to say.

But her voice was drowned out by Joy's high-pitched scream of horror.

chapter

4

The Ghost Boy

Still shrieking, both her hands tugging at her hair, Joy leapt up from the table. Her chair toppled over backward, clattering noisily against the bare wooden floor.

"Joy, what *is* it?" Marla screamed. "What?"

Trembling all over, Joy removed one hand from her hair and pointed a trembling finger at her salad plate.

Claudia leaned over and peered at the plate. She made a disgusted face when she saw the fat brown worm crawling on a lettuce leaf.

Sophie had jumped up and wrapped her arms around Joy's shoulders. "What's wrong? What's the matter?"

"It's a worm," Claudia said quietly. "A big brown one."

Joy covered her face with her hands. "I-I'm

sorry," she stammered. "I didn't mean to frighten you. But you know how I get. I mean, you know I have a thing about bugs and worms."

Sophie hugged Joy tighter. Marla was calling loudly for Alfred.

"I've had a thing about bugs," Joy repeated, "ever since—ever since camp."

None of us has been the same since camp, Claudia thought sadly.

Not since the accident last summer.

But she didn't want to think about that now. She wanted to enjoy this week, to have fun with her friends—and not think about what had happened last summer.

Alfred came bouncing into the room, concern on his pink face. "Is there a problem, miss?"

"Joy found a worm in her salad," Marla replied, pointing.

Alfred's mouth dropped open for a second. Then he quickly regained his composure. "I am so sorry," he said, scurrying to gather up the plate. He held it close to his face, searching for the worm. "The lettuce is locally grown," he said, and quickly disappeared with the plate.

When he was gone, Sophie laughed. "Was that an explanation? That it was locally grown?"

Claudia and Marla laughed too.

"I guess the worm was locally grown too!" Claudia joked.

"Sometimes Alfred is weird," Marla said, shaking her head. "I wish he'd get glasses. He'd serve up fewer worms if he did."

Joy bent to pick up her chair. She seemed to be

recovered as she pushed her black hair back and sat down, her green eyes flashing to life.

Joy was always the most emotional, the most dramatic of the group, Claudia remembered, watching her friend. She guessed that's why she'd always liked her so much. Joy was so completely different from her. Claudia was so calm, so in control all the time. I never show my true feelings, she thought.

Lost in her thoughts, Claudia realized with a start that Marla had asked her a question. "I'm sorry. What did you say?"

"I asked you about that boy," Marla repeated. "You said something about a boy digging you out of the sand."

"Yeah, tell us about him," Sophie said eagerly, pushing her glasses up on her nose. "Are there boys around here?"

Alfred returned, carrying an enormous silver tray stacked high with hot cheeseburgers. He returned in a moment with a bowl of french fries and a tray of condiments for the cheeseburgers.

The girls helped themselves before Claudia answered Marla's question. "He said his name was Daniel. He had been for a swim, and then he saw me buried there."

"Been for a swim? On our beach?" Marla cried, narrowing her eyes. "What did he look like?"

"Not bad," Claudia replied. "Tall, very good-looking actually, black hair. A great bod, like he worked out."

"And he said his name was Daniel?" Marla demanded.

Claudia nodded.

"Strange. I've never seen him around," Marla said thoughtfully. "In fact, I never see any boys on our beach."

"You *must* know him," Claudia insisted. "He knew the code to open the back gate."

Marla dropped her cheeseburger onto her plate. "Huh?"

"He let me in," Claudia told her.

"No way. That's impossible," Marla insisted. Her blue eyes revealed some fear. "A strange boy knows the code to our gate? Come on, Claud. How long were you out in the sun?"

"A long time, thanks to you," Claudia replied, surprised by her own anger.

"You hallucinated this Daniel," Marla told her.

"Hallucinate one for *me!*" Sophie joked.

Everyone laughed.

"He was real," Claudia insisted. "He saved my life." She took a bite of cheeseburger. The tomato slid out from the bun and dropped into her lap. "Not my day," she muttered, struggling to pick it up.

"But there *are* no boys around here," Marla said heatedly. "There couldn't be a boy who knows the code. There couldn't be a boy who—"

She stopped in midsentence and uttered a silent gasp, raising a hand to her mouth at the same time. Her blue eyes grew wide, and her forehead became lined in a fretful frown.

"Marla, what's the matter? Did you find a worm too?" Joy demanded anxiously, holding her cheeseburger in front of her with both hands.

"Oh, wow," Marla muttered, ignoring Joy and her question. Marla shook her head. "Wow." She raised

20

her eyes to Claudia's and stared intently at her across the table.

"What? What is it?" Claudia asked, reaching for Marla's hand.

"It wasn't a boy," Marla told her in a hushed whisper. "I know who it was, Claud, and it wasn't a boy."

"Marla, what do you mean?"

"It was a ghost," Marla said, her hand trembling under Claudia's. "It was the Ghost Boy."

chapter

5

Shadows

Claudia laughed. "Get serious, Marla. That boy was real. He told me his name was Daniel."

"I thought he was real too," Marla replied softly, her expression solemn. "I thought he was real the times I saw him. But he isn't. He's a ghost."

Joy's green eyes sparkled to life. "You mean—your house is haunted?" she asked.

Marla nodded and pointed to the tall window that faced out the back. "He lives in the guest house, I think," she told Joy. "That's where I've seen him the most."

"You've seen him a lot?" Joy asked.

Sophie shoved her plate away and stared intently across the table at Marla. Claudia's mouth was twisted in a skeptical smile.

"Once I saw him on the tennis court," Marla said,

her blue eyes darting from girl to girl. "He was dressed in white, in old-fashioned clothes, very starched. He was holding a weird tennis racket, made of wood, I guess. He had the saddest look on his face. I waved to him."

"Did you play tennis with him?" Claudia asked sarcastically.

Marla shook her head, ignoring Claudia's tone. "He turned toward me and realized I could see him. He stared at me for a second, that sad expression on his face—then he disappeared." She snapped her fingers. "Poof. Into thin air."

Claudia narrowed her eyes and studied Marla. "You're serious—aren't you?" she said.

"Yes. It's all true," Marla told her.

"But this boy had to be real!" Claudia protested. "He shoveled away the sand with his hands. He pulled me to my feet. I *touched* him, Marla. I had my arm around his shoulders. Solid shoulders. Real shoulders."

"And he didn't feel strange to you?" Marla asked.

"Well . . ." Claudia hesitated. "His skin *was* very cold. But—"

"See?" Marla slapped her hand triumphantly on the table. "His skin was cold because he's dead, Claud."

Claudia's mouth dropped open. "He told me he had just been swimming," she said, thinking hard. "His skin was cold from the ocean."

"No." Marla shook her head. "That was his excuse. He's dead, Claud. He's been dead for a hundred years."

"How do you know that?" Joy asked excitedly,

twirling a strand of black hair into a corkscrew and tugging it over her forehead. "Have you talked with him?"

"No," Marla replied, turning to Joy. "The real estate agent told us about him when he sold us this place. He said a boy had been murdered in the guest house a hundred years ago. The murderer was never found. The agent said that since then, the boy had been seen haunting the grounds, going for solitary swims, walking in the gardens."

Marla took a long drink of ice tea, then continued in a hushed voice. "I've seen him three times. The last time, he came very near. I think he wanted to tell me something, but he acted very shy. I said hello to him, and he disappeared."

"Wow," Joy muttered, shaking her head.

"He's very handsome," Marla said, "in an old-fashioned way."

"Weird," Sophie muttered, obviously a little frightened.

"I want to see him," Joy declared. "I really do believe in ghosts. I've always wanted to see one."

"His skin was so cold," Claudia admitted thoughtfully. "Even in the hot sun, his skin was cold. Cold as death." She shuddered. "I can't believe a ghost saved my life this afternoon."

To her surprise, Marla laughed. "Then *don't* believe it!" she cried.

"Huh?" Claudia was bewildered by Marla. "What do you mean?"

"I made it all up!" Marla confessed, and uttered a gleeful laugh, her blue eyes glittering.

"You *what?*" Claudia and Joy cried in unison. Sophie pushed her glasses up on her nose, stunned.

"I made it all up!" Marla told them, unable to hide how pleased she was. "The whole story. There *is* no ghost boy. No murder in the guest house. No boy on the tennis court with a sad expression."

"Marla!" Claudia screamed angrily. She stood up, grabbed Marla by the neck and pretended to strangle her. Marla collapsed in gales of laughter.

"I believed her! I really did!" Joy confessed.

"Me too," Sophie said, shaking her head.

"Wish I had my camcorder," Marla cried gleefully. "The expressions on your faces! So serious!" She turned to Claudia. "I'm really surprised at you, Claud. At camp, you were always the one who could scare us with your crazy ghost stories. You were always the one with the wild imagination. How could you fall for my stupid little story?"

Claudia could feel her face grow red. She couldn't decide if she was more angry or embarrassed. "A boy really did help me!" she insisted shrilly. "Daniel. He really did rescue me. And he really did vanish into thin air!"

"Yeah. Really!" Marla cried, and began laughing again.

Well, Daniel, Claudia thought, frowning, if you aren't a ghost, then who are you?

Claudia pushed back the white lacy curtains and peered at the night through the French doors of her room. Even with the doors closed, she could hear the steady wash of ocean waves against the shore.

Spotlights sent out yellow cones of light over the back lawn. The tennis court and rectangular swimming pool were nearly as well-lit as they would be during the day.

After dinner the girls had watched a tape of *Bye Bye, Birdie* that Marla had rented. The old musical was a riot, Claudia thought. The girls had hooted with laughter at the funny way the fifties-style teenagers were dressed and at the hilariously sexist attitudes.

"Those girls were so *dumb!*" Sophie had exclaimed. "They only cared about pleasing boys!"

"Yeah. Not at all like today," Claudia replied, rolling her eyes.

After the movie they said good night and made their way upstairs to their rooms. Feeling sleepy, her face burning from her sunburn and chills running down her back, Claudia had taken a hot bath. Then she changed into a long nightshirt and carefully applied more cream to her face.

Now, yawning, she found herself leaning against the glass door, taking one last peek at the back lawn before tucking herself in. It was all so beautiful, so luxurious. Listening to the faint roar of the ocean beyond the cliff, she felt as if in a fantasy world.

She uttered a little gasp when she saw the light flicker on in the guest house window.

Raising her hands to the sides of her face, she narrowed her gaze and squinted hard.

Yes.

A shadow was moving in the guest house window.

A pale light flickered there.

Someone is in there, Claudia thought, staring hard, her nose pressed against the glass.

SUNBURN

For a brief second she thought she recognized the shadow figure.

Is it Daniel? she wondered.

Is it the Ghost Boy?

Then an icy hand, cold as death, gripped Claudia's shoulder.

27

chapter

6

A Shock

Claudia cried out in fright.

She spun around, gasping for breath to scream again.

"Oh. Sorry. I didn't mean to scare you," Marla said, lowering her hand.

"Marla! I—I—" Claudia stammered, breathing hard. She could still feel the chill of Marla's cold hand.

"You were concentrating so hard on what's outside that you didn't hear me call you," Marla said, her blue eyes locked on Claudia's.

Claudia stepped back to pull the curtains over the glass door. "I saw the shadow of someone," she told Marla. "In the guest house."

"Huh?" Marla appeared surprised. She moved toward the glass door and pulled the curtain back.

"A light. In the guest house," Claudia repeated.

"No way," Marla said, shaking her head. "There's no one staying there, Claud. The guest house has been empty all summer."

"But I saw someone—" Claudia began.

"Probably a reflection," Marla said, moving back. "Those spotlights are so bright. Daddy had them installed to discourage prowlers. But they throw so much light. You must have seen a reflection in the guest house window. That's all."

"I guess," Claudia replied doubtfully.

"I just came in to see if you needed anything," Marla said.

"No thanks. I'm fine," Claudia replied. She yawned. "The sun really knocked me out."

"Such a bad burn," Marla said.

Something about the way she said it struck Claudia as odd. Marla hadn't sounded sympathetic. She sounded *pleased*.

No. I'm just overtired, Claudia scolded herself. I'm starting to get really paranoid.

She said good night to Marla, turned off the light, and climbed between the satiny sheets of the enormous, four-poster bed.

A few seconds later she drifted off to sleep, the dark, handsome face of Daniel, the Ghost Boy, floating in her mind.

When Claudia awoke the next morning, she stretched luxuriously in her bed.

Morning sunlight filtered in through the lacy curtains covering the French doors. One door had been left ajar a few inches, and she could smell tangy salt air and hear waves falling onto the shore. Any place in this house, I can always hear the ocean, she thought, smiling.

She pushed back the sheet and light summer comforter and sat up, enjoying the elegantly furnished room.

A cherrywood dressing table and mirror stood directly across from the bed. Beside them was a matching chest of drawers. On the adjoining wall a small, ornate desk, complete with writing paper and a fountain pen. A cut crystal vase filled with fresh flowers was on the corner of the desk, and the dressing table held tiny vials of perfume.

A door beside the desk led to a private bathroom. Claudia thought she liked the bathroom best of all. The night before, lying back in the deep bathtub, she had raised her eyes and realized that the entire ceiling was painted with pictures of mermaids.

This guest bedroom was a long way from the cramped room on Fear Street that she shared with her younger sister, Cass. I could get used to this luxury, Claudia decided.

What was it like for Marla to live like this all the time? Did she even notice how beautiful it all was?

Claudia didn't know very much about Marla's family, but she knew that her father, Anthony Drexell, was a financial wizard. He made his money buying up companies around the globe, and it seemed Marla usually communicated with him by phoning Vienna or Stockholm or Barcelona.

Mrs. Drexell was, in Marla's words, a socialite. She

accompanied her husband everywhere, and spent most of her time making the rounds of international benefits.

It must get lonely for Marla, Claudia thought. No wonder she wanted company for a whole week, rather than be alone in this big house. Alfred seemed like a nice guy, but he wouldn't be much company.

Claudia got out of bed and sat down at the dressing table to examine her sunburn. Her skin was still an alarming shade of red, and it hurt to raise her eyebrows or wrinkle her nose, or even smile.

"What's wrong with you, Claudia?" she asked her reflection. It was the first time in years she'd gotten burned. She'd been crazy to agree to let the others bury her in sand, and crazier still to fall asleep in the sun—though the antihistamine had had something to do with that.

Why hadn't one of the girls awakened her? She couldn't believe they'd forgotten. They knew how easily she burned. How could they have left her to fall asleep like that?

Claudia smoothed some aloe gel onto her face and then hurried to get dressed. She put on a yellow T-shirt, black spandex shorts, and white sneakers, and headed downstairs past Joy's and Sophie's rooms. Their doors were still shut.

Claudia checked her watch. It was nine in the morning. They'd all turned in fairly early the night before. How could they sleep late with all that bright sunlight streaming in? she wondered.

Downstairs, she found Marla in the kitchen, wearing crisp white shorts and a pale pink top. "Alfred fixed us a fruit salad, biscuits, and some sausage," Marla said, motioning to a row of blue and white china serving dishes on the counter. "Help yourself."

"I guess Joy and Sophie are still asleep," Claudia said.

"Joy hates getting up before noon," Marla reminded her.

"And Sophie loves doing whatever Joy does," Claudia added with a smile.

It was true. At Camp Full Moon, Sophie had practically worshiped Joy, copying her every move.

"How about a game of tennis before they wake up?" Claudia suggested, spooning fruit salad into a bowl. Tennis was Claudia's sport. At camp, she remembered, she and Marla had been fairly evenly matched. But Marla said that her father was going to get her a private coach, so she was probably terrific now.

"Well, okay," Marla replied reluctantly. "A short match. You don't want to get too much sun, Claud."

"I'll be careful," Claudia replied. Once again she had the uneasy feeling that Marla was gloating about her sunburn. She dished up the fruit salad and tried to ignore it.

The tennis match was not what Claudia had expected.

Marla couldn't do anything right. She had never had a problem with Claudia's serve at camp, but today she failed to return ball after ball.

"The sun is in my eyes," she explained, shaking her head, kicking at the red-clay court.

They traded sides.

To Claudia's surprise, Marla misjudged balls,

swung wildly, and hit the ball high in the air as if she were a beginner.

Those private lessons have wrecked her game! Claudia thought. She was winning in straight sets and hadn't even worked up a sweat.

"It's just not my day. My muscles are tired or something," Marla cried unhappily. Angrily, she threw her racket down.

"You'll probably beat me easily next time," Claudia said, jogging over to her.

Marla scowled and studied her toes, avoiding Claudia's eyes. "I'm out of practice," she muttered. "I haven't had time to play this year."

Claudia stepped up beside her as they headed slowly back to the house. She placed a hand lightly on Marla's shoulder. "Maybe you're upset seeing us again," she said softly.

Marla turned to her, her blue eyes wide. "Upset?"

"You know," Claudia insisted. "You haven't seen us since the accident. Since your sister died."

Marla's face turned bright red. She tugged the hairband out of her hair and shook her blond hair free. "I don't want to talk about Alison," she replied, still avoiding Claudia's eyes.

"It's on all of our minds," Claudia said. "We know how you must feel, Marla. We—"

"I *told* you," Marla shouted shrilly, "I don't want to talk about that." She turned abruptly, her eyes narrowed into slits, her cheeks bright scarlet, and stormed angrily toward the house.

When Claudia finally returned to the house, she was pleased to see that Marla had calmed down. Joy,

Sophie, and Marla were seated at a white umbrella table on the terrace, chatting as they ate their breakfast. Behind them Alfred was humming pleasantly as he pruned a row of rhododendrons near the guest house.

"How was your tennis game?" Joy asked Claudia as Claudia pulled a canvas chair into the shade of the umbrella.

"She let me win," Claudia joked, glancing at Marla. "She wants me to get overconfident, then she's going to *slaughter* me."

Marla forced a smile. "Claudia's game has really improved," she said, and poured herself a glass of orange juice from a tall glass pitcher.

"Looks like a great beach day," Joy exclaimed, raising her eyes to the cloudless, blue sky.

"I can't wait!" Sophie declared.

"Alfred packed us a picnic lunch," Marla told them. "We can carry it down and have lunch on the beach."

"I hope there are good waves," Joy said to Marla. "I want to try out one of your boogie boards."

"The waves are always pretty strong," Marla told her. "There aren't any sand bars or anything to break them up." She took a long drink of orange juice, then turned to Claudia. "Do you want to stay up here and avoid the sun?"

Claudia hesitated. "No. I thought I could take a beach umbrella down to the sand and just stay in the shade."

"Good idea," Marla replied. She shouted to Alfred to fetch a beach umbrella from the equipment shed.

A short while later the four girls were making their way across the back lawn toward the steps leading down to the ocean. Claudia carried a yellow- and white-striped beach umbrella over her shoulder. Ahead of her, Marla and Joy each gripped one handle of the large Styrofoam cooler that held their lunch. Sophie led the way.

As they neared the cliff edge, the roar of the ocean grew louder. Shielding her eyes from the bright sun, Claudia could see the dark *V* of a sea gull soaring high above them against the bright blue sky.

Not yet eleven, and it was already hot. The air hung wet and heavy, without a breeze.

I'm going to take a short swim, Claudia thought, shifting the weight of the beach umbrella on her shoulder. If I slather my face with sunscreen, my burn won't get worse.

They hesitated at the metal gate.

"Just turn the handle," Marla instructed Sophie. "It'll open."

Balancing the beach umbrella, Claudia watched Sophie grab the oval handle on the gate.

Then she watched Sophie appear to freeze as a loud crackling burst from the gate.

Claudia uttered a horrified gasp as Sophie's body shot backward and she slumped to the ground.

chapter

7

Surprise Visitors

Marla was the first to move.

She dove toward a control panel hidden behind some low shrubs and tugged down a switch.

Claudia tossed down the beach umbrella and lowered herself to the ground beside her fallen friend.

Sophie stared up at her with unfocused eyes. Her glasses had flown off, and Claudia picked them up from the ground.

"Sophie? Are you okay?" Claudia demanded, holding the glasses.

"Yeah, I guess." Sophie blinked once, twice. The color began to return to her ghostly white face.

Marla knelt beside Claudia and leaned over Sophie. "You had a nasty shock," she said, shaking her head.

Sophie seemed confused as she started to sit up. "My whole body is buzzing."

Marla gently helped her up. She turned toward the house and yelled for Alfred, cupping her hands into a megaphone.

The servant must have gone into the house because there was no sign of him.

"I don't get this," Marla declared, raising her eyes to Claudia. "I just don't get this. The electrical system is supposed to turn itself off during the day."

Sophie groaned. "Ow," she muttered, and began to rub the back of her neck. "It hurts back here. The muscles are all tight."

"Are you sure you're okay?" Joy demanded, still lingering several feet away. "Do you feel dizzy or anything?"

"I'm okay," Sophie answered, still rubbing the back of her neck. "Ow. That really did hurt, though."

"You could've been killed!" Joy shrieked, her shoulders beginning to tremble under the loose top she wore over her bathing suit.

"Joy, please," Marla muttered impatiently. "Sophie is all right. Don't carry on and make it worse."

Joy muttered an apology.

"How do you feel, Sophie?" Claudia asked softly. "Better?"

"Yeah." Sophie nodded. "I'm just afraid the shock made my hair even more frizzy!"

Everyone laughed except for Marla.

She rose to her feet and began pacing in front of them, her hands balled into tight fists at her sides. "I don't understand this," she kept muttering. "That system is not on during the day. It goes off automatically."

"Maybe the timer is broken," Claudia suggested, helping Sophie to her feet. Sophie took her glasses from Claudia and slipped them on with a shaky hand.

"She could have been killed!" Joy repeated.

Marla flashed Joy an impatient look. Then her expression softened as she turned back to Sophie. "I'm so sorry. Really. I'm so sorry. Do you want to go back to the house?"

"No. No way!" Sophie declared, motioning for Marla to stop. "I'm okay. Really. My heart is racing a little, but I feel fine. Let's get down to the beach. Let's not spoil this beautiful day."

"But the shock—" Joy began.

"It just woke me up, that's all," Sophie said, forcing a smile. "Really. We have only one week together. I don't want to spoil it."

"If you're sure . . ." Marla said, studying Sophie's face.

"Tell you what," Sophie said. "I'll stay in the shade with Claudia. Okay? I'll rest for a bit in the shade. My body's just tingling a bit. I'm a little shaky, that's all."

Marla stared at Sophie thoughtfully, then shrugged. "Well, okay. But if you start to feel weird, let us know?"

Sophie agreed.

Joy had finally calmed down and hoisted the heavy cooler up by herself.

"We're all getting *cooked* here!" Claudia joked. "First I get barbecued by the sun. Now Sophie nearly gets fried by the gate."

Claudia meant it as a light remark, but Marla took it to heart. "They were accidents—right?" Marla snapped angrily as if challenging Claudia.

"Yeah, of course," Claudia replied quickly, her voice rising. "Of course they were just accidents, Marla."

"Don't worry. When we get back, I'm going to speak to Alfred," Marla proclaimed in a low voice filled with menace.

They made their way down the wooden stairs slowly, with Marla leading the way. Far below, Claudia could see the sparkling, blue-green ocean ending as white froth on the sandy shore.

The air grew cooler, saltier, but the hot sun still burned down on Claudia's shoulders.

By the time Claudia had descended the stairs and stepped onto the beach, Marla was spreading the blanket. Joy had set the heavy cooler down. She spread out a brightly colored beach towel of her own. Then she pulled off her top, revealing a shiny green bikini underneath, and immediately began to brush out her long, black hair.

Well, that was one thing that hadn't changed from camp, Claudia thought dryly. Joy is still brushing her hair at every opportunity.

Marla had spread the blanket out a good distance from the stairs. As Claudia trudged toward it with Sophie at her side, she felt burning grains of sand slide through her thongs and onto her feet.

What a scorcher! Claudia thought, gazing up at the sun, which seemed to fill the entire sky.

At Marla's direction she stood the beach umbrella up at the edge of the blanket, then buried it deep in the sand, bearing down with all her weight.

As soon as the umbrella was spread, Sophie lowered

herself into its shade and stretched out on her stomach. Claudia reached for the beach bag and began covering her sunburned face with a thick layer of pink sunscreen.

"You look gorgeous, dahling!" Joy trilled.

"Oh, shut up," Claudia muttered, laughing. Adjusting the straps of her purple, one-piece swimsuit, she began to apply the pink sunscreen to the rest of her body.

Joy, meanwhile, had put down her hairbrush and was rubbing a light tanning oil over her already tanned body.

Claudia turned her eyes to Marla, who was still working at getting the blanket perfectly smooth. How strange, Claudia thought, her eyes on Marla's slender back. *Marla isn't tan at all. In fact, she's very pale.*

It struck Claudia as strange because Marla had told them she'd spent most of the summer here at the beach.

How has she managed to avoid the sun for the entire summer? Claudia wondered.

Her thoughts were interrupted by a low cry from Joy. Claudia saw Joy sitting up on the blanket, shading her eyes with one hand and staring out at the water.

"I think we've got company," Joy declared.

Sure enough, two boys were stepping out of the water. They were wearing blue, sleeveless wet suits and carrying pink and black surfboards under their arms.

Claudia raised her hand to her mouth to cover a startled gasp.

One of the boys, she saw, was Daniel. Daniel, the Ghost Boy.

chapter

8

"Let's Party"

*T*he two boys stepped onto the sand, water dripping off their wet suits.

Shielding her eyes from the sun with her arm, Claudia realized the boy wasn't Daniel at all. It was another tall, dark-haired boy.

What's happening to me? Am I getting really messed up? She asked herself, watching the boys approach.

She studied them as they tossed down their surfboards. They were about seventeen, both with strong, muscular builds.

The one Claudia had thought was Daniel was slim with dark, razor-cut hair and gray eyes. He grinned at the girls, his eyes lingering on Claudia. She had a sinking feeling that what was making him grin was the sight of her face covered in pink sun block.

41

"We've got to get rid of them," Marla whispered, adjusting the top of her red bikini.

"How come?" Claudia heard Joy whisper back. "They're cute."

"Hey, how's it going?" the second boy called out. He had longish blond hair and a more compact build, almost like that of a wrestler.

His friend gazed down the shoreline toward Summerhaven. "I have a feeling we're way past the bird sanctuary."

"You girls see any birds around here?" the blond guy asked. His grin, Claudia saw, revealed about four hundred teeth.

"Just a couple of Dodos," Marla said nastily.

Claudia was surprised by Marla's meanness. Why was she on their case?

Joy had climbed to her feet and was brushing back her hair and smiling at the two boys. Sophie remained under the shade of the umbrella, but she too seemed pleased by the surprise visitors.

The boys' grins faded. The blond-haired boy sauntered toward the blanket. "We were just taking out our boards and got caught in a really strong riptide." He pointed out to the water. "It runs along the shore. It was amazing. Pulled us out here to the Point before we even knew it."

"How fascinating," Marla replied sarcastically.

Claudia watched Joy roll her eyes. "Marla, will you please chill?" she whispered, her dark eyes on the boys.

The dark-haired one followed his friend toward the blanket. "Watch out if you go swimming," he said very seriously. "If you get caught in that riptide, you could get pulled out beyond the Point."

Marla stood with her hands on the hips of her red swimsuit. "Thanks for the safety tip," she said coldly. "It was very nice of you to come warn us, but this is a private beach." She pointed toward the sanctuary and Summerhaven. "If you want to surf, the public beach is down there."

The dark-haired boy grinned at Marla. "I thought all beaches were public," he said, studying her. He raised his eyes to the stairway that led up to her family's estate. "Has your family bought the ocean too?"

The other boy sat down on the beach blanket and smiled at Sophie. "Hi. Are you always this quiet?"

Sophie giggled. She pulled off her glasses and smiled at him. "Not always."

"Don't you think you should go now?" Marla asked, frowning unpleasantly.

"Depends on what you have for lunch," the blond boy told her. He slid the cooler over and lifted the lid.

His friend held a hand out to Claudia. "I'm Carl, this is Dean, and thanks for inviting us to lunch."

"Well . . ." Claudia found herself speechless. She glanced at Marla, who was fuming.

Why is Marla so unfriendly? Claudia wondered.

Does she know something about these boys? Is she really scared of them?

"Wow, you must really hate the sun!" Carl exclaimed, staring at Claudia's lotion-covered face. He laughed, shaking his head.

43

Claudia could feel herself blushing underneath the thick layer of goo. "I—I got a bad burn yesterday," she stammered.

Kneeling on the blanket, Dean had begun emptying the cooler. "There's plenty here," he said. "Fried chicken. Potato salad. Lots of little sandwiches. Picnic time!" He raised his eyes from the cooler and smiled at Marla, a shark's smile.

Carl joined his friend, dropping down on the other side of the cooler. "Is there enough for the girls too?"

"Yeah. We can share," Dean replied, grinning his many-toothed grin.

Marla, her hands in tight little fists, a furious expression on her face, started to say something. But Joy cut in. "There's plenty of food," she told Marla. "Why not share with them?"

Carl grinned at her appreciatively and offered her the plate of sandwiches. "What's your name?"

"Joy. Joy Birkin." She took the plate and sat down next to Carl.

"I'm Sophie Moore," Sophie offered brightly, moving out from under the umbrella to join them. "Mmmm. The chicken does look good. I'm starving even though we just ate breakfast."

Marla stormed off to the water's edge, where she angrily ignored them all.

"Don't mind Marla. She's just a little shy," Joy said.

"How about you?" Carl asked Claudia, his voice mocking. "Are you shy too?"

"That's why she's hiding behind that pink stuff," Dean teased, chewing on a chicken leg.

Claudia knew she shouldn't care, but she was dying

of embarrassment and knew she looked like a total dork.

"You should try that pink stuff," Dean told Carl. "It would be an improvement on *you!*" He tossed his chicken bone on the sand and grabbed for a sandwich.

"Hey, don't litter," Carl scolded his friend. Then he added, "This is a private beach, remember?"

The two boys laughed heartily, slapping each other high-fives.

Joy asked them questions about surfboarding. It was obvious to Claudia that she was flirting with them. Obvious to the boys too.

After a while Sophie and Carl moved under the umbrella, where they chatted quietly, sipping on cans of soda.

The sun had moved higher in the sky. The ocean waves were lined with gold.

"This isn't a bad picnic," Claudia said, feeling a little strange about the situation.

"Too bad the princess over there won't join us," Dean said.

Claudia saw Marla heading back toward them, taking long strides over the fine sand, her features set in anger. "Did you save me a sandwich or something at least?" she demanded.

"There are some left," Dean replied. "But you'll have to ask nicely."

Marla uttered an angry groan and crossed her arms over her chest. "I'm going to ask you nicely one more time to *leave!*" she said through gritted teeth.

Dean jumped up and stepped in front of her. "Hey, give us a break," he pleaded, a mocking grin spreading over his face. He pushed a lock of blond hair off his tanned forehead. "Carl and I are great guys. Why the attitude?"

"I'm warning you," Marla fumed. "Just go— okay?"

Dean took a defiant step closer to her. "Don't spoil the party, Marla. Is that your name? Marla?" He glanced quickly back at his friend, who had come out from under the umbrella. Carl was staring at Dean warily, as if expecting trouble.

"Carl and I were hoping that after lunch, we'd all go up to your house and—you know—party." Dean took another step toward Marla, who stepped back.

Uh-oh, thought Claudia, climbing slowly to her feet. This was getting tense.

"Get back. Go away!" Marla cried, contempt in her eyes.

"No. Really," Dean insisted. "Carl and I are great guys. Let's go up to the house. It's too hot down here, don't you think?"

Carl was standing there, his smile fading, his features hardening.

Are these guys just playing at being tough? Claudia wondered, drawing back. Or are they really looking for trouble?

"I—I have an attack dog," Marla warned, glancing up at her house. "An Irish wolfhound. Have you ever seen an Irish wolfhound? They're huge."

"Oooh, I'm shaking all over!" Dean cried, shaking his arms and legs. "How about you, Carl?"

"Chill," Carl said edgily. "Let's just go, Dean."

"All I have to do is call the dog," Marla warned.

"Dogs like me," Dean boasted. "I'm not scared."

He turned to Claudia and the other girls. "You want Carl and me to come up to the house, right?"

"I—I think you'd better go," Claudia stammered, moving over to stand beside Marla.

Dean moved closer, his expression menacing. "You're not going to invite us up?" he asked Marla, his eyes cold, his tone challenging.

"No way," Marla insisted.

Then, before Claudia realized what was happening, she saw a blur of motion.

And heard a loud *smack*.

Marla staggered back with an angry cry.

It took Claudia a long moment to realize that Dean had slapped Marla.

Oh no, Claudia moaned, suddenly afraid. *These boys are going to be trouble.*

chapter

9

Return of the Ghost

Marla quickly regained her balance and glared at Dean, her face bright red.

"It was a horsefly," Dean told her. "On your shoulder."

"Huh?" Marla cried, a little stunned.

"A really big horsefly," Dean repeated. "Those things can bite."

"But—" Marla's expression softened.

"I didn't mean to slap it that hard," Dean said softly. "Sorry if I scared you."

Claudia breathed a sigh of relief. Behind her, she could hear Joy and Sophie giggling nervously.

"We'd better get going," Carl said, picking up his pink and black surfboard.

"Yeah. Okay," Dean agreed. He cast another apologetic look at Marla. "I really didn't mean to scare you or anything," he said. Then he blurted out, "My dad used to work for your dad."

"He *what?*" Marla demanded.

But the boys had hefted their surfboards, tucked them under their arms, and started off down the beach in the direction of town. "Thanks for lunch!" Carl called back.

"It was great!" Dean added.

Claudia watched them walk along the shoreline, kicking up wet clumps of sand as they made their way.

"Let's pack up and go back to the house," Marla said, frowning. "It's too hot down here anyway."

"Marla, why'd you give those guys such a hard time?" Claudia demanded.

Marla was shaking out the beach blanket. She stopped and turned to Claudia. "My parents made me promise," she told her.

"Promise what? No boys?" Joy asked.

"My parents made me promise it would be just the four of us this week," Marla replied. "If they found out there were guys with us, they'd ground me forever."

"It's not like they were sleeping over!" Joy protested. "I mean, they just happened to wash up on the beach."

"I don't need any trouble," Marla replied, and began folding the blanket.

That's an odd thing to say, Claudia thought, helping Sophie and Joy load up the cooler. But then she realized that what had happened with the two boys really wasn't that much different from the way Marla had treated guys at camp the previous summer.

Marla had been very standoffish around guys then. As far as Claudia knew, Marla had had only one boyfriend, a guy named Michael, and they had gone together for only a few months.

Joy, on the other hand, flirted as easily as she breathed. And Sophie worked hard to copy Joy, although she was less outgoing.

As for herself—Claudia had gone out with a few guys, but she'd only had one real boyfriend. The problem, she'd decided, was that she didn't make much of an impression on guys. She met them and they forgot her.

She smiled, realizing that wasn't true with Dean and Carl. She knew she'd made an impression this time. They'd probably remember her forever—as the Girl with the Really Gross Pink Goo on Her Face.

Later that day the three girls were up in Claudia's room. Joy and Sophie, in shorts and sleeveless T-shirts, were sprawled on top of the quilted coverlet on the four-poster bed. Claudia stood at the open French doors, staring down as the long, late afternoon shadows spread out across the back lawn.

"Does anyone here think Marla is acting a little weird?" Joy asked. "Raise your hands."

Both Claudia and Sophie obediently raised their hands.

"She's so tense," Sophie remarked, lying on her back, hands behind her frizzy brown hair.

"She's always been a little tense around boys," Claudia said.

"But she wasn't just tense. She was angry," Joy declared. "Angry that the boys were there."

50

"She never gave them a chance," Sophie agreed.

"I thought Carl was kind of cute," Joy said, grinning.

"Kind of," Claudia said from the window. "But they were kind of tough too. I think Marla was frightened. I know I was a little bit."

"Marla was a lot more relaxed at camp," Sophie offered.

"A lot has happened since then," Claudia said wistfully. She walked over and sat down on the edge of the bed at Sophie's feet. "Are you feeling better?"

Sophie shrugged. "I'm still a little weird. Kind of light-headed."

"What did it feel like?" Joy asked. "Did it hurt?"

"Yeah, it hurt," Sophie told her. "It was sort of like being punched in the stomach. I couldn't breathe, and—oh, I don't know."

"What a weird two days," Claudia commented. "We're supposed to be having fun, enjoying the beach and this incredible house. So far, it hasn't exactly been fun in the sun! You nearly got electrocuted. I got buried—"

"And don't forget that disgusting brown worm in my salad," Joy interrupted. "That was so gross!"

Claudia and Sophie laughed.

"I have to tell you something, Claud," Sophie said, abruptly sitting up and cutting her laugh short. "I meant to tell you before, but I didn't have a chance."

"What?" Claudia demanded, rubbing her hand over the smooth bedspread. "Why so serious all of a sudden?"

"Well . . ." Sophie seemed hesitant to talk, then all at once the words burst out of her. "Joy and I wanted

51

to go back for you yesterday afternoon, but Marla wouldn't let us."

Claudia stared at Sophie, not quite understanding what Sophie was telling her.

"When we got back from our walk, Marla insisted you had gone up to the house," Sophie continued, lowering her voice to a whisper, her eyes on the bedroom door. "We took the other path, the one up from the dunes. But Joy and I wanted to go back down to make sure you weren't still buried in the sand."

"Yeah. We were worried about you," Joy added.

"But Marla said she was sure you had left the beach. She insisted we go up to the house with her," Sophie whispered.

"Weird," Claudia muttered.

"Then she acted so surprised when you came staggering up from the beach, burned to a crisp," Joy said.

Claudia automatically touched her face. Her cheeks and forehead were hot and still a little swollen. She walked over to the makeup table to get more aloe lotion.

"I guess Marla was confused," Claudia said thoughtfully. "If you went up on the other path, there was no way you could have seen me."

"I think she's messed up," Joy said, lowering her feet to the floor and turning to face Claudia. "I think the accident last summer—"

"That's the other thing," Sophie interrupted. "She never mentions her sister. She hasn't mentioned Alison once. Don't you think that's strange? I mean, we were all there last summer. We all shared it. I mean, Alison *was* Marla's sister. But we all—"

"Poor Alison," Joy said in a low whisper. "That poor kid."

"Well, it's on my mind all the time," Sophie admitted heatedly. "I'm sure it's on *all* of our minds, but Marla acts as if it never happened. I mean—"

"She told me she doesn't want to talk about it," Claudia interrupted. The fresh lotion felt cool and soothing on her forehead.

"You *asked* her?" Joy demanded. "You mentioned Alison?"

"We were playing tennis this morning before you guys woke up. I mentioned the accident—and Marla snapped at me. She told me she didn't want to talk about it."

"But it's so—*unnatural* not to!" Sophie protested. "I feel like I'm bottled up. I mean . . ." Her voice trailed off.

"I guess Marla just wants us all to have a great time this week, and forget about what happened," Claudia said thoughtfully. She stared at her burned face in the mirror. "And if we could all stop being so accident prone, I'm sure we *would* have a great time. . . ."

That evening the four girls had dinner in the big, formal dining room again. Sitting scrunched together at one end of the long table made the huge room seem even bigger than it was.

But everyone was in a good mood. Joy told hilarious stories about her attempts to break up with a thick-headed boyfriend who refused to get what she was saying to him. The story had the girls roaring with laughter.

Then Marla told a funny story about her father showing up in the wrong country for a business meeting and being totally confused as to why everyone was speaking Italian!

Then, as Alfred began to clear the dishes from the table, Joy turned to Marla. "So," she asked, "what's there to do in Summerhaven at night?"

"Not much," Marla admitted. "We can see a movie, maybe. There's one old movie theater in town. It smells like cats, but sometimes they show good films. Or we could hang out on the boardwalk."

"Boardwalk? You mean like an amusement park?" Joy asked excitedly.

"Yeah." Marla nodded.

"Let's go!" Joy cried. "I love rides!"

"Me too," Sophie added enthusiastically. "We've got to do bumper cars—and the house of mirrors. I love seeing myself skinny!"

"How about you, Claud?" Marla asked.

"Sounds good," Claudia replied. The idea of getting out of the Drexell mansion for a while and seeing other people appealed to her. She thought of the things she liked best about amusement parks. "I want to ride the Ferris wheel."

"No way! Not me!" Joy blurted out. "Ever since last summer, I'm afraid of heights!"

"Oh!" Sophie cried out, her mouth dropping open.

Joy immediately realized what she'd said. She turned bright red. "Oh, I'm sorry, Marla. I—I wasn't thinking." She lowered her eyes to the table.

"No problem," Marla said in a flat, dry voice, her eyes blank, her face completely without expression.

* * *

A short while later the four girls were in the Mercedes, with Marla at the wheel, driving toward Summerhaven. Again Claudia was struck by how isolated the mansion was on its remote point of land. The house was miles from any humans.

About twenty minutes later Marla pulled into a parking space at the edge of town, and the four girls stepped onto the boardwalk.

What a change! Claudia thought. She felt as if she were a thousand miles from the Drexell estate. The beach in town was a much narrower strip of sand. It was flat with no dunes, and even the waves seemed tamer. There were no cliffs. The sound of human voices, laughing and screaming on the rides, drowned out the sounds of the ocean and the gulls.

The girls joined the crowds on the boardwalk. Neon lights flashed everywhere, and the mixed aromas of popcorn, hot dogs, and cotton candy floated through the air.

It's crowded and noisy—and friendly, Claudia found herself thinking. She realized she felt an unexpected sense of relief at being in the middle of it.

They went to the House of Laffs first and spent about fifteen minutes trying to find the mirror that would make Sophie look skinny. Claudia laughed at her reflection. She and Marla both appeared at least eight feet tall. But somehow, even in the distorting mirrors, Joy managed to look perfectly proportioned and sexy.

Next they rode the Sizzler, and, after standing in line for nearly twenty minutes, the bumper cars. Joy, in her usual cool way, slid her car right through all traffic jams, her long, black hair flying loosely behind her.

To Claudia's surprise, Sophie turned into a demon driver, intent on ramming everything in sight!

After the bumper cars, they made their way along the food stands that lined the boardwalk. Claudia stopped to buy a giant cone of pink cotton candy.

She had just taken her first careful bite when she heard a familiar voice behind her. "You have a thing for pink, don't you?"

She turned to see Carl smiling at her. Dean stood beside him, his blond hair catching the light from a street lamp. The boys had changed into faded jeans, torn at the knees, and sleeveless muscle shirts. Claudia was again aware of how good-looking both boys were, in a rough sort of way.

She raised the cone of pink cotton candy. "Yeah. I'm going to rub it all over my face," she told Carl.

The boys laughed.

"What are you two doing here?" Marla demanded, sounding more surprised than hostile.

"We live here," Carl said, grinning.

"Yeah. Right here on the boardwalk," Dean jumped in. "That's my bedroom over there." He pointed to a bench between two food stands.

"Very cozy," Joy said, moving close to Carl.

Sophie immediately imitated Joy, moving in on Dean.

"You guys want to do the bumper cars?" Joy asked. "We just did them a few minutes ago. They're fun!"

"Yeah. Sure," Carl agreed quickly.

Marla started to protest, but she found herself swept along as everyone hurried to get in line.

"I'll meet up with you in a bit!" Claudia called to her. Claudia decided she'd had enough bumper cars for the night. She wanted to explore the boardwalk, and she needed a little time to herself.

Besides, she thought, Joy and Sophie were obviously going to monopolize the boys. And she was sure Marla would go with them just to make sure they didn't invite Carl and Dean back to the house.

So why should she tag along?

Taking a bite of her cotton candy, Claudia made her way past a row of games and a small video-game arcade. The noise on the boardwalk was so loud, it drowned out the roar of the ocean, even though the beach was right beneath them.

Beyond the arcade the crowd thinned out. The lights grew dimmer. Claudia took a last lick of the empty paper cone, then tossed it into a trash basket.

She licked her sticky fingers and gazed up at the sky. Slender wisps of gray cloud swam over a pale full moon high in the sky. Away from the game booths and food stands and crowds, the air felt cool and wet.

I'd better turn around and go find my friends, she thought.

As she turned, she saw that someone was standing nearby, staring intently at her.

Startled, Claudia stopped and focused on him.

She recognized his straight, dark hair and his intense dark eyes at once.

Daniel.

"The Ghost Boy!" she cried aloud.

57

chapter

10

Death on the Boardwalk

"What did you call me?" He moved quickly toward her, a smile forming on his handsome face.

"I—uh—nothing," Claudia stammered, embarrassed.

"Did you say I was a ghost?" he demanded, his black eyes burning into hers as if looking for the answer to his question.

"No. I—" Claudia didn't know *what* to say.

Impulsively, she grabbed his hand and squeezed.

The hand was cold.

As cold as yesterday on the beach, she thought, surprised.

As cold as death. The thought creeped into her mind.

"No. You're real," she told him, letting go quickly,

smiling at him, her heart thudding. "At least, you feel real. I mean—"

"I guess that's a compliment," he said with a shrug.

"It's just that when you helped me, you vanished before I could thank you," Claudia said awkwardly. "You vanished like a ghost, and—well . . ."

"Your name is Claudia, right?" he asked, shoving his hands into the pockets of his denim shorts. He wore a white Gap T-shirt with a gray sweatshirt tied around his waist.

Real clothing, Claudia thought, feeling a little guilty.

So what made me believe he was a ghost?

What could I have been thinking of?

"Yes," she said. "Claudia Walker."

"Your burn doesn't look too bad," he said, his eyes examining her forehead. "Do your friends do that to you a lot? Bury you in the sand and leave you there to roast?"

"Not a lot," Claudia told him. "They thought I had gone up to the house."

"Great friends," Daniel said, shaking his head.

"They're okay," Claudia replied, feeling defensive. What right did he have to put down her friends? He hadn't even met them. "It was an accident, a mistake," she said.

They had been ambling back toward the amusement area. Claudia found herself doing most of the talking. She told him how the girls had been in the same bunk at camp the summer before, and how surprised she was to receive Marla's invitation to come visit for a week.

Daniel listened attentively, making quiet comments. He seemed shy to Claudia. Not uncomfortably shy, just shy. As they walked, his arm bumped hers softly. His dark eyes studied her.

They stopped at the Ferris wheel. As it twirled, the bright yellow lights on its frame rose up against the black night sky like shooting stars.

A cool breeze floated in off the ocean, fluttering Claudia's hair. "Beautiful night," she murmured, smiling at Daniel.

He held up his hand. "Look. I have two tickets," he said, his eyes on the Ferris wheel. "The line isn't very long. Let's go."

"Okay. I love Ferris wheels!" she declared.

"I know," he said mysteriously, taking her hand and leading her to the line.

Why is his hand so cold? Claudia wondered.

"What do you mean? How could you know?" she demanded playfully.

"I'm a ghost, remember? I know all things." He grinned at her, a mischievous grin.

A few moments later Daniel handed the tickets to the young man running the ride. An empty seat rolled around. The wheel stopped. They stepped along a short ramp and climbed into the seat.

As soon as the safety bar was pushed down in front of them, the seat lurched backward and, with a jolt, they rose up off the ground.

Claudia leaned back against the plastic seat. She was a little surprised to find Daniel's arm around the seat back. She rested her head against it, the breeze off the ocean cool against her face, and stared up at the sky.

"It's such a clear night," she said. "We'll be able to see everything. The ocean. The entire boardwalk . . ."

He smiled. "It's a full moon," he said softly, pointing with his free hand.

"Do you turn into a werewolf in a few minutes?" Claudia teased.

He growled at her. "Make up your mind," he said. "Am I a ghost or a werewolf?"

"Do you live in town?" she asked.

"No." He shook his head. A wave of black hair fell over his forehead.

"Well, where do you live? What are you doing here?" Claudia asked.

"I live everywhere. I float through the night sky," he replied, grinning. He leaned very close to her, lowering his arm from the seat back to her shoulders. "I haunt people," he whispered with mock menace, bringing his face close to hers.

"Have you ever been all alone in the dark with a ghost before?" he asked, lowering his voice to a whisper. "Have you ever been this close to a ghost, Claudia?"

Is he going to kiss me? Claudia wondered.

Do I want him to?

Yes.

She felt disappointed when he pulled back against the seat. "Wow. Look at the ocean," he said. "It's unreal."

As they rose higher, the ocean coming into view on their right. The full moon cast a wash of pale light over it, making the tossing waters sparkle like silver.

Beneath them stretched the crowded, noisy boardwalk. Turning to her left, Claudia could see the lights of Summerhaven, tiny and twinkling, as if the town were some kind of toy.

"You've been here longer than I have," she told Daniel, enjoying the weight of his arm around her shoulders. "Point out the sights to me."

"Well—okay," he agreed reluctantly, leaning across her to see out the left side. He pointed. "That's a building of some kind over there. And that's a red light. And that's a street. And there's a yellow light." He grinned at her, his face inches from hers.

"You're a great tour guide," she teased.

"I told you, I don't live here," he said, staring hard into her eyes.

He's so good-looking, Claudia thought. And funny. And nice.

Impulsively, she leaned forward and kissed him.

He seemed startled at first, then returned her kiss.

He's real, she found herself thinking. He's not a ghost. His lips are warm.

The car suddenly rocked and came to an abrupt start.

"Oh!" Claudia cried out, pulling away from him. She gazed down. They were at the very top.

"Why'd we stop?" Daniel demanded, leaning over the safety bar to stare straight down, rocking the car gently.

"They're letting on more people," Claudia replied, the taste of his lips still on hers. She smiled at him. "I like it up here. Look how big the moon is."

"I'll bet I could touch it," he said, following her gaze. He stood up, rocking the car violently. "Here. I'll grab it," he said, reaching up with both hands.

"Daniel—sit down!" Claudia cried.

SUNBURN

Leaning over the safety bar, he pretended to grab the moon.

And as he reached, the seat jolted hard—and tilted all the way forward.

Claudia stared in horror as Daniel, his arms still outstretched, went sailing over the safety bar and fell head first to his death.

chapter

11

Alison's Tragic Accident

*B*efore she could cry out, before she could even *breathe,* Claudia realized she wasn't watching Daniel fall.

She was watching Alison.

Alison. Poor Alison had been on Claudia's mind since arriving in Summerhaven.

Now, once again, she was reliving the tragic accident that had taken Alison Drexell's life.

Like a life flashing before a person's eyes, the tragedy of the previous summer appeared to Claudia, the stark horror of it washing over her as Daniel rocked the Ferris wheel car.

Once again it was the previous July and she was back at Camp Full Moon. . . .

Claudia stretched out on her bunk, feeling limp from the damp afternoon heat. She swatted listlessly at a fly. She was convinced the insects liked Bunk 12's peculiar combination of scents—a mix of bug repellent, deodorant, and Marla's rosewater perfume.

It was just after lunch, "free time" when everyone was supposed to be in her bunk writing letters home. Luckily, Caroline, Claudia's counselor, was in love with the waterfront counselor, so Caroline was never around and none of them ever had to write letters.

That afternoon Claudia, Marla, Joy, and Sophie were playing a lazy game of Truth or Dare. It was Joy's turn. She gave Claudia a sly look. "Truth," she said. "Tell us how many zits you have today."

Claudia blushed as she realized Joy must have seen her in the latrine that morning examining her face.

"Would you rather have a dare?" Joy asked idly as she applied pale pink polish to her toenails.

"Three," Claudia confessed, staring at the wooden floorboards. "Big deal. So I don't have your flawless skin."

The girls all laughed.

Suddenly the screen door banged open and Alison, Marla's younger sister, bopped in. Alison was a year younger than her sister. Like Marla, she was long and slender, with blond hair. But to Claudia she was much less sophisticated. Alison didn't have her sister's easy grace or natural athletic skills, and she wasn't the least bit likable.

"What are you guys doing?" Alison asked.

"Nothing you'd be interested in," Joy assured her.

Marla didn't even look up. "Go away, fish face."

Even Claudia, who had tried hard to like Alison, had to admit she was a world-class brat. She never hung out with the kids in her own bunk. She acted desperate to be accepted by Marla's friends and become part of Marla's group.

Which might have been okay if she weren't a snitch and a spy. Alison was always reporting their minor sins to the head counselor, always doing her best to get them in trouble.

"I want to play," Alison announced, dropping down on Marla's bunk. "Can I play? I'm bored."

"You don't know what we're playing," Joy pointed out, frowning.

"Truth or Dare," Alison said smugly.

"You're too young for it," Claudia told her.

"Go out and play in the traffic," Marla said coldly. "You don't belong in here, Alison."

"I'll report you all," Alison threatened. "You're supposed to be writing letters home."

"Fine," Marla said. "You want to play? Then tell us about the time Mother caught you kissing Michael Jennings up in your bedroom."

"Huh? I never did," Alison insisted. "That's a filthy lie!"

"Wasn't he *your* boyfriend?" Claudia asked Marla, unable to conceal the surprise in her voice.

"He *was* my boyfriend till Alison saw him," Marla said, scowling.

"You're lying!" Alison insisted shrilly. "You're a filthy liar!"

"Oh, yeah. Right," Marla replied sarcastically, rolling her eyes. "Come on, Ali. You want to play the game? Tell my friends what you did to me. Come on. Details."

"This is fascinating and all," Joy said in a weary tone, "but couldn't Alison maybe leave so we can enjoy our game?"

"Yeah. Take a hike, Alison," Sophie said.

"Come on, Alison. Truth," Marla insisted. "Either tell the truth or take the dare. Truth, Ali. What happened between you and Michael?"

Alison stared at the floor, then raised her eyes defiantly to her sister. "I'll take the dare."

"You don't have to. You could just leave," Claudia pointed out. She suddenly didn't like the atmosphere in the small cabin. She had a bad feeling creeping up from her stomach, one of dread.

"I said I'll take the dare!" Alison insisted, standing up angrily.

"Then I dare you to go back to your own bunk and stay there," Claudia suggested, grinning at Joy and Sophie.

"No," Marla objected, her blue eyes lighting up. "I have a better dare. Either tell us the truth, or tonight you cross Grizzly Gorge under the full moon."

Alison glared angrily at her sister, her face drained of color. They all knew she was terrified of heights. And she wasn't exactly the most coordinated girl in the world. There was no way Alison could cross the log over the gorge—especially at night.

Finally Marla had come up with a way to make Alison leave them alone.

"All right," Alison said softly, her blue eyes locked on her sister's. "I'll do it."

"What are you saying?" Sophie cried. "You will not, Alison!"

"What time do you want to meet there?" Alison asked, ignoring Sophie.

Marla shrugged nonchalantly. "How about after lights out. At ten."

"No problem. See you there," Alison said, and stalked out of the bunk.

That night, just before ten, when they were sure Caroline was down by the mess hall with her boyfriend, the four girls crept out of the bunk one by one. It was a cool night, with the full moon yellow and low in a purple sky. Crickets chirped loudly. The trees whispered as they swayed in the soft breeze.

They were halfway down the dirt path that led to the deep gorge—when a bright light bobbed through the woods, catching Marla in its beam. They heard Caroline's stern voice. "All right, Drexell. You're busted. Where are your pals?"

Marla, muttering under her breath, stepped fully into the circle of light from the counselor's flashlight. The others remained silent. Not moving. Trying not to make a sound.

Claudia crouched behind a tree, sure that her breathing would give her away. Caroline searched for them, moving the light along the trees that lined the path. But she quickly gave up and contented herself with marching Marla back to the bunk.

"Should we go back?" Sophie whispered when Caroline and Marla were out of sight.

"Yes. This is dumb," Claudia said, lingering by the big oak tree that had hidden her.

"No," Joy insisted. "Caroline will only be waiting for us at the bunk. Besides, what if Alison is already at the gorge? We'd better go get her."

They found Alison standing on the lip of the gorge, staring down at the Grizzly River below. It was at least a twenty-foot drop, Claudia knew.

A single log had been set across the gorge, its rough surface gleaming under the bright moonlight.

"Alison, go back to your bunk. This is crazy," Claudia told her, stepping up behind her. One look at her face and Claudia could see how frightened Alison was.

"Yeah. It's okay if you wimp out," Joy said, her hands shoved into the back pockets of her jeans. "It's too far down. If you fall . . ."

"Don't do it, Alison," Sophie added, standing at the edge, peering down at the white foam of the rushing river.

Alison ignored them. "Where's my sister?" she demanded, eyeing them tensely.

"Caroline caught her and made her go back," Claudia replied. "We should go back too."

"You'll have to tell Marla I did the dare," Alison said in a tight, choked voice.

"No, please!" Joy cried.

"*You've* done it, haven't you?" Alison snapped. "You've all crossed the log. What makes you think I can't do it?"

"We did it in the daytime," Sophie told her. "And we're all very athletic—"

"And we're not afraid of heights," Claudia added.

"Come on, Alison," Joy begged.

Alison didn't say another word. Biting her lower lip, her eyes narrow with determination, she stepped out onto the log.

"No!" Claudia gasped.

The gorge was narrow—no more than thirty feet across. But if she fell, Alison would land on huge rocks in the shallow river, with current strong enough to carry her away.

"Alison—whoa!" Joy called, her hands pressed against her cheeks.

"I can't look," Sophie declared, turning away from the gorge.

Slowly, her legs trembling, Alison inched her way out onto the log.

"Alison—enough!" Claudia called. "You proved your point. You did it. Come back."

"Yeah. Come back!" Joy pleaded.

Alison ignored their frightened words.

Then, about two-thirds of the way out, she stopped, her knees buckling. She struggled to regain her balance.

"Oh, help," she said softly. "I'm going to fall."

"No, you're not," Claudia told her, moving to the edge of the log. "You're fine. Just sit down, turn around, and scoot back."

Just then Claudia saw darting, weaving circles of light play against the trees. It took her a moment to realize the light was coming from flashlights. Then she heard footsteps. Voices.

"It's Caroline!" Joy cried. "And some of the other counselors!"

"Run!" Sophie shouted. "Come on! We'll be caught!"

"Come on, Alison—hurry!" Claudia urged.

"I'm coming," Alison answered. Then the girls were running breathlessly, running back through the woods, away from the darting lights, away from the counselors.

Claudia thought that Alison was right behind her. Claudia thought that Alison was running too.

She didn't see Alison fall.

She didn't hear the hard *crack* as Alison dropped into the boulder-strewn river, the splash as she was tossed into the rushing water.

She honestly believed Alison was right behind her.

And so she ran from the counselors' lights, ran through the dark woods.

Ran through the cold black shadows . . .

Ran . . .

Now Claudia felt a hand on her shoulder.

She swallowed hard and gazed into Daniel's eyes. "You okay?" he asked softly.

She blinked, startled to discover that she wasn't in Camp Full Moon. She was sitting next to Daniel in the Ferris wheel car. And the wheel was moving smoothly again, carrying them down to the brightly lit park.

"You didn't fall?" she blurted out.

He shook his head, his eyes narrowing in confusion. "Fall? You mean out of the seat?" He laughed.

"I thought—" Claudia felt dizzy. The ground was rushing up to meet her. It took her a while to realize it was the movement of the Ferris wheel.

"I'm a ghost, remember," Daniel teased. "I fell out, but I floated back in."

She forced a smile.

Alison. You've been in the back of my mind all this time, Alison, Claudia thought with a shiver.

That's why I saw you just now. You fell. Not Daniel. You fell, Alison. Such a terrible accident . . .

A short while later the chair stopped on the platform, swaying gently. Daniel helped Claudia out. "That was cool," he said, his dark eyes sparkling.

"Yeah. It was great," Claudia agreed, still a little shaky. "Thanks, Daniel."

They started walking along the boardwalk, nearly colliding with two boys whirring rapidly toward them on rollerblades.

"I've got to find Marla and the others," Claudia told him. "Do you want to come along? I want to prove to them that— Hey!"

He was gone.

Vanished again.

What is going on here? Claudia wondered.

"Claudia! Claudia! Over here!" familiar voices called.

Claudia spun around to see her friends waving to her from in front of a brightly lit dart-game booth. Joy was carrying a hideous pink teddy bear. Dean and Carl gave Claudia a wave and took off. Her three friends came hurrying over to Claudia.

"Where did you run off to?" Marla demanded.

"Yeah. We all had a great time," Joy gushed. "The boys are nice, when you get to know them."

"Have you just been wandering around by yourself?" Marla asked, her eyes studying Claudia.

"Uh—yeah," Claudia told them. "I enjoyed it. Really. I just like watching people at places like this, you know?"

"Look what Carl won," Joy cried, holding up the ugly pink bear. "He gave him to me. I'm going to name him Carl."

"Looks just like him," Marla said dryly.

Chattering excitedly, the four girls headed to the car to go home.

Later, Claudia lay in bed, thinking about Daniel, about their kiss, about how handsome and mysterious he was. A soft breeze floated in from the open glass doors and gently cooled her skin.

She realized she hadn't learned a thing about Daniel. She didn't know where he lived or what he was doing at the beach this summer. She didn't even know his last name.

She had just drifted into a light sleep when the shrill screams awoke her.

Claudia jerked straight up, breathing hard.

The screams, she realized, were coming from Joy's room.

chapter

12

Torture

*J*oy's room was across the hall from Claudia's.

Claudia pushed open her door and fumbled for the light switch.

"Help me! Help me!" Joy was shrieking at the top of her lungs.

The ceiling light clicked on, revealing Joy sitting up in bed, her skin bright red under a sleeveless night-gown. Her black hair fell in wild tangles around her face. Her features were twisted in horror. Her arms thrashed wildly above her.

"Help me! Claudia—help me!"

Sophie and Marla burst into the room behind Claudia.

"Yuck! Joy! What are those things on your arm?" Sophie screamed.

"Help me! Please—help me!"

The three girls ran to her bed.

"Leeches!" Claudia declared.

Three enormous black leeches were stuck to Joy's right arm just below the shoulder.

"Get them off! Get them off!" Joy shrieked hysterically.

"Joy, calm down!" Marla shouted.

"How did they get on you?" Sophie demanded, nearly as hysterical as Joy.

"Stop moving around and we'll pull them off!" Claudia said, grabbing Joy's shoulder.

"Help me! Help!"

"Joy—stop thrashing about!" Claudia shouted.

"How did leeches get in her bed?" Sophie demanded of Marla.

"How should I know?" Marla cried impatiently.

Marla grabbed Joy's wrist and held it down on the bed.

With a trembling hand, Claudia struggled with the leeches. As Joy cried and shook, Claudia pulled the leeches off one by one and tossed them in a wastebasket.

"Ow! I'm bleeding! I'm bleeding!" Joy cried.

"The bleeding will stop in a minute," Claudia said, trying to reassure her.

Joy's entire body convulsed in a shudder of horror, and then was racked by another. She pulled the sheet up to her chin, shaking violently, tears streaming down her cheeks.

"Remember last summer at camp?" Sophie asked Claudia. She squinted at her. She had run into Joy's room without putting on her glasses. "Remember that day Joy was swimming in the lake and got the leech on her leg?"

"Stop!" Joy pleaded. "Don't remind me!"

It took all day to calm her down, Claudia thought unhappily.

"How did they get in here?" Marla asked angrily. She stared into the wastebasket. "How?" she demanded of no one in particular. "How could leeches get into an upstairs bedroom?"

"Someone was in here!" Joy cried, wiping away tears with her sheet.

"Huh?" Marla reacted with surprise.

"Someone put them on my arm!" Joy cried. "They weren't there when I went to bed. They weren't in the bed. Someone had to bring them in."

"How do you know that?" Claudia asked, laying a soothing hand on Joy's heaving shoulder.

"Because I checked the bed!" Joy told her. "You know how I am about bugs and worms. I pull back the covers and check the bed every night before I get into it!"

Marla strode to the window and peered out. She became very pale and worried-looking. "Who would come in here? Who would put leeches on your arm, Joy? It—it doesn't make any sense."

Joy uttered a low moan. "They're so disgusting. I felt something pinching my arm. They—they sucked my blood. They—"

"Please, Joy, try to calm down," Claudia said softly, her hand still on Joy's shoulder. "You're okay now. You're okay."

"Did someone *know* Joy has a thing about bugs?" Sophie asked.

"No one was in here," Marla said firmly, turning away from the window. "No one can get in. You know that, Sophie."

"Then how did leeches get on her arm?" Sophie demanded in a high-pitched voice.

Marla shook her head and closed her eyes. Her blond hair fell loosely over the shoulders of her white nightshirt. She tugged at a strand of hair, pulling it to her mouth and chewing on it as she thought.

"There are always lots of bugs in the summer," she said finally, brushing the strand of hair back, talking to herself. "Mice too. But there's no way leeches could get up here. Leeches don't live in the ocean, so . . ." Her voice trailed off.

"Someone had to stick them on me!" Joy declared, only a little calmer.

"I'm going to speak to Alfred about this right now!" Marla declared. Shaking her head, she strode from the room.

Claudia listened to her footsteps pound down the stairs. "This certainly is a mystery," she said to Joy. "Are you feeling a little better?"

"Know what I think?" Joy asked, ignoring the question. She pulled herself up straighter against the quilted headboard. "Know what I think? I think Marla invited us here to torture us!"

"Huh?" Both Claudia and Sophie reacted with surprise.

Sophie dropped down onto the edge of the bed and squinted hard at Joy. Sophie was wearing silky striped pajamas. Claudia remained standing next to Joy.

"What on earth do you mean?" Sophie demanded.

"You heard me," Joy snapped. "These things that are happening here—they can't all be accidents."

"Joy—what are you saying?" Claudia demanded.

Joy wiped her runny nose with the sheet. "I'm saying that Marla invited us here to torture us," she replied darkly. "Because of Alison."

"I'm sure Marla doesn't blame us for what happened to Alison," Sophie said, her voice revealing uncertainty.

"Let's not get totally paranoid," Claudia said softly.

"Paranoid? I'm not paranoid!" Joy replied angrily. "Do you really think it was an accident that Marla left you buried in the sand to fry?"

"Yes, I do," Claudia told her.

"And what about Sophie?" Joy asked with a shudder. "It was Marla who asked Sophie to touch the electrified gate. Sophie could've been electrocuted. And now me! Leeches stuck to my arm. I'm telling you, Claudia—I'm not paranoid. I—"

"Sshhhh!" Sophie whispered, raising a finger to her lips.

They all heard Marla's footsteps in the hall. Marla entered the room, a concerned expression on her face. She swept her hair back over the shoulders of her nightshirt. "Alfred is just as baffled as we are," she announced in a low voice.

The room fell silent. No one knew what to say next. The high-pitched whistle of crickets drifted in from the open window.

Sounds like camp, Claudia thought with a shiver.

Sophie yawned loudly.

Joy had stopped crying and had pulled the bedspread up to her chin.

"Let's go back to bed," Marla suggested, frowning. "Maybe we'll be able to figure it out in the morning."

After saying good night to Joy and making sure she was calm enough to be left alone, Claudia made her way across the hall to her room. Feeling chilled, she pushed the French doors shut. She had started to climb into bed, picturing again the three big leeches on Joy's arm, when she realized her mouth was dry.

"Water, water," she groaned aloud.

A glass of cold water from the refrigerator would help a lot, Claudia thought.

Walking as silently as possible, so she wouldn't disturb the others, she made her way down the long hall. Then crept down the stairs to the kitchen.

She stopped in the doorway, surprised to find a dim light on over the long counter. The tile was cool under her bare feet.

A shadow moved.

Someone else is down here, Claudia realized.

"Marla? Is that you?" she whispered.

No.

She could just make out a tall figure half hidden in the shadows near the back pantry.

"Daniel!" she cried. "What are *you* doing here?"

chapter

13

Riptide!

"Daniel—how did you get in here?" Claudia demanded, her voice a whisper.

His dark shadow moved against the wall.

Frozen in the doorway, Claudia squinted against the dim light, struggling to see his face.

The shadows darkened.

No one replied.

For a brief moment the dim light from the counter played over his face. Claudia could see his expression. Troubled. Frightened.

"Daniel—?" she called, taking a few steps toward him and shivering from the cold tile. "Hey, wait—"

But he had vanished silently into the shadows.

"Daniel . . . ?"

Silence. No footsteps.

A door creaked somewhere. A gust of wind set a tree branch tapping at the kitchen window.

Claudia could hear her heart pounding as she continued to search for him in the shadowy kitchen.

But he was gone.

Why didn't he answer me? she wondered.

Why didn't he say anything?

Why did he look so frightened?

"He isn't a ghost," she said aloud. "He *can't* be. I touched him. I kissed him."

But then how had he gotten into the house? How had he gotten past the electrified fence?

"Oh!" Claudia cried out as the bright ceiling lights clicked on.

"Hello?" a voice said.

Claudia spun around to see Alfred. Dressed in dark trousers and an undershirt, his suspenders drooping down at his sides, Alfred seemed as startled to see her as Claudia was to see him.

"Oh, hi," Claudia managed to choke out. "I came down for a glass of water."

Alfred nodded. "Me too. I'll get some for both of us." He pulled open the big refrigerator and squinted for a long time at the top shelf. Finally he reached for a bottle of water.

"I—I saw someone," Claudia stammered.

"What did you say?" He turned to her, the refrigerator door still open.

"I saw someone in here. In the kitchen. A boy."

He narrowed his eyes at her suspiciously. "Are you sure?"

"Yes," she insisted, leaning against the counter on one elbow, her hands clasped at her waist. "Yes. It was dark, but I saw him. I mean, I recognized him. He—"

"But that's impossible," Alfred said, scratching his

bald head. He set down the bottle of water and pushed the refrigerator door shut, keeping his eyes on Claudia. "No one could get in here."

"Is someone else staying here maybe?" Claudia asked.

Alfred shook his head. "No one else."

"There's no one in the guest house? I thought I saw a light in there last night," Claudia said.

"A light?" He tilted his head, staring intently at her. "That's impossible, miss. I cleaned the guest house today. Dusted and vacuumed it. I clean it every week. It's empty. Completely empty. No sign of anyone being in there."

"But I saw this boy's face," Claudia insisted heatedly. "His name is Daniel. I saw him at the boardwalk tonight. He—"

"How would some strange boy get in here?" Alfred interrupted. Still scratching his head, he crossed the room and peered out the window, squinting hard. "The electrified fence is on. The guard dog has been let out of his pen. Miss Drexell changed the alarm system code herself this evening."

"Marla changed the alarm system?" Claudia asked.

Alfred nodded. "Yes, she did. There's no way. No way a boy could get through all that without our knowing."

"Oh," Claudia replied flatly and let out a long breath.

Alfred poured out two glasses of water and handed her one. He seemed to be uncomfortable, and his eyes avoided hers.

Is he hiding something? Claudia wondered.

Does he know more than he's saying?

And then, as she sipped the cold water, a frightening thought flashed into her mind:

Was Daniel upstairs? Had he put the leeches on Joy's arm?

Why? Why? Why?

The next morning, after a restless sleep, Claudia hurried down to breakfast. She couldn't wait to tell the others about seeing Daniel in the kitchen.

Sophie teased her. "The Ghost Boy!" she cried. "Come on, Claud. Now you're seeing ghosts in the house?" Sophie started to laugh, but stopped when she saw the serious expressions on everyone's face.

"*Someone* came up to my room with those leeches," Joy said with a shudder. "That was no *accident*. Maybe it was this boy Claudia saw."

"He seemed like a nice guy," Claudia told them. "But—"

Marla interrupted by jumping up from the table. "I don't believe in ghosts. If there *is* some boy hiding in this house, I want to find him," she declared, frowning.

She started toward the kitchen. At the doorway, she turned back to her guests. "I'm going to have Alfred call the police," she said. "I want them to search the estate from top to bottom. They can do it while we're out waterskiing this afternoon."

Shouting for Alfred, she disappeared from the room.

Claudia had looked forward to waterskiing. But with her face still scarlet and starting to peel, she decided she'd better protect her skin more than she normally would.

First, she covered herself in number 30 sun block. Then she changed into an iridescent blue one-piece bathing suit. Over her suit she pulled on a pair of light drawstring pants and a long-sleeve T-shirt. She topped the outfit off with one of her brother's baseball caps that her mother had insisted she take.

There, she thought with satisfaction. I look like a total jerk, but the sun won't get near me!

By the time she reached the Drexell's dock, the other three girls were already in the boat, wearing bright orange flotation belts. Marla was perched up front at the wheel, Joy in the back in the spotter's position, and Sophie hanging over the side, running her hand through the water.

"Whoa! Claudia, you're going to melt," Marla predicted as Claudia stepped onto the dock.

"Probably," Claudia agreed as she strapped a life belt on over her T-shirt. A cool wind played over the water, but the sun beamed down hot and strong from a cloudless sky. Waves lapped quietly at the dock. The boat rocked gently, pulling against its line.

"Who wants to ski first?" Marla asked.

"I'll go," Sophie volunteered, raising her hand as if she were in school.

Marla and Joy both showed their surprise. "You're the one who never liked to water ski," Joy said.

"Weren't you the one who didn't believe in getting in water that was colder than your body temperature?" Marla teased.

"I've changed," Sophie assured them. "I'm a much stronger swimmer than I used to be. Ever since I found out I was a Pisces and water was my sign, I've had a much better relationship with swimming. You'll see. I've become a great swimmer. I'm a fish! Really!"

It was a typical Sophie explanation, Claudia thought with a smile. Next, Sophie would probably discover she'd been an eagle in a past life and she was, like, meant for hang-gliding.

"Do you want a dock start or a water start?" Marla asked Sophie.

"Water," Sophie said. "I'm a little out of practice."

"Okay," Marla said. "Just one thing. If you go down, hold up your right arm to let us know you're okay."

"No problem," Sophie said. She climbed out of the boat and sat on the edge of the dock to put on the long skis. Claudia helped her tighten them, checking that they were on properly.

Sophie swung her legs around so that the skis were out over the side. Then she pushed herself off the dock, squealing as her body hit the cold water.

Claudia untied the boat from the dock and jumped in. The motor started with a pleasant roar. Marla pulled the boat out a short distance from the dock, and Joy threw Sophie the tow line.

Slowly, Marla took the boat out until the line was drawn taut. Claudia saw that Sophie had her knees drawn up in perfect position, the tips of the skis above the water, the wooden handle of the tow rope between her legs.

"Ready?" Marla called back.

Sophie nodded to Joy at the back of the boat, who called to Marla, "Ready!"

After a moment's hesitation the boat shot forward, its bottom slapping against the dark green swells.

Claudia's eyes were riveted on the back of the boat, where Sophie stood up smoothly, then bounced across the glassy waves, perfectly balanced on her skis.

"She *has* improved," Joy cried out over the roar of the motor.

"For sure!" Claudia agreed, watching Sophie confidently release one hand from the rope and wave at them.

Marla swung the boat in a wide arc, and Sophie leaned into the curve, laughing and happy. Her short, fuzzy hair bobbed freely.

Watching her friend, Claudia could feel herself getting impatient for her own turn.

As if reading her thoughts, Joy called, "Do you want to go next?"

Claudia nodded. She hurriedly took off the baseball cap and then the flotation belt, so that she could remove her pants and T-shirt.

I can't wait to get into the water! she thought. I'm sweating to death under all these clothes!

She peeled off her T-shirt and pants and was reaching for the flotation belt again when she heard Joy's cry over the noise of the motor: "Marla—stop. Sophie's gone down!"

Claudia turned her eyes quickly to the water.

Sophie was definitely down.

She watched for Sophie's right arm to shoot up, the signal that she was okay.

No signal.

Squinting hard and shielding her eyes from the sun, Claudia saw something bob to the top of the waves.

Sophie?

Claudia felt her throat tighten as she realized it was a ski. One lone ski.

"Where *is* she?" Joy shouted.

"There!" Claudia cried, pointing as she spotted Sophie's head float to the surface.

As Claudia was pointing, Sophie sank again and then resurfaced, flailing her arms and legs frantically.

"Marla—turn the boat around!" Claudia screamed. "Sophie's in trouble! She must be caught in the riptide!"

"It—it's taking her out to sea!" Joy cried, her eyes wide with horror.

Claudia gasped at the sudden silence.

The boat slowed, then drifted with the waves.

She could see Sophie kicking and thrashing, struggling desperately to free herself from the powerful current.

"Marla—go after her!" Claudia screamed in a shrill voice choked with fear.

"I—I can't!" Marla shouted back, her hands frantically working over the controls. "The boat—it stalled out! It won't move!"

chapter

14

Swept Away

"**S**ophie's drowning!" Joy shrieked, leaning over the side of the boat, shielding her eyes with one hand from the glare of the sun. "Marla—do something!"

"It won't start!" Marla shouted, both hands stabbing wildly at the controls. "What can I do? What can I do?"

The boat bobbed helplessly on the rocking waves.

Claudia saw Sophie struggling frantically as the powerful current swept her farther and farther away.

"What can I do? What can I do?"

The panic in Marla's voice spurred Claudia to action. Without realizing what she was doing, Claudia dove over the side of the boat.

The shock of the cold water made her gasp. Choking, she rose to the surface.

My flotation belt! she thought. It's still in the boat!

The sun made the rolling waves sparkle all around her. Spinning around, she searched for Sophie.

Where are you? Where are you?

Her heart pounding, she finally spotted Sophie in the near distance and saw her arms still flailing wildly.

Taking a deep breath, Claudia began swimming toward her with a strong, steady crawl, moving against the pull of the waves. She knew she had to stay parallel to the riptide—without getting caught in it.

Sophie's head went under. Then, a few seconds later, it appeared on the diamondlike surface again.

"Sophie! I'm coming!" Claudia shouted. But the wind and the waves blew her voice back behind her. "Sophie!"

She tried to swim faster, but the current was pulling hard the opposite way.

"Marla— Where are you? Marla, please hurry!" she said frantically to herself.

She listened for the roar of the boat motor as it caught. But the only sounds she could hear were the steady wash of the waves and her labored breathing as she pulled herself through the water.

Glancing back over her shoulder, Claudia could see the boat, bobbing silently far behind her.

"Marla—*please!*"

How could a boat just stall out like that?

Claudia's shoulders began to ache. She cried out as a cramp shot up her right leg.

Her eyes burning from the saltwater, she squinted hard, searching for Sophie.

Where are you? Where are you, Sophie?

Keep swimming. Keep struggling.

Yes. Claudia could see her up ahead.

I'm coming. I'm coming, Sophie.

Claudia suddenly realized that she was swimming much faster, gliding easily now over the tossing waves.

The leg cramp eased. She seemed to be moving with the current now instead of against it.

With the current.

The current.

To her horror, Claudia realized she had swum into the riptide.

"No! No—please!"

She was caught.

Caught in the powerful rush of current.

Helpless.

Being swept away, out to sea.

chapter

15

"She's Trying to Kill Us!"

I'm going to drown, Claudia realized.

The thought made her spin around to search frantically for the boat.

Marla, where are you?

She couldn't see the boat anywhere.

A tall wave rose over her, tossing her forward. She gasped and started to choke again. She could feel herself being pulled under the surface.

I'm sorry, Sophie. I tried.

I'm so sorry. . . .

Her arms throbbed as she struggled to pull herself free from the current. Her leg cramp returned, shooting paralyzing pain up the length of her right side.

I'm going to drown now, she thought, gasping out a sob.

I'm going to die.

The wash of the water became a loud hum.

The hum became a roar.

I'm sinking, Claudia thought. Sinking into the roar.

Her arms were too heavy to stroke now.

Her legs ached with shooting pains.

She could feel herself sinking into the deafening roar.

And then, unexpectedly, hands were circling her arms.

She felt strong hands grasp onto her and pull.

That roar wasn't inside her head.

The roar was the sound of a motor. A boat's motor.

And she was being lifted out of the water. Two people were working to lift her, to pull her onto the boat.

Beside Sophie.

Sophie smiled at her. Trembling all over, her entire body shivering and dripping wet and covered with goose bumps, Sophie had her arms crossed in front of her—and was smiling at her.

"Are you okay? Claudia, are you okay?" another voice, not Sophie's, asked.

Claudia stared up into the worried face. Tried to focus on the dark hair tossed in the strong ocean wind. Tried to focus on the dark eyes.

"Carl!" she cried.

"Carl and Dean to the rescue," he said quietly, a smile forming on his tanned face.

Claudia turned to see Dean at the wheel. She rolled onto her knees on the deck of the boat, her wet, auburn hair falling over her face. She pushed the hair back with a trembling hand. "Sophie, are you okay?"

Sophie nodded. "Yeah. I just can't stop shaking."

"Close one," Claudia managed to mutter.

"We'll take you to the Drexell's dock," Carl said, his hand warm on her shoulder.

Claudia nearly toppled backward as the small boat roared forward. She struggled to keep her balance. Wiping water from her eyes, she saw that they were in a small fiberglass powerboat.

She searched the horizon for Marla's boat but didn't see it. The tiny boat roared loudly, bouncing over the waves.

Claudia scooted close to Sophie. "What happened?" she shouted. "Did you let go of the rope?"

"I don't know," Sophie told her, still shivering despite the hot sun that burned down directly above them. "One minute I was up. The next, I was down. I was still holding onto the bar. But—but the tow rope— I don't know! I wasn't connected to the boat anymore. I don't know what happened, Claudia. I got caught in the riptide and—and—"

Claudia wrapped a comforting arm around Sophie's trembling shoulders. She could see the white dock up ahead.

We're okay, she thought.

We're okay.

Claudia's legs were shaking as Carl and Dean helped her onto the dock a few moments later. Sophie offered both boys a relieved smile as they pulled her from the boat. "You guys are heroes," she told them.

"Hey, we do this all the time," Dean told her, grinning.

The roar of another boat's engine made them all turn toward the water. Marla and Joy were both waving wildly as Marla's boat bounced up to the dock.

A few seconds later Joy leapt off the boat and, shrieking happily, came running over to throw her arms around Sophie and Claudia.

Marla tethered her boat, then jumped ashore, a broad smile on her face. "I'm so happy!" she cried. "My stupid boat. I've got to get a new motor. Joy and I saw that you were safe. Then I finally got my motor to turn over. I think I'd flooded it or something!"

There were more hugs and cries of thanks to the two boys. Carl and Dean tried to act casual, but Claudia could see how pleased they were with themselves. Even Marla thanked them again and again, which seemed to be a special triumph for them.

"We've got to get the boat back," Carl said finally. "We, uh, sort of borrowed it."

Everyone laughed.

"Maybe we'll catch you later," Dean said, smiling at Sophie.

"Yeah. Catch you later," Carl repeated.

The four girls watched the boys roar off in the tiny boat.

"Let's get up to the house," Sophie cried, smiling at Marla. "I'm starving!"

"Close calls always make me hungry too!" Joy declared, her arm around Sophie's shoulders.

"What on earth happened, Sophie?" Marla asked, her smile fading. "Did you lose your grip on the bar, or what?"

"I don't know—" Sophie started.

But Claudia interrupted. She had reached into the water and pulled up the end of the nylon tow rope. "Look at this!" she called to the others.

She held up the end of the rope for them to see. Her

hand began to tremble as she realized what she had discovered.

"What are you showing us?" Marla asked as the three girls huddled around Claudia.

"Look at this tow rope," Claudia said softly. "It isn't frayed. It didn't tear."

"Huh? What do you mean, Claud?" Joy demanded, bewildered.

"The rope had to be cut. Look how smooth the end is. It had to be cut so that it would snap under pressure."

"You mean—" Sophie started, raising a hand to her mouth.

"I mean someone did this deliberately," Claudia said, turning to Marla.

Marla tossed back her blond hair, her blue eyes staring hard at the end of the rope. "That's impossible," she said shrilly. "My father and I took this boat out waterskiing last week. The rope was fine. I really don't think—"

Marla's mouth dropped open. She turned her gaze to the boat. "Whoa!" she cried. "Hold on a minute . . ."

"What?" Sophie demanded. "What are you thinking, Marla?"

"The boy you saw in the kitchen, Claud. I wonder—"

"Daniel?" Claudia cried. "Why would he cut the tow rope?"

"I have another idea," Marla replied thoughtfully, pointing in the direction the boys' had headed. "Carl and Dean. They were on the beach yesterday. I wouldn't be at all surprised if *they* cut the rope."

"Huh?" Joy cried out. "How can you accuse them, Marla?"

"Yeah! They *saved* us!" Sophie declared heatedly.

"We would've drowned!" Claudia agreed. "Those boys—"

"How did they know to be here?" Marla interrupted. "Don't you think it was a little too convenient? How did they know just when to come riding in to the rescue?"

"Marla—" Sophie started.

Marla cut her off. "They cut the rope after we left the beach yesterday. Then they probably watched from the Point, waiting for someone to start skiing and go down. I'm telling you, Sophie, they did it so they could be heroes. Their showing up like that is just too big a coincidence."

"No, it isn't," Joy said loudly, her green eyes lighting up.

"Huh? What do you mean?" Marla asked.

"It wasn't a coincidence," Joy confessed. "I told them to come around today."

"You *what?*" Marla cried, hands on her hips.

"Can we please get up to the house?" Sophie cried. "I've got to get changed. And I'm *starving!*"

"Yeah. Let's go," Joy eagerly agreed, starting toward the stairs that led up to the back lawn. Frowning thoughtfully, Marla followed.

Only Claudia lingered behind, holding the cut tow rope out of the water, staring at the smooth end.

"Now I know I'm right!" Joy declared, whispering.

"Right? Right about what?" Claudia demanded.

It was right after lunch. They were in a dark wood-paneled den, huddled together on an enormous red leather couch. Marla had disappeared to make some phone calls. Across the room, a mounted moose head hung over a redbrick fireplace stared at them with mournful brown eyes.

"Joy, what are you talking about?" Sophie asked, whispering too, her eyes on the den doorway.

Joy pushed herself off the couch, crossed the room, and closed the door before replying. She wore a white sleeveless top over white tennis shorts, which emphasized her tanned skin.

"Just what I said before," she whispered, her expression troubled, "about the reason for this little Camp Full Moon reunion. Marla brought us here to torture us." She swallowed hard. "Maybe even to—kill us."

"Joy—really! You need a reality check," Sophie said, rolling her eyes. She turned to Claudia for support, but Claudia didn't say a thing. "Anyone can have a waterskiing accident," Sophie insisted. "You can't blame Marla—"

"Yes, I can. Claudia was right about the tow rope," Joy continued, tugging at her ponytail. "You saw it, Sophie. That rope was cut."

"But, Joy—"

"And do you really believe that Marla's boat cut out just at the moment it was needed to rescue you?" Joy continued, her nostrils flaring. "Do you really believe it stalled out just when you were about to drown?"

"I—I don't know," Sophie replied, shaking her head. She pushed her wire-framed glasses up on her nose, frowning.

"I'm right. I *know* I'm right. The leeches on my arm weren't an accident. None of the accidents here have been accidents. Marla has to be responsible. Alfred reported that the police searched and didn't find any trace of Claudia's Ghost Boy. It *has* to be Marla. Marla brought us here to torture us."

Claudia raised her eyes to Joy's. "But why?" she demanded. "What's her reason, Joy? Why would she want to do that to us?"

Joy leaned forward, all the light fading from her green eyes. "Because," she whispered, "Marla must know that Alison's death wasn't an accident."

chapter

16

The Truth About Alison

Claudia uttered a silent gasp as Joy's words burned into her mind. She sank back against the soft red leather of the sofa and closed her eyes.

Alison's death—it had to be an accident, she thought.

A horrible accident.

But Joy's words had cleared a path in Claudia's mind, a path that had been closed off since the previous summer.

Joy's words brought the frightening memories rushing out from their dark hiding place in a corner of Claudia's mind.

And for the first time in nearly a year, Claudia allowed herself to remember what had really happened that night at Grizzly Gorge. . . .

* * *

99

Claudia, Joy, and Sophie watched fearfully as Alison balanced on the log, halfway across the gorge, her slim body illuminated by the full moon. The sound of the river rushing beneath her echoed up to them. Her arms straight out at her sides, Alison slowly inched across the thick log.

Claudia, Sophie, and Joy huddled together back near the thick bushes. "I can't believe she's really doing it," Sophie whispered.

"I tried to stop her," Claudia whispered back. "But she's so stubborn."

"I'm glad Marla isn't here," Joy said, her arms crossed in front of her chest. "She'd have a heart attack."

"Are you kidding?" Sophie exclaimed, her eyes riveted on Alison. "Marla would shake the log! She can't *stand* her sister!"

"That's not true," Claudia insisted. "Marla cares about Alison. But you know Marla. She doesn't like to show that she cares about anyone."

Just then Alison cried out. She appeared to have stumbled. Her arms flew up as she struggled to regain her balance. "I'm going to fall!" she cried.

"Keep going," Sophie urged. "You're almost there."

"Don't turn back," Joy told her. "Keep going!"

"I mean it." Alison's voice became panicky. "I—I can't do it. I'm going to fall!"

"Alison—stop messing around. Hurry up before someone comes," Joy told her impatiently.

And then all three girls saw the darting lights, flashlights in the woods. Footsteps approaching. Counselors' voices.

"Come on, Alison!" Sophie called. "We're going to be caught!"

"Hurry!" Claudia shouted. "Let's go!"

And then the three girls were running into the darkness of the woods, running away from the approaching lights.

Was Alison running too? Was she following them back to the bunks?

Claudia didn't bother to check.

As she ran, her sneakers crunched loudly over twigs and dry leaves. So loudly that she could barely hear Alison's high-pitched squeal; "Help me!" And she didn't hear the *thud* of Alison's body hitting the rocks, or the splash of the water swallowing her up.

When Alison's counselor discovered Alison was missing, they searched for her. Her blood-soaked T-shirt was found the next morning, clinging to a jutting rock near the riverbank.

Her body was never found.

Claudia, Joy, and Sophie never told anyone they had been there when Alison fell. They never told anyone that Alison had asked for help, that they had run away instead, that they had never checked to make sure Alison was safely back on solid ground.

Maybe we could've saved her, Claudia thought, overcome with guilt.

Maybe we could've walked out and helped her off the log.

Maybe she didn't have to die.

"She was fine when we ran off," they told Marla later. "We thought she was right behind us. We really did."

Marla believed her friends' story.

It didn't take the three girls long to believe their story too.

It was easy to believe.

Easier than the truth.

It was a nicer version of a horrifying death.

And, Claudia realized, they had all clung to the story because it offered a much nicer version of themselves.

We probably could have saved Alison, Claudia knew.

Instead we let her fall to her death.

The memories of that dreadful night roared through Claudia's mind faster than the rushing river at the bottom of Grizzly Gorge.

It seemed so long ago.

And so long since she had faced the truth.

Claudia opened her eyes and leaned forward on the soft leather couch. She raised her eyes to her two friends. "We have to get out of here," she said in a low, steady voice. "I think Joy is right. I think Marla has decided that we could have saved Alison but didn't that night at Camp Full Moon. I—I think she brought us here to torture us. Maybe worse."

Sophie gasped, her eyes open wide. "But how? What do we do? How do we get away from here?"

"Marla won't let us get away," Joy muttered, standing and pacing. "She won't, Claud. I know it!"

Claudia got to her feet and crossed to the desk. She lifted the phone receiver. "I'm going to call my mom and tell her to come pick us up," she told them. "When she shows up, Marla will have to let us go."

Claudia punched in her home number and turned toward the wall to talk to her mother.

When she turned back to her friends, her expression was troubled. "She can't come till the day after tomorrow," she told them.

"What do we do till then?" Joy demanded shrilly.

"Lay low, I guess," Claudia replied, replacing the receiver.

"We can make it for one more day," Sophie said. "We'll just have to be careful. No dangerous water sports. And we'll act as if everything's okay."

"Sophie's right," Claudia quickly agreed. "We'll just be careful until my mom arrives. We'll pack and be ready to go. And—"

She turned toward the figure in the den doorway.

Marla!

Claudia was startled to see Marla silently standing there, one hand raised against the door frame, staring intently at her. A frown hardened Marla's features.

How much did Marla hear? Claudia wondered.

Did she hear their whole conversation?

Did she know they were planning to leave?

Marla's expression softened as she stepped into the den. She held up a flat gold box in one hand and made her way toward the three girls.

"Would anyone like a chocolate?" she asked, lowering the box. "They're very good."

chapter

17

Down, Boy!

Staring up at the white glare of the after-noon sky, Claudia adjusted her purple swimsuit, brushed sand off her back, and gazed down the butterscotch beach.

I'll go for a long run, she decided.

Despite the tension the three girls felt, the day had gone pretty well. Joy and Sophie had played tennis most of the morning. Marla had slept late, then said she had chores to do.

After lunch Joy had gone into town with Carl. Sophie announced she was taking a long nap. Marla had letters to write. Claudia had ventured down to the beach.

Splitting up is a good idea, Claudia thought. We'll get through this day. Then my mom will be here bright and early tomorrow, and we'll be out of here.

Barefoot, Claudia started to run south, in the direction of town. She stayed close to the shoreline, where the sand was wet and compact. The waves splashed up against her bare legs, cold and salty.

Watching the sea gulls make their soaring V's against the gray-white sky, she lost track of time. The waves splashed against her. Her feet kicked up chunks of wet sand as she jogged.

Before long, Claudia found herself running on the beach that cut past the bird sanctuary. She also realized that once again she'd misjudged the intensity of the summer sun.

Even though it barely poked through the high cloud cover, she could feel her skin burning. She wished she'd taken a water bottle and worn something more protective than the one-piece bathing suit. She wished she was the type of person who tanned instead of fried.

Should I turn around and go back? she asked herself.

No. It feels so good to run. I'll just go a little bit farther.

A jetty of dark boulders broke the water a short distance ahead. She decided to jog as far as the jetty and then go back.

Her eyes on the preserve, Claudia sensed that something was wrong. She could hear her own footsteps, her breath coming in hard pants, and the sound of breakers hitting the shore.

But the air had suddenly gone very still.

Claudia stopped.

What's wrong here?

What feels so weird?

It took her a while to realize that the *quiet* was what was wrong.

What had happened to the sounds of gulls and sandpipers and the other sea birds?

She listened.

Silence.

This was a bird sanctuary, right?

So where were the birds?

She squinted into the distance and, to her surprise, saw another person running near the edge of the beach. It looked like Marla—no one else had that strawberry-blond hair and perfect, slender figure.

"Marla!" Claudia called, cupping her hands around her mouth.

The girl in the distance didn't stop or even look back.

It must be someone else, Claudia thought.

Forgetting the girl, Claudia searched the trees for birds.

None in sight.

And no chirps or whistles.

Why would all the birds have suddenly vanished? Why?

She could think of only one answer.

And the answer made a cold chill run down her back despite the heat of the sun.

Something had frightened the birds away.

A predator.

There must be a predator—a large one—nearby.

Seconds later Claudia's guess was confirmed by a low growl directly behind her.

She turned to see an enormous white Irish wolfhound. It stood eyeing her. Its narrow snout was lowered, and its matted, wiry fur appeared to be standing up on its back.

The dog stared menacingly, its teeth bared, revealing long, pointed fangs. It snarled out a warning.

"Down, boy," Claudia muttered in a low, trembling voice. "Easy now. Go home. Go home, boy, okay?"

The rumble in the dog's chest deepened in reply.

"Nice dog," Claudia tried, desperate, her heart thudding in her chest. "Nice doggie. Go home, boy."

Saliva dripped from the wolfhound's mouth. Its snarl changed to a loud, frightening growl.

Slowly, her eyes trained on the dog, Claudia began to back away.

In response, the wolfhound loped toward her with alarming speed.

Claudia wheeled around and started to run, her feet kicking up large clods of wet sand.

She turned to see the dog running after her, its teeth bared, its eyes eager for the chase.

What little she knew about Irish wolfhounds flashed through her mind as her feet pounded the sand. Even bigger than Great Danes, they were bred for speed and aggressiveness, bred as the ultimate hunters.

They were bred to tear apart wolves.

The dog was gaining on her, Claudia saw.

Closer.

Closer.

Until she could hear the snap of its teeth and feel its hot breath on her legs.

What can I do?

What can I do?

She had no other choice.

With a desperate cry, she lunged into the water. Taking a deep breath, she dove under the waves.

She came up, swimming hard, stroking out from the shoreline.

Got to get away.

Got to swim away.

She screamed as the surge of pain shot up her leg.

Thrashing hard, she stared down—and saw the dog's teeth clamped around her ankle.

chapter

18

No Escape

Claudia screamed as the dog bit deeper into her ankle.

"Let go! Let go!"

She tried to kick at it with her free leg, but only succeeded in forcing her head under the water, her arms thrashing desperately.

The dog let go, but the throbbing pain remained, shooting up Claudia's side.

The huge dog lunged at her, snarling, its teeth snapping ferociously.

Sputtering, Claudia tried to stand, to kick the animal away.

"Help!"

With a desperate, shrill cry, she fell again.

Choking, struggling to breathe, she kicked at the growling creature.

Blood stained the water. *Her* blood. Claudia's ankle throbbed with pain.

I'm going to pass out.

I can't bear the pain.

"Help me! Somebody—help!"

Her screams rang out across the beach. The empty beach.

The dog's teeth snapped near her leg again. She struggled to pull back, but each attempt sent pain stabbing up through her entire body.

Claudia's head sank under the water. She fought her way to the surface, gasping for air.

"Help me! Can't somebody help me?"

With a desperate lunge, she heaved herself into the tossing waves.

Snarling furiously, the dog snapped at her hand. Missed. Snapped again.

Got to get away. Got to get away from him.

Her heart pounding, and sobbing with each breath, Claudia dove under the surface and began to swim. Dragging her injured leg, she pulled herself away, using all of her remaining strength, pulled herself away from the shore, away from the snapping dog.

She stayed under the surface until it felt as if her lungs would burst. Then, lifting her head, she took in deep, hungry breaths.

The saltwater stung her open wound, and her leg burned as if it were on fire.

Gasping for breath, she looked back and saw the dog paddling toward her, its dark eyes locked on hers.

I have to get away.

I have to wear him out.

She turned toward the open sea and dove under once again.

Dragging her leg still, she swam hard.

I can outswim it. I know I can.

If I go out far enough, the dog will have to turn back.

Pulling herself through the dark waters, Claudia urged herself on.

But then, a few moments later, she surfaced again, sucking in deep breaths of air. As the water rolled off her eyes, she stared into the near distance—and lost all hope.

A single, blue-gray fin was cutting smoothly through the water. Not wavering to the left or right, it was moving toward her with unnerving speed.

A shark!

chapter

19

Dead in the Water

"Nooooooo!"

Claudia's wail rose over the tossing waves.

Watching the dark fin skim so smoothly through the water, she panicked.

She tried to swim, but her arms failed her. Salt water rushed into her nose and mouth, choking her.

Coughing, struggling to breathe, she felt herself being pulled below the surface by the undertow.

No!

Got to get control!

Get control!

Sputtering and sobbing, Claudia fought her way back up to the surface again. Her throat and nose burned from the water she'd taken in. Her leg sent fiery pain straight up through the top of her skull.

Got to think.

Think clearly.

Taking a deep breath and holding it, Claudia forced herself to fight down the panic that rolled through her body.

Think. Think!

She'd read that sharks were drawn to struggle and violent movement. Which meant she had to stop moving around.

The shark might get her anyway—she knew it would be drawn to her blood—but she could try to slow her movements and not guarantee a quick death.

Exhausted and terrified, Claudia forced herself to do a slow, even breaststroke. She remembered Steve, the waterfront counselor at Camp Full Moon, telling them, "Your legs and arms should move so smoothly in the breaststroke that they barely make the water ripple."

So smooth.

So smooth . . .

Swimming without making a ripple was all Claudia had to hold on to.

Smooth.

Smoother.

Ignoring her pounding heart, the blood pulsing at her temples, the throbbing pain in her ankle, she swam as smoothly and calmly as she could, counting silently to a measured rhythm.

One, two, three, four . . . Two, two, three, four . . . Three, two, three . . .

I'm too tired.

I can't swim another stroke.

Exhaustion swept over her. Her arms suddenly weighed a thousand pounds each.

I can't make it.

I can't swim anymore.

The shark wins. . . .

Now she was fighting for every breath. Fighting to stay afloat.

And then suddenly, miraculously, the swimming became easier.

What's happening?

I'm moving again!

It took her a long time to realize what had happened. And when she realized, an ironic laugh escaped her lips.

I've swum straight into the riptide.

It's carrying me away from the shark.

But would it carry her fast enough?

Sucking in deep breaths, Claudia didn't allow herself to look back. With renewed energy, she kept swimming, grateful for the pull of the tide that carried her along.

The anguished squeal of pain made her stop.

"What was *that?*" she muttered aloud.

She turned in time to see the wolfhound's long white snout thrashing furiously above the water, its front legs shooting straight up.

A wave of pure horror swept over Claudia.

The dog squealed again.

The shark was attacking it from below, Claudia realized.

As Claudia gaped in horror, a geyser of blood boiled up from beneath the water. The foamy crest of a wave turned pink. The metallic smell of blood floated out over the tossing waves.

Even from where she swam, Claudia could see the water darken with the wolfhound's blood.

A surge of nausea made her stomach heave.

The dog uttered a final weak yelp.

Claudia shut her eyes.

But she opened them wide when something coarse bumped against her.

Treading water, Claudia goggled at the disgusting object.

She opened her mouth to scream, but no sound came out.

What is it?

What *is* it?

She didn't want to look at it—but she couldn't pull her eyes away.

She soon realized that it was a hair-covered chunk of meat.

Part of the dog.

The water all around her was black with blood.

Glancing around, she could see no other sign of the dog or shark.

Claudia couldn't stop the horrified scream that unexpectedly burst out of her. All of the terror of the last twenty minutes racked her body.

Again she slipped beneath the surface. She was never going to get back to shore, she realized. If the shark didn't take her, the riptide would.

I've got to swim, got to force myself to swim.

Was the shark gone? Was it really gone?

Had the dog satisfied the shark's appetite?

A biology lecture came absurdly to mind: "Sharks are among the most efficient predators ever designed."

It was a fact Claudia had memorized for a quiz. Now she understood its true meaning.

If the shark did come after her, she wouldn't have a chance.

Her eyes searching the bobbing, dark waters, Claudia took another deep breath.

Just swim, she told herself. Keep it smooth.

She was so tired now, it was an effort to move her arms. But she turned toward shore and forced herself to swim, stroke after painful stroke.

Stroke. Stroke.

I—can't.

Her entire body throbbed. Her foot was numb now. Her chest tightened, about to burst.

Water rushed over her.

The beach. Where is the beach?

Horror gripped her as she had the frightening feeling she'd been swimming in the wrong direction.

Why can't I see the beach?

She whirled around in the water, panic sweeping over her.

Where is the beach?

Her arms gave out. She couldn't move.

The tide carried her now.

Everything went bright red. Red as blood.

And then black.

chapter

20

The Truth About Marla

"Claudia? Claudia?"

Strong hands pushed at Claudia's shoulders.

"Claudia? Can you hear me?"

Claudia groggily realized that she was sprawled on her stomach. She tried to raise her head, to see through her soaked and matted hair, which covered her eyes.

"Claudia, are you okay?" the voice demanded.

Claudia groaned and made another attempt to push herself up.

"Claudia?"

"Am I alive?" Claudia asked weakly, rolling onto her back.

She pushed the hair off her forehead and squinted at the blurred figure in front of her. "Marla?"

Marla knelt beside her, her face twisted in fear. "You—you're okay?"

"Marla, what are *you* doing here?" Claudia blurted. She adjusted the top of her purple bathing suit. The sun had disappeared behind thick storm clouds, she saw. The late afternoon sky had darkened to charcoal-gray. Cool winds swirled over the beach.

She shivered, pain stabbing at her foot.

"I—I saw you," Marla stammered, placing a warm hand on Claudia's cold, wet shoulder. "I ran as fast as I could. The water had carried you onto the sand. You—you were just lying there. I thought . . ." Her voice trailed off.

"My foot," Claudia said. She pulled herself to a sitting position to examine it. The cut was deep, but not as wide as she'd imagined while struggling with the dog. The saltwater had stopped the bleeding.

"It's lucky I came along," Marla gushed. "I was going for a swim and—and I saw you wash ashore. And—"

With a loud groan, Claudia pulled herself to her feet.

"Can you walk?" Marla asked, holding on to her.

Claudia gingerly put some weight down on her injured foot. "I think so," she told Marla uncertainly. The sand tilted up to meet her. Long blue shadows stretched toward her. "I-I'm a little dizzy," she confessed.

"What *happened?*" Marla demanded. "How did you cut your foot?"

"It—it was so horrible!" Claudia cried. "A dog chased me. And then a shark—" Her breath caught in her throat. "My ankle—"

"Easy. Just take it easy. I'll get Alfred to treat it

immediately," Marla said. And then frowned. "Oh. I forgot. It's Alfred's day off. Well, we'll take care of it ourselves."

She started to help Claudia toward the stairs.

Leaning against Marla, Claudia gazed up at the gathering black storm clouds, and all sorts of dark thoughts began running through her mind.

Marla didn't just happen to be on the beach, Claudia thought, as they started up the stairs toward the back lawn. Marla was the girl on the beach. The stranger I saw running away.

The Irish wolfhound was Marla's guard dog.

Marla brought the dog to the beach, then ran away.

The dog was kept locked up in a wire-mesh dog run. It was never allowed out except to guard the property at night. Never!

Claudia shuddered as she pulled herself up the wooden stairs. "Almost there," Marla said. Claudia heard a rumble of thunder behind her over the ocean. "It's really going to storm," Marla remarked softly.

She brought the dog down to the beach to attack me, Claudia thought.

She wanted the dog to kill me.

She wanted me to die.

Marla bent down to the low shrubs, pushed the keypad inside the metal box, and the gate swung open.

Claudia leaned on Marla as they made their way past the swimming pool and tennis court and toward the house.

Claudia stopped a short distance from the guest

house. "I—I need to catch my breath," she told Marla.

Marla's eyes examined Claudia intently. "Poor thing. I just don't believe this happened," she said in a low voice. "You have to tell me the whole story when we get inside."

Another rumble of thunder over the ocean. Closer this time.

"I'll run into the house and try to find some antiseptic cream and bandages," Marla offered sympathetically. "Can you make it on your own?"

"Yeah. No problem," Claudia told her, wincing from the pain in her ankle. "Let me catch my breath. I'll be there in a second."

She watched Marla run across the terrace and enter the French doors at the back of the house. When she was certain Marla was out of sight, Claudia turned and, limping, made her way across the lawn with long, determined strides.

The dog run where the Irish wolfhound was kept came into view at the side of the wide, four-car garage. Hobbling badly, Claudia hurried toward it.

She had to see for herself.

I have to know that I'm right, she thought warily.

She stopped a few feet from the wire-mesh gate.

The gate was open a few inches. The padlock, unlatched, was hanging beside the gate.

Yes, she was right, Claudia realized, shaking her head grimly.

The dog didn't break out. The dog was let out.

The lock was removed. The gate was opened.

Marla had deliberately set that attack dog on her.

"This proves it once and for all. We really are in danger here," Claudia muttered out loud.

Turning to the house, she hurried toward the sliding French doors. Another low rumble of thunder crossed the sky. Claudia felt a few cold raindrops on her bare shoulders.

I know what we have to do, she thought unhappily. We can't wait any longer. We have to get out of here—now!

Joy, Sophie, and she had to get away—as fast as they could.

Breathing hard, Claudia hobbled into the house. She pulled the door shut, glancing around for Marla. No sign of her.

Claudia quickly made her way through the back hall, toward the stairs. Then, leaning heavily against the polished wooden banister, she pulled herself up the stairs.

Where are Joy and Sophie? she wondered.

We've got to get packed. Got to get out. *Now!*

Sophie's room was the first on her right. She knocked softly on the door. "Sophie—are you in there?"

Sophie pulled open the door before Claudia could knock again. "What happened to *you?*" Sophie demanded, eyeing Claudia's matted, sandy hair.

"Never mind," Claudia whispered urgently, pushing past Sophie into the room. "Pack up, Sophie. Hurry. We've got to go!"

"Huh?" Sophie's mouth dropped open.

"We have to hurry! Really!" Claudia insisted. "Pack up."

"But, Claudia—your mom. I thought—tomorrow—"

"Where's Joy?" Claudia demanded breathlessly. "We have to tell Joy."

"But—but—" Sophie stammered. "But, Claudia," she said in a low, trembling voice. "Joy is gone."

chapter

21

A Dead Girl

"Joy's gone? Where *is* she?" Claudia demanded shrilly.

Sophie gaped at

motioned to Sophie's bed. "You've got to keep the weight off it."

Claudia obediently moved to the bed. She could feel Sophie's questioning eyes on her. But she knew there was no time to explain.

No time for anything.

The three of them had to get away.

As soon as Joy returned, Claudia would ask Marla to drive them to the train or bus station. And if Marla refused . . .

If Marla refused, they'd *walk* to town—storm or no storm. Or they'd call the police.

Thinking about all the "accidents" that weren't really accidents during the past few days, Claudia allowed Marla to cleanse and bandage her ankle.

Marla tsk-tsked as she worked—but she didn't ask what had caused the wound.

That's because she knows, Claudia thought angrily.

into sheets against

her, her eyes wide behind her glasses.

Rain pattered against the window. Lightning streaked through the nearly black sky.

"She's still in town," Sophie said. "With Carl."

"Still? When's she coming back?" Claudia asked frantically.

Sophie shrugged. "Before dinner, I think."

"Well, start packing," Claudia instructed.

Sophie frowned. "I don't get it. What happened?"

Before Claudia could reply, the door swung open and Marla hurried in, loaded down with bandages and ointments. "So *there* you are," Marla said to Claudia. "I've been looking all over for you. Sit down." She

She knows.

Gusts of wind flattened the rain the window.

Marla must have been so disappointed when she saw me wash up on shore, still alive, Claudia thought bitterly.

A bright flash of lightning made the shadows leap in the room.

Please get back soon, Joy, Claudia thought anxiously. Please hurry back. She stared out at the storm, wondering if the hard rain would keep Joy from getting back. She jumped when the thunder boomed.

"There. All better," Marla said, smiling at Claudia. "How does that feel?"

"Good," Claudia replied distractedly.

Marla glanced at her watch. "Almost dinnertime. It's Alfred's day off, but he left us a picnic basket. I thought it'd be fun to have dinner out in the gazebo."

"But it's pouring!" Sophie protested.

"It doesn't matter," Marla replied, heading to the door. "The gazebo is closed in. It'll be fun to sit inside it and have a candlelight dinner and watch the storm over the ocean." She stopped at the doorway and turned around. "Hope Joy gets back in time. See you out there around six, okay?"

Joy burst into Sophie's room a few minutes before six, her black hair plastered to her head, her yellow sundress drenched from the storm.

"How's it going? Is everyone okay?" she asked nervously.

"I had a close call," Claudia told her, lowering her eyes to her bandaged ankle.

Joy gasped. "Did Marla—"

"Pack up, Joy. Quick. You were right about Marla," Claudia said, climbing to her feet. "This afternoon, she set her guard dog on me."

"No!" Joy cried, raising her hands to her face.

"I saw her on the beach. Marla doesn't know I saw her. You were right, Joy. She's trying to kill us."

Joy shivered. "Let me change. Then we can go."

"Change, then pack up," Claudia instructed. "Then we'll tell Marla we want a ride to town."

"What if she refuses? What if she tries to stop us?" Sophie demanded in a shrill voice. "What if she—"

"It's three against one," Joy said, hurrying to the door as a blaze of light lit the sky outside.

"If she won't drive us, we'll walk," Claudia said firmly.

A deafening thunderclap provided an exclamation point for her declaration.

The three girls dropped their suitcases in the front hall. Claudia slid open the coat closet door and pulled out three umbrellas.

As they made their way through the hallway toward the back of the house, the lights flickered.

"Uh-oh," Sophie cried softly. "Hope the lights don't go out."

"Are you sure Marla's in the gazebo? Isn't it kind of crazy to be there now?" Joy demanded in a whisper.

The lights flickered again, but didn't go out.

"She said it would be fun to eat out there and watch the storm," Claudia told her.

"She probably had some plan for us to be struck by lightning," Joy muttered dryly.

"I still don't think she's going to let us go," Sophie said.

They opened one of the French doors that led to the back terrace. The lawn was illuminated by spotlights that automatically came on at dark. The sheets of rain shimmered in the bright light.

The three girls stepped quickly out onto the terrace and opened their umbrellas. The terrace was puddled with rainwater. Claudia's umbrella nearly blew out of her hands.

A long streak of lightning was followed by an immediate roar of thunder. The spotlights flickered, then shone steadily.

"Is she there? At the gazebo?" Sophie asked anxiously, lingering behind the other two girls.

"I can't see very well through the rain," Claudia replied.

"I think I see a light at the gazebo," Joy reported, holding the umbrella handle steady with both hands.

"The wind is so swirly, I'm getting soaked!" Sophie complained.

Their sneakers squishing in the grass and soft ground, they made their way past the guest house and the tennis court, the red-clay court nearly as bright as day under bright white spotlights on tall poles.

A light flickered in the gazebo near the fence at the back of the lawn. The roar of the heavy rain drowned out the rush of the ocean just beyond the fence.

Claudia hesitated near a small, white shed at the edge of the lawn. "What's that awful smell?" she asked.

Despite the falling rain, a heavy, sour smell, like decaying meat or rotten eggs, floated into her nostrils.

"Ugh. I smell it too," Joy cried with disgust.

"Gross!" Sophie agreed.

The woodshed door was slightly ajar.

"That's strange," Claudia commented. "I thought Alfred was always so careful about locking everything up."

"Whatever it is, it sure stinks!" Joy declared. "Let's get to the gazebo and then *out* of here."

"No, wait." Claudia held Joy back with one hand.

On an impulse, she moved toward the open shed door. The other two girls followed close behind.

127

The sour odor grew heavier as they approached the shed.

Gripping the umbrella in one hand, struggling to keep it steady in the swirling rain, Claudia pulled open the shed door.

All three girls screamed as Marla's lifeless body toppled out.

chapter

22

Who Killed Marla?

Marla's body had tumbled stiffly into the harsh glare of a spotlight.

Before Claudia could turn away and cover her face, she saw that Marla's skin was purple. Her eyes had sunk deep into her skull. Her jaws were frozen open in a permanent scream of terror.

"Noooooo!" Sophie uttered a low howl of horror and disbelief.

Joy spun away from the gruesome sight and buried her head in Claudia's shoulder. "It can't be. It can't be," she repeated.

"We just saw her a couple hours ago," Claudia said, thinking out loud. "How can she be dead?"

"She was m-murdered!" Sophie stammered. She had let her umbrella drop to the ground and stood with her hands covering her face, the rain drenching her short hair and her sweatshirt.

"Alfred!" Joy cried, pulling away from Claudia. "We have to tell Alfred!"

"He isn't here. It's his day off, remember?" Sophie said.

"Who killed Marla?" Claudia asked, feeling dazed and shaky. She stared into the yellow cone of light from one of the spotlights and watched the steady downpour. The sound of the rain pushed by the wind drowned out the ocean behind them.

Was it Daniel? Claudia wondered, dread sweeping through her body. Was he still around?

"There's no one here but us!" Sophie cried.

"So who killed Marla?" Claudia repeated, trying to force away the fluttery feeling of panic, trying to slow her racing heart.

"We've got to call the police—now!" Joy declared. She glanced down at Marla's stiff, unmoving body for a second, then turned away.

"Yes! Come on!" Sophie agreed.

Limping on her bad ankle, Claudia followed the two girls around the deep puddles in the lawn, back to the house. She tossed her umbrella down at the doorway. Once inside, she shook her head hard, as if trying to shake away the hideous picture of Marla's purple face.

Shuddering, with rainwater soaking through her clothes, Claudia hurried to catch up to the others in the kitchen.

She stopped at the doorway. The lights flickered once again, but didn't go out.

Joy was standing by the counter, the phone receiver in her hand. She uttered a short cry of dismay.

"What's wrong?" Sophie asked, wiping the rainwater off her glasses with a paper towel.

"The line. It's dead," Joy replied softly.

Sophie gasped. "We can't call the police?"

Joy shook her head and replaced the receiver on the wall.

"We've got to get out of here," Claudia said, her eyes darting from Joy to Sophie. "Whoever killed Marla—maybe they're coming after us next!"

"No!" Sophie screamed, her face bloodless in the overhead fluorescent light.

"We've got to get to town. We've got to tell the police," Claudia said. She could feel panic tighten her throat.

"How can Marla be dead?" Joy wailed, gripping the back of a tall kitchen stool. "We just saw her. How did it happen?"

A loud crack of thunder made all three of them jump.

"We'll take some rain gear from the front closet," Claudia said. "We'll get out on the road and start walking, unless one of you knows where the car keys are kept." Neither girl answered. "Maybe someone will come by and give us a lift to town."

"Her face—it was so gross!" Joy exclaimed. "And her mouth—it was frozen open as if she'd died screaming."

"Joy—stop!" Sophie pleaded, even more pale.

"Yes. Stop," Claudia agreed. "Try to get Marla out of your mind. We've got to get out of this house. We've got to get the police."

Lightning crackled outside the kitchen window. As

the thunder roared, the three girls made their way to the front and searched the coat closet for rain gear.

Claudia found a yellow slicker, two sizes too small, but she pulled it on anyway. Joy pulled a long silk scarf from a shelf and wrapped it around her head. Sophie pulled a light blue jacket on over her drenched sweatshirt.

"Ready?" Claudia asked.

"I guess," Joy replied quietly.

"Let's go," Sophie muttered, her eyes revealing her fear.

Claudia pulled open the front door and peered out over the wide front lawn. Bright spotlights illuminated the front lawn too. The rain had slowed a little, she saw, although the lightning and thunder continued.

"Let's go!" Claudia called. "Once we get on the road, someone may come by."

"I just want to get *out* of here!" Joy cried.

They ran out into the rain, bending low as they ran, their sneakers splashing up water and sinking into the soft grass as they made their way down the lawn.

At the end of the grass a tall metal fence rose up, hidden from the other side by a high, perfectly manicured hedge.

Claudia started to reach for the gate handle.

"Stop!" Joy screamed, pulling Claudia's arm back.

Joy pulled off the scarf she had taken from the coat closet and tossed it at the gate.

Sparks flew as electricity plastered the scarf against the fence.

"Oh, wow! I forgot!" Claudia cried. She turned to Joy. "Thanks!"

"Now what?" Sophie cried miserably. "Now what do we do? We don't know where the controls to the fence are!"

"We're trapped," Joy muttered.

"We can't get out," Claudia agreed, staring hard at the electrified fence. "We're trapped here until it shuts off in the morning."

"But—what about the killer?" Sophie stammered.

chapter

23

A Ghost

The rain shimmered down like silver coins in the bright spotlights. Lightning streaked high over their heads.

"We have to find the controls," Joy said breathlessly. "There's got to be a way to shut off the fence."

"But it's all automatic, remember?" Sophie said in a tight voice. Drops of rainwater shone on her glasses. "It's on a timer."

"Then we've got to find the timer," Joy replied.

"It's probably in the basement," Claudia said with a shiver.

"I'm not going in the basement!" Sophie shrieked. "No way!"

Claudia had an idea. "I bet we can shut off the fence in back," she told them. "There's some kind of switch near the gate that leads down to the beach. I remember seeing Marla pull it. Near the control pad you have to push to open the gate."

"You mean we should go down to the ocean?" Sophie demanded shrilly. "In this storm?"

"No," Claudia told her, holding the yellow slicker over her head. "We just get out. Go through the gate. Once we're on the other side of the fence, we can follow it around the side of the house and head back to the front."

"Yes," Joy said. "That sounds good."

"You're sure we can shut off the gate in back?" Sophie demanded skeptically.

"I'm not sure, but we can try," Claudia said.

Bending low against the driving rain, they made their way around the side of the house, their sneakers sinking deeply into the soft mud as they walked. Joy slipped and fell against the house, but quickly pushed herself up and regained her balance.

The back of the house came into view. Rain splattered noisily against the flagstone terrace. Water poured out like a waterfall from the gutter.

"Do we have to go by the shed?" Sophie asked in a tiny voice.

"No. We can go on the other side of the guest house," Claudia told her. Her leg was burning with pain again, and she felt an agonizing jolt every time she stepped down on her foot.

Joy said something, but her words were muffled by the roar of the rain.

They were nearly to the guest house when a figure stepped out into the glare of a spotlight.

"Oh!" Claudia cried out in surprise.

All three girls froze.

The figure wore a trench coat pulled tight at the waist. A wide-brimmed straw hat covered her head, throwing her face into shadow.

What was that gleaming object she was raising in her hand? Claudia wondered.

Was it a pistol?

She pulled the brim of the hat back and revealed her face. Her cold blue eyes reflected the spotlight as she glared angrily at the three girls.

"Marla!" Joy managed to choke out. "But Marla—you're dead!"

chapter

24

"Who Wants to Die First?"

*T*hey backed out of the rain and under an overhang of the sloping guest-house roof. The pistol continued to gleam in the bright light. Marla raised it to her waist. "Surprised, huh?" she asked bitterly.

"We saw your body in the shed," Claudia managed to choke out. "We thought—"

A bitter smile formed on Marla's lips. "Well, Claudia, you're the one who believes in ghosts. I guess I'm a ghost too."

Claudia took a step toward Marla. "The gun—" she began, staring hard at it, feeling cold fear sweep over her.

Thunder roared over the ocean. Wind pushed the rain against their backs.

"You all look so confused," Marla observed, the bitter smile still playing over her lips. Her blue eyes sparkled in the rain-filled light.

"We're so glad you're alive!" Joy cried.

"But Marla isn't alive," came the startling, even-toned reply. "Marla is dead. I killed her a week ago. Before you even arrived."

"Huh?" Claudia cried out.

Joy uttered a cry of surprise. Sophie remained frozen, her eyes on the gleaming silver pistol.

"Marla's been dead for a week! Couldn't you tell by the smell?"

"Then—then—" Claudia started. Her legs suddenly felt weak, and she could feel the blood pulsing at her temples.

"That's right. I'm not Marla. I'm Alison." She tossed the straw hat into the rain. Her blond hair fell wildly about her face. Her eyes burned into Claudia's. "I'm Alison, back from the dead. And now Marla's the one who's dead. Surprise, surprise."

Claudia and the other two girls stared at Alison in silent shock. No one moved.

The spotlights flickered.

Alison gripped the pistol tightly, aiming it at Joy.

"You all look so confused," Alison said, shouting over the rain. "Not like at camp, where you thought you knew it all." She uttered the words slowly, bitterly.

"But, Alison—" Claudia started.

"Perhaps you'd like me to clear up your confusion," Alison continued, ignoring her. "Marla didn't know I was alive, you see. Marla thought her poor sister had died in the gorge. She didn't know I was alive until I showed up here last week and killed her."

"But why?" Joy interrupted in a high-pitched voice. "Why did you kill Marla?"

"Because she watched me fall into the gorge. After you three ran away. Marla's face was the last face I saw, staring at me from the edge of the woods, staring at me *with a smile!*"

"No!" Claudia cried. "She couldn't—"

"Marla was smiling," Alison shouted, brandishing the pistol. "She didn't care about me. No one in my family cared if I lived or died. No one cared about me. So when a family pulled me out of the river, all broken and beat up and half drowned, and they were so nice, so caring, I decided to stay with them. I pretended to have amnesia—"

"You *what?*" Joy interrupted, gaping at Alison in disbelief.

"I pretended that I'd lost my memory," Alison cried, "so I wouldn't have to go back to my disgusting family. I decided this was my chance. To start a new life. To be with a happy family. So I pretended I didn't know who I was, and I stayed with them."

"But wh-what do you want with us? Why are you doing this?" Claudia stammered.

"Because the hatred built up," Alison shouted bitterly. "My anger didn't go away. Over the past year, it grew. I couldn't get Marla's smile out of my mind, that horrible smile as I fell off the log. I knew I had to come back to kill her.

"I made my way back here, not knowing what I'd find," Alison continued. "Mom and Dad were away, of course. They always are. I hid in the pantry. I heard Marla talking with Alfred, telling him she had invited you three for a camp reunion."

Alison grinned. "Perfect timing on my part. I killed Marla, hid her body in the shed, and took her place.

Poor nearsighted Alfred didn't have a clue. And now, here we are, girls, having our gala camp reunion. Are you enjoying it so far?"

"Alison—put down the gun. Please!" Claudia pleaded.

"Uh-uh. No way." Alison's grin faded. The hand holding the pistol trembled.

"Alison, listen—" Claudia began.

"You shouldn't have let me fall," Alison cried with a surge of emotion. "You shouldn't have run away. You should've helped me. One of you should have helped me. One of you should've *cared* about me just a little."

With a loud sob, she pointed the gun from girl to girl. "Okay. I guess the party's over. It's been great. Really."

"Alison—stop! We'll help you! We care about you!" Joy cried, her eyes on the pistol.

"This time it's *my* turn," Alison said, ignoring Joy's plea. "This time I get to stand and watch while *you* die." She narrowed her eyes, her jaw set hard. "Who wants to die first? How about you, Claudia?"

Claudia gasped as Alison pointed the pistol at her chest.

chapter

25

A Second Death

*L*ightning flashed close by. A white streak just beyond the tennis court.

Claudia heard a pop as the lightning struck the ground.

She cried out, thinking she'd been shot.

Thunder shook the ground.

Claudia brushed her wet hair off her forehead and stared at the raised pistol quivering in Alison's hand.

And as she stared, the door to the guest house swung open.

"Oh!"

Claudia's cry made everyone turn.

A dark, hooded figure stepped out of the guest house and into the light.

Squinting through the rain, Claudia saw that the hood was part of a dark blue plastic windbreaker worn over dark jeans.

A gust of wind tossed the hood off his head.

Claudia saw his dark eyes, his thick black hair.

She recognized him at once. The Ghost Boy!

"Daniel!" she cried.

Alison's mouth dropped open. She turned the pistol on the new arrival. "Hey—who are you?"

He didn't reply. His dark eyes locked on Alison, he stepped toward her.

"Who *are* you?" Alison demanded, shaking the gun in his direction.

He took another step toward her.

"It's the Ghost Boy!" Claudia cried. "The ghost from the guest house!"

"Huh?" Alison reacted scornfully. "I made that story up. Are you *crazy?*"

Daniel took another step, rain sliding down the front of his windbreaker, his eyes on Alison.

"Hey—stay away! Stay away!" Alison cried, her anger suddenly giving way to panic. "Don't come any closer! I'm warning you!"

But the Ghost Boy continued his slow, steady walk toward her.

"I'm warning you!" Alison cried shrilly. "Stay away!"

Her eyes grew wide with terror.

With a loud cry, the Ghost Boy dove at Alison, tackling her around the waist.

Claudia froze for a second. Then seeing Alison start to fall, she darted forward, her hand outstretched, and grabbed the pistol from Alison's hand.

A streak of lightning hit with a pop near the swimming pool.

This time the lights went out.

The girls shrieked, startled by the sudden total darkness.

Claudia turned her gaze to the house. "The lights are out everywhere!" she cried.

She heard a struggle below her on the ground.

"Let go!" she heard Alison cry.

Then, as her eyes adjusted to the darkness, Claudia could see Alison running across the back lawn, past the tennis court and pool, running through the pouring rain at full speed toward the gate.

"No—Alison! No!" Claudia screamed, starting after her.

"It's electrified!" Joy screamed. "Stop! The gate is electrified!"

"The power is off, idiot!" Alison screamed back.

All three girls were running now, running after Alison.

Too late.

Claudia heard a generator hum on—just as Alison grabbed for the gate.

She heard the crackle. Saw Alison's arm catch in the wire mesh. Saw Alison struggle to free herself as a white streak of electricity encircled her body.

Alison screamed once. Then her body jerked and tossed inside the bright white electrical flame that appeared to dance around her.

I'm watching her die again, Claudia thought, horrified.

I'm watching Alison die a second time.

A jolt of current shot Alison off the fence, her body sprawling facedown in the muddy ground.

Twitching.

Then still.

By the time the girls knelt beside her, Alison was dead.

The bright spotlights flickered on. The wet grass sparkled green again.

Claudia stared down at Alison. Alison who was so frail and tiny. Her blond hair, matted flat to her head, shone golden under the harsh light.

She was so pretty, Claudia thought. So pretty.

How horrible to hate your family, to want to forget them. What a horrible life Alison had.

Claudia glanced toward the house and gasped.

She had forgotten all about the Ghost Boy.

He was advancing toward the three girls, his dark eyes trained on them in an eerie stare.

chapter

26

Not a Ghost

"**I**s she—is she dead?" The boy asked, staring down at Alison's body.

Claudia nodded, her eyes trained on him as he advanced. "Yeah."

Behind her, Joy and Sophie were hugging, trying to comfort each other from the horrors of this night.

"Who are you? What are you doing here?" Claudia demanded, rising to her feet, pushing her soaked hair off her forehead.

"I'm not a ghost," he replied, a grim smile forming on his handsome face. "I told you, my name is Daniel."

"Daniel who?" Claudia asked suspiciously.

Joy and Sophie turned to listen.

"Daniel Ryan," he replied, standing beside Claudia. "I'm Alfred's son."

The three girls reacted with surprise.

Daniel pointed to the guest house. "I'm on summer break from college. Visiting my dad. Dad let me stay in the guest house, but we didn't want anyone to know. The Drexells aren't the most generous people in the world. They wouldn't approve. I didn't want my dad to lose his job." He turned to Claudia. "That's why I've been so mysterious. Sorry."

"That's okay," Claudia replied softly, feeling relieved.

"The rain is slowing. Maybe the phones are working again," Joy said.

"We'd better try to call the police," Sophie said.

Joy and Sophie began jogging toward the house, their sneakers splashing through the marshy lawn.

Claudia lingered behind. She raised her eyes to Daniel's.

"Now both sisters are dead," Claudia said sadly, shaking her head.

Daniel put a comforting arm around her shoulders. "It's a horrible night. A horrible night," he muttered.

Claudia nodded in silent agreement.

"Did you really believe I was a ghost?" he asked, pulling her nearer.

"Maybe," she replied softly.

He smiled. "How can I prove that I'm not a ghost?" he asked, his dark eyes lighting up.

Claudia raised her face to his and kissed him.

"You pass the test. You're not a ghost," she told him. "Now let's get out of this rain."

Walking side by side, they made their way to the house.

About the Author

"Where do you get your ideas?"

That's the question that R. L. Stine is asked most often. "I don't know where my ideas come from," he says. "But I do know that I have a lot more scary stories in my mind that I can't wait to write."

So far, he has written nearly three dozen mysteries and thrillers for young people, all of them bestsellers.

Bob grew up in Columbus, Ohio. Today he lives in an apartment near Central Park in New York City with his wife, Jane, and thirteen-year-old son, Matt.

The Nightmares Never End . . .
When You Visit

Next: *THE FEAR STREET SAGA*
A Three-part FEAR STREET
Miniseries

Why do so many horrifying things happen on Fear Street? The burned-out Fear Mansion is all that's left of the powerful Fear family . . . or is it? What really happened to the Fears—and why does their evil live on?

Coming in August 1993

THE BETRAYAL: It begins when an innocent young girl is burned at the stake for witchcraft . . . and it escalates into a bloody feud that lasts for 200 years. Only Nora knows the whole story. Can she tell it before it's too late?

Coming in September 1993

THE SECRET: The nightmare continues as the curse haunts each new generation. Then Simon Fear learns a powerful secret. Can he conquer the evil legacy once and for all?

Coming in October 1993

THE BURNING: The terrifying conclusion. Simon Fear is rich and powerful—but that won't save his teenage daughters' lives. Is there any escape from the deadly curse? And will Nora be the evil's last victim?

FEAR STREET®

R.L. Stine

- THE NEW GIRL................74649-9/$3.99
- THE SURPRISE PARTY....73561-6/$3.99
- THE OVERNIGHT.............74650-2/$3.99
- MISSING.........................69410-3/$3.99
- THE WRONG NUMBER.....69411-1/$3.99
- THE SLEEPWALKER.........74652-9/$3.99
- HAUNTED.......................74651-0/$3.99
- HALLOWEEN PARTY........70243-2/$3.99
- THE STEPSISTER............70244-0/$3.99
- SKI WEEKEND.................72480-0/$3.99
- THE FIRE GAME...............72481-9/$3.99
- THE THRILL CLUB.............78581-8/$3.99

- LIGHTS OUT.....................72482-7/$3.99
- THE SECRET BEDROOM.....72483-5/$3.99
- THE KNIFE.......................72484-3/$3.99
- THE PROM QUEEN............72485-1/$3.99
- FIRST DATE.....................73865-8/$3.99
- THE BEST FRIEND.............73866-6/$3.99
- THE CHEATER..................73867-4/$3.99
- SUNBURN........................73868-2/$3.99
- THE NEW BOY..................73869-0/$3.99
- THE DARE........................73870-4/$3.99
- BAD DREAMS ....78569-9/$3.99
- DOUBLE DATE ....78570-2/$3.99
- ONE EVIL SUMMER ....78596-6/$3.99

FEAR STREET SAGA
- #1: THE BETRAYAL.... 86831-4/$3.99
- #2: THE SECRET.........86832-2/$3.99
- #3: THE BURNING.......86833-0/$3.99

SUPER CHILLER
- PARTY SUMMER......72920-9/$3.99
- BROKEN HEARTS.....78609-1/$3.99
- THE DEAD LIFEGUARD
  ....86834-9/$3.99

CHEERLEADERS
- THE FIRST EVIL.........75117-4/$3.99
- THE SECOND EVIL....75118-2/$3.99
- THE THIRD EVIL.........75119-0/$3.99

99 FEAR STREET: THE HOUSE OF EVIL
- THE FIRST HORROR ....88562-6/$3.99
- THE SECOND HORROR.........88563-4 /$3.99

WHERE THE MAGIC OF THE MOVIES...
MEETS THE THRILLS OF A LIFETIME!

By combining the fantasy of motion pictures, with the excitement of world-class theme parks, the Paramount Parks provide the ultimate in family entertainment. From state-of-the-art roller coasters, dazzling musical productions, and interesting shops to refreshing water attractions, magical children's areas and dining opportunities galore, the parks offer something for everyone!

CAROWINDS.
CHARLOTTE, NC ★ (800)888-4386

GREAT AMERICA
SANTA CLARA, CA ★ (408)988-1776

KINGS DOMINION
RICHMOND, VA ★ (804)876-5000

KINGS ISLAND
CINCINNATI, OH ★ (800)288-0808

Parks are open weekends in the spring and fall and daily during the summer. Operating dates and times, admission prices and policies vary. Call the parks directly for more detailed information.

- -

Paramount Parks

Fear Street "Sunburn" Readers SAVE Up To $16 In 1993

A Paramount Communications Company